One Special Summer in *Tenerife*

Ian Wilfred

One Special Summer in Tenerife
Copyright © 2023 by Ian Wilfred

ISBN: 9798378289936

Cover Design: Avalon Graphics
Editing: Laura McCallen
Proofreading: Maureen Vincent-Northam
Formatting: Rebecca Emin

For Ron

Acknowledgements

There are a few people I'd like to thank for getting *One Special Summer in Tenerife* out into the world.

The fabulous Rebecca Emin at Gingersnap Books for organising everything for me and who also produced both kindle and paperback books. Laura McCallen for all the time and effort she spent editing the book, Maureen Vincent-Northam for proofreading, and the very talented Cathy Helms at Avalon Graphics for producing the terrific cover.

Finally for my late mum who is always with me in everything I do.

Chapter 1

'Have you fastened your seatbelt, Sophie? It looks like we're ready to take off. How exciting is this? In just a few hours we will be in Tenerife – our first time abroad together for ten years as the last time was for your eighteenth birthday. This is going to be so lovely, darling. Eight months of sunshine and being together, mum and daughter bonding... Ok, we'll be working, but that will be fun and we both have our own part to play so there will be no stepping on each other's toes, which I'm sure you will be glad about. It's going to be a summer we will never forget!'

It wasn't the stepping on toes Sophie was worried about, it was being with her mother the perfectionist, Madeline Mundey, for all that time. They would be going from seeing each other three or four times a year (and even then, just for weekends) to this – living and working together, and in another country on top of that! Sophie worried she'd made a mistake. She should have said no to her mum when Madeline suggested it. Ok, Sophie had just been made redundant and needed a job, but this? Running a holiday home for large groups of holiday makers? This was madness. But it was too late now.

'Yes, Mum. So how long do we have to get everything ready before the first guests arrive, and how long does each group stay for?'

'Oh, Sophie. I gave you the file with all the details of everything in! Haven't you read it? I'm so disappointed in you. Here, have my copy. I suggest you spend the flight reading and digesting it thoroughly. And to answer your question, we have three weeks before the first guests arrive. That should give us plenty of time to get prepared. Now, start reading and make sure you take it all in as I will be asking you questions on it later.'

As Sophie opened the notes her first thought was that she now had to think of this as a proper job because after all, she and her mum were being paid to run the villa for the summer. As she started to flick through the pages – of which it seemed there were quite a lot – she came across an unopened envelope. Why was it there and why was it still unopened? Perhaps it had been mistakenly put with the villa paperwork and forgotten about?

'Mum, what's this letter for you? It's marked urgent but you haven't opened it. From the return address it looks like it's from a television company...'

'Oh, yes, I forgot. It's probably another request to do an interview – they have been sending them to me for the last six months. It will all be to do with that drama I was in before I gave up acting to have you – *The Village Green* – because the thirtieth anniversary of the show's premiere is coming up. As I don't have an agent anymore they send the requests directly to me. Pass it here and I'll have a look. Now, darling, please read the file, it's very important.'

Madeline was right, Sophie should have read the file earlier, but if she had then she would likely have talked herself out of coming. So, here goes. One thing was for sure, every minute detail would be written down. Madeline was nothing if not meticulous.

- *Villa Kennal is located in the coastal town of Los Kalanchoe, just a short drive from Costa Adeje.*
- *Sleeps twelve people in six bedrooms (all en suite).*

- *Has one kitchen/lounge plus separate TV room and a heated outdoor pool.*

Sophie's responsibilities:

- *Clean each room and bathroom every day (between eleven a.m. and three p.m.) with a bed change every third day. Clean towels only when they have been left on the floor by guests.*
- *Serve dinner to guests when required and clear up afterwards.*

Madeline's responsibilities:

- *Liaise with guests to make sure they have everything they need to have the perfect holiday, including arranging transport and bookings as needed.*
- *Fulfil any food shopping requests.*
- *Cook dinner when requested.*
- *Supervise and quality check of housekeeping.*

So basically, Sophie was a dogsbody. Ok, she knew she would be cleaning, that wasn't a problem, and her mum would cook if the guests needed it, but hopefully most nights the people would go out.

Flicking through all the other paperwork Sophie noted that there was a page for each group of guests with lists of their requirements. All the names and addresses seemed to be from the UK and Europe and looking at the calendar there didn't seem to be much of a gap between parties, but it all appeared to be well organised, with clear timings laid out to ensure everything that needed to get done, got done. They were talking about Madeline here though – Sophie wouldn't expect anything less.

Unfortunately there weren't any specific details about where Sophie and her mum would be staying. She daren't ask about it though because no doubt her mum had already told her and she had simply not been paying attention. All Sophie knew was that it was some type of bungalow.

Right, think of a question, Sophie, about something that's not in the file that might lead to Mum revealing more hints about our accommodation.

'This all seems very well organised, Mum. It looks like we're going to be very busy! I see one group is booked in for the whole of August, which will be good. Can I just ask a couple of questions? You still haven't said how all this came about, so how have you and I ended up running this holiday rental? Do you know the owner? Is it a friend? And why did they want someone from England to take on the job? Surely a couple who already live in Tenerife and speak Spanish would be better? Not that I'm saying we aren't capable...'

'So many questions! I forgot how you need to know the ins and outs of everything. There's really no need to worry. We can manage the property just fine for the next eight months and I promise we are the best people for the job.'

'Yes, Mum, I agree that we can do it, but why us specifically? And why does it all have to be a mystery?'

Sophie thought she might have flummoxed her mum, but Madeline couldn't walk away or make an excuse as they were stuck on an aeroplane heading for Tenerife. She was going to have to tell Sophie the whole story and although she felt bad about cornering her mum, Madeline needed to realise Sophie was part of this set-up and deserved to know who was paying their wages.

'Ok, I will tell you how all this has come about, but first let's have a drink. When the hostess gets to us I'll be ordering a nice double gin and tonic.'

Gin in hand, Madeline finally explained that the villa complex was owned by an old actor friend who she had known for over thirty years. The man's name was Kennal Scott and when he was a big TV star back in the seventies, he'd bought the property so he had somewhere to escape to. As his fame and the acting work fizzled out, he had had time to do the place up and had started renting it out, but this year he'd been cast in a new show that was filming in America, and so needed someone else to oversee the villa and the vacationers.

Sophie's mum had also dabbled in real estate when she gave up acting to have her, investing what money she had in property – a little two up, two down row of terrace houses, which were rented out to students – and after a while she had quite a few. It brought in a good income – and still did – and so she had never returned to acting.

Sophie was a bit shocked as she'd never heard her mum talk about this Kennal before. Ok, she claimed he was in her past, but Madeline seemed to know a lot about his life in the present – the way the house was a wreck when he bought it and how he did it up using money from the odd acting jobs he took on – and she had neglected to mention that they'd been in contact before now. Did he just phone around everyone he knew until someone agreed to come to Tenerife and look after it for him? Sophie wanted to ask more but was aware that if she pushed her mum too far she would likely turn the tables and ask why Sophie was so secretive about her own life. That was easy – because up until Sophie was eighteen, she wasn't allowed to make any decisions for herself. Every aspect of her life was planned by Madeline, but she had reached breaking point and put her foot down. That was one of the reasons they'd never had a holiday together since then. Sophie realised her mind was wandering; she needed to memorise the file because, like her mum had said, questions would be asked.

Sophie had to admit that the house did look lovely in the photographs and although it wasn't a holiday for either of them, if the guests didn't need feeding every day she and her mum would be able to get on with life in their own way without living in each other's pocket. Perhaps this wouldn't be the disaster she was expecting it to be?

Notes read, everything was clear in Sophie's head. She knew what her and her mum's responsibilities were to be and exactly what they were each being paid to do.

'All done, Mum. Ask me any question you'd like and I promise I'll have the answer. One thing first though, where will we be living? You said in a bungalow, but is it far from the villa?'

'No, darling, it's within the villa complex. It's where Kennal lives when he rents out the main house. It has bushes and trees to separate it so it's very private and though we obviously won't be able to use the swimming pool when guests are there, the beach is only a few kilometres away. Oh dear, not now after all these years! The timing couldn't be worse...' Madeline muttered, looking at the letter she'd opened while Sophie reviewed the file.

'What's wrong, Mum?'

'Darling, it's this letter. The TV company want to make twelve episodes of *The Village Green* as a celebration of the anniversary of the original run and they have offered me the lead roll – the part I played thirty years ago!'

'That's wonderful, Mum, how exciting!'

'Yes, darling, but filming starts in four weeks and to be honest, from the moment I gave up acting to have you I have never had the desire to go back to it. I closed the door on it and moved on. I thought my acting career was well and truly gone for ever. Could I really go back?'

Chapter 2

How much longer before these cases appear on the conveyor belt? Sophie needed something to break the silence.

She could tell her mum wanted to go back to the UK to film this series – even though she had said she'd closed the door on that part of her life, they both knew she would never get an opportunity like this again. Sophie had already told her till she was almost blue in the face that Kennal would understand because even though Sophie didn't know him, she did know he was an actor and if he was in her mum's position he would most likely jump at the opportunity. Anyway, it shouldn't be too hard for him to find two other people to take over from them and then they could head back to London. It was kind of a shame though because, in a way, Sophie was finally starting to look forward to the summer here on the island of Tenerife – and it did open up another problem as it meant Sophie would need to find another job ... and quickly. Oh, why did she have to quit so suddenly rather than just taking the promotion? She knew she would have been able to do the job and would have enjoyed it, but she also knew she couldn't stomach the prospect of working beside someone she couldn't face seeing ever again, even if it was only on a monthly basis.

'Look, Mum, they've started to put the cases on. I can see them coming through and... what a bit of luck! I can see mine already.'

****

Fifteen minutes later they were heading out of the arrivals hall and looking for their names on a board – they'd been promised that a taxi driver from Los

Kalanchoe would be waiting for them.

'There we are, darling. Ooh! He looks very handsome and thankfully not hot and sweaty.'

'He's a taxi driver, Mum, not a blind date.'

After the introductions, Ramon the driver put the cases in the boot of the car and they headed off. Even though they would only be here a couple of weeks, just until Kennal could find someone to take over from them, Sophie found she wanted to know everything there was to know about Los Kalanchoe and what better person to ask than a taxi driver.

'So you are staying at Kennal's villa? It's lovely – he's worked very hard making it look so nice and everyone who stays there is very happy. Also, you are only a short distance from the beach and of course you have great restaurants on your doorstep.'

'Are there a lot of places to eat in the town? I don't think my mum and I will be doing a lot of cooking, if we can help it.'

'There are a few but the best restaurants are in the bigger towns – Playa Del Duque, in particular, has some really nice ones. They are a little bit more expensive but it's the "in" place as it's very glamorous. It's also easy to get to – buses go there every half an hour – and it only takes a short journey, or it's a nice walk along by the sea, and as for the food, it's the best in the area! But saying that, along the coast there are also so many lovely little villages. If you are looking for somewhere a little quieter there is La Caleta – it still has holiday makers and can get busy but it's very quaint with gorgeous restaurants that are very traditional, but then I am a little biased as that's where I come from.'

'Oh, we aren't here for a holiday, we've come to work! My daughter and myself are looking after the villa for eight months while Kennal is in America,' Madeline explained.

'Well, in that case, I will give you my phone number and if there is anything you need you must give me a call. Also, if your guests need a taxi, I can prioritise them.'

'Actually we might not be staying that long—' Sophie began.

'Darling, we will discuss that other thing later. Now, Ramon, tell me about yourself. Are you married? And have you lived here long?'

As per usual, her mother was back in control of the conversation, any thoughts of the acting job seeming to have gone right out of her head. Why Sophie was surprised she didn't know.

For the rest of the journey Ramon chatted about his life in La Caleta, telling them his mum had a shop there where she sold beautiful gifts as well as lovely soft furnishings. Madeline said he was the perfect advertisement for his mum's business and he laughed and said he tried, but he didn't need to do much as one look in the shop window and people fell in love with everything on offer. Madeline was of course full of questions, one being: was he single? But he was saved having to answer as they were now very near to the villa.

'Welcome to Los Kalanchoe! This is the start of the town and Kennal's villa is at the other end but as you can see it's a very pretty area. It's built in a circle with the little shops and restaurants in the centre.'

With that, Ramon turned up a side street and then on to what looked like nothing more than a dirt track, and there on a wall in front of them, next to a pair of huge wooden gates, was a sign saying 'Villa Kennal'.

'Oh look, darling,' Madeline said as they got closer to the villa, 'that young man must be the one with the keys. You go and introduce yourself to him – his name is Luis – and tell him I won't be a couple of minutes. Now, how much do I owe you, Ramon?'

Sophie couldn't help but notice the unwelcoming scowl on Luis's face as she approached.

'You are late. Your flight landed a while back and I was expecting you at least an hour ago. I'm Luis. I keep an eye on the property when Kennal is away. You must be Madeline,' he said briskly, with a trace of contempt.

'Hi, no, Madeline is my mum. I'm Sophie. Thank you for bringing the keys for us and I'm really sorry we've kept you waiting but we weren't in control of the plane or the journey from the airport,' Sophie said, trying to keep her annoyance at his unfriendly manner under control.

'I'm in a hurry to start work so I haven't got time to go in with you and show you around as I had planned, but I've written down my phone number and put it in the bag of keys so if you need anything just give me a call. But know that I am very busy so don't assume when you call that I can drop everything and come running.'

With that, Luis handed over the bag of keys, got on a scooter and left. Sophie couldn't help but notice that he was handsome – even though he had an attitude – and he had a lovely tan. And those gorgeous eyes... She wanted to just dive into them. Shame about his bad manners.

As Sophie waited for her mum to stop chatting to Ramon, she noticed a lane that went up the side of the villa and spotted a man with a cat in his arms, both of them looking at her. She gave a little wave but the man ignored her and walked away, passing through a gate. *I've been here two minutes and already two people have been rude to me,* she thought to herself.

The taxi fare paid, Ramon lifted their cases out of the boot, Madeline and Sophie picked up their hand luggage, and they all headed for the gate.

Thankfully, it was very straightforward as each key had a tag on it explaining what it was for. Once inside the villa complex, mother and daughter waved Ramon goodbye.

'Luis was very good looking, wasn't he, Sophie? Why did he go off in such a hurry? I feel rude I didn't introduce myself to him.'

Sophie explained that there was nothing to worry about it as it was Luis who was rude and though he had to head off to work, he had left his phone number. What she didn't say was that she was secretly hoping he would have to come back soon.

Now through the gate, the two women took in the villa and the surrounding land properly. It was stunning. To the right was a gorgeous swimming pool surrounded by a terrace and then up a path directly in front of them was the villa itself. Sophie couldn't wait to get in and open up the shutters.

'I've locked the gate, Mum, so we can safely leave our bags and cases here. Let's go and investigate.' When Madeline stayed unusually silent, Sophie turned to her. 'Mum, come on, did you hear what I said? Let's go and have a look around! Are you ok? You've gone all quiet...'

It was clear that Madeline was miles away and Sophie briefly wondered if perhaps there was more to this villa than she was letting on... But enough of that for now, time to find the key to get into the villa itself.

Having dragged Madeline up the path Sophie tried to pull her out of her reverie. 'Here we go, Mum, let's go in and see what's on offer.'

As they walked up the steps to the front door they took in the huge terrace, which would be perfect for enjoying the evening sun. Once through the front door, they saw that, as advertised, the main floor was one big room. To the right was a kitchen with a dining table in front, which looked like it had enough chairs around it to seat dozens of people, then to the left of that, on the other side of the front door, were huge, welcoming sofas with coffee tables dotted around them. A corridor led off the main room with five doors and as they peeked into each room they saw they were bedrooms. There would be plenty of time to investigate each one later so they continued on to the back of the property, where they found another lounge area. It wasn't as big as the main room but it did have a television on the wall. Looking over to the corner they spotted a little staircase. For some reason, Sophie hadn't realised it was two storeys high. Madeline suggested it must lead to another bedroom so off they went up the stairs to try and confirm her suspicion.

'Oh, Mum, how fabulous is this?'

They were both blown away with what they found at the top of the stairs. Not just another bedroom and bathroom, but a huge lounge that looked down to the pool and managed to be both incredibly cosy and airy at the same time.

'Welcome to Villa Kennal, Sophie! This is what this property is all about. Imagine waking up and sitting here with a coffee looking at that view. The couples who have the bedroom up here will be very lucky. Just put a little kitchen in the corner over there and I could live up here for ever!'

'Yes, Mum, it is a very special villa. I can't see how anyone couldn't have a lovely holiday here. Right, now, I have a few more keys in this bag. Let's find out more about where we are going to be living.'

Back outside Sophie was still blown away by the place. It wasn't a bit like she'd thought – nothing 'holiday let' about it at all. Ok, it was very minimalist, but it still felt like a home and would be so easy to keep clean, and if that was the standard of the villa, surely their bungalow would be on par with it? They'd soon find out, but first they had to find it. Madeline had said it was hidden from the view from the villa by bushes and trees so they followed a little path that led to the side of the main house and looked as if it went behind the villa. The keys in the little bag said things like 'store room' and 'laundry' and 'pool room' and one marked as 'the den' – that had to be it, though hopefully it was more than a den...

'This way, Mum. Look, there's a little gate in between those two trees – I think we've found the bungalow. Oh my goodness! It looks so small... Perhaps it goes back further? On a positive note, it has a lovely veranda. I can see us eating there. Actually, I think that's where we'll spend most of our time. It's so private and the guests in the villa won't be able to see us. Let's go in. As long as there's a kitchen and bathroom, and the bedrooms are ok, we'll cope.'

'Darling, before we go in, I think there is something I should mention... You're right, it is small and though the kitchen looked quite modern in the photos I saw and the bathroom is lovely, with a nice big shower, there is one rather significant downside. I should have said but I thought if I had you wouldn't have agreed to come. I'm sorry, Sophie, but there is only one bedroom. We will have to share.'

Chapter 3

So, here goes, Sophie's first morning waking up on the island of Tenerife. She had to admit that there were a lot worse places to be getting up in. She supposed it helped that she had persuaded her mum to sleep in the gorgeous upstairs bedroom in the villa so she could wake up to the amazing view of the pool ... and Sophie could have the bed in the bungalow to herself. It just seemed daft, them both being in the bungalow when the villa was empty until the first guests arrived in a few weeks. The bungalow was perfect ... but really just for one person. There was no denying it was gorgeous – Sophie loved that it was modern but with old world charm in the old bits of pottery in the kitchen and Kennal's knick-knacks dotted about the place. But her favourite part? It had to be the veranda. She could see herself sitting there when she wasn't working – coffee in the morning, wine at night... It would definitely do her for the summer, thank you very much! And it could be just Sophie if she could convince her mum to go back to England and do the acting job. Last night she was still saying she wouldn't take it as she didn't want to leave Kennal in the lurch, but if Sophie could come up with a solution for the cooking of the guests' meals, she was sure Madeline would agree to let her take the job on by herself.

Settling down for a coffee on the veranda, Sophie was thinking how happy she was that it was quiet and so private, but then something moved behind her and she turned quickly, finding a cat walking towards her.

'Oh, hello, Mr Cat ... or is it Miss Cat? Where have you come from? I must say, you don't look like a stray. Please don't tell me you live here with

Kennal and you need looking after. I've never had a cat but then again, they do say a cat owns you not the other way around, so maybe it won't be all that difficult? I'm sorry, I don't have any food, and... Yes, you can curl up and go to sleep,' Sophie said, watching with amusement as the cat did just that, taking no further notice of her.

Wait, is this the cat that the man I waved to yesterday had in his arms when he went into the property up the lane?

'Good morning, Sophie; you're up early. How did you sleep? Oh! Where did that cat come from?'

'Great, thanks, Mum. He or she just appeared! Kennal didn't mention he had pets, I suppose? By the way, what was it like waking up to that gorgeous view?'

'It was lovely, darling, I'm glad you convinced me to stay over there and no, he didn't mention a cat.'

'Very odd. Shall I make us both a coffee?'

Madeline nodded and the cat followed Sophie inside the bungalow and then back out again.

'There you go, Mum, one coffee. Did you enjoy the meal last night? I don't think I have ever had such a lovely pizza and only a five minute walk from here! I'm glad I've come with you, this is just what I need for the summer – a complete switch off from everything.'

'Sophie, what is "everything" and why would you need to switch off? Sorry, darling, I know it annoys you when I pry and ask too many questions, but there is something I've noticed that is a bit odd so I might as well ask and get it out the way. Since we landed at the airport yesterday, I've not seen you look at your phone once. In fact, I've not even seen you with it in your hand. When we have weekends together at home you are on it every five minutes. What's going on?'

16

It was true and Sophie knew she was going to have to give her some kind of answer, but there was no need for her mum to know the real reason. That was all in the past – and certainly none of her business – but Sophie would have to think quick if she wanted to stop this line of questioning because history had told her that her mum wasn't going to let it drop until she had an answer.

'You're right, Mum. I was on my phone all the time but it was always work things I was dealing with. My boss worked twenty-four-seven and he never thought twice about sending emails out to the staff day and night asking for reports or saying we needed to be at this meeting or that. Since I've been made redundant, there's no need for me to check my phone as the only person that would need to contact me is you.'

'Ok, I will accept your answer for now, Sophie, but I will say that I don't entirely believe you. For one because I know there's more to your job situation than what you're telling me – I know you took redundancy rather than the promotion you were offered, which is unusual – and for another because there is clearly something else bothering you. I just hope one day you will feel able to tell me what it is. Now, on that note, I'm off to have a shower and grab my notes outlining what we have to do. I will be back here in an hour so we can make a plan.'

Well, that had told her. Sophie wasn't daft, she knew that wasn't the end of it as her mum wouldn't give up until she knew everything, but that conversation could wait for another day. No, today was all about getting her mum to go back and film the TV series. Sophie really thought it would be good for her because she knew Madeline missed acting and – if she was being honest – she still felt a bit guilty knowing that her mum's departure from

17

showbiz was down to her. Madeline had wanted to create a stable home life for them both, and thankfully she was able to with her house rentals, but now that Sophie was grown and didn't need her mum as much, it would be daft for Madeline to miss out on this opportunity. Acting had been her first love and this was the perfect time to fall back in love with it.

****

Three hours later they were walking around the little town of Los Kalanchoe and neither the acting job nor the disastrous break-up Sophie was hiding from her mum had been mentioned. Surprisingly, though, everything had been going ok. After focusing on the reason they were here in Tenerife – to run Villa Kennal for the next eight months – and making a plan of action for completing their individual tasks, they had been to the little supermarket and come to the conclusion that everything the holiday makers would need could be bought there. They had also found the bus stop, the doctors' office, and the chemist. Madeline had been making notes the whole time, which made Sophie feel a little guilty, but she was just too busy taking it all in.

They stopped for a coffee and a pastry in the little bakery cum café and when Madeline's phone rang she looked at who it was and didn't hesitate to take the call. Sophie instantly realised it was Kennal, given the pleasantries being exchanged – Madeline saying how lovely the villa was and describing the journey from the airport and reassuring him everything was fine and saying how excited they were to be here on Tenerife. Then Madeline stopped talking and her face went very serious. There were the odd 'yes' and 'no' but that was it for the next fifteen minutes. Finally she said goodbye to Kennal and promised to call him back later that evening.

'Is everything ok, Mum?'

'Yes, darling, it was Kennal just checking we've arrived ok and that the bungalow suits us. Also, he said he's had an email from a mutual friend who mentioned to him about the TV programme and his question to me was have I been asked to go on it. Well, I couldn't lie. He said he was pleased for me and thinks it could lead to lots of good things in the future. The odd thing was, he never asked if I was going to go back and do it ... he took it for granted that I would and simply asked if you would be able to cope here by yourself, running things. Apparently he's even come up with a solution for the cooking for guests if they need it! He knows a woman in Los Cristianos who would be able to help out so really you would just be doing what you came here to do. Darling, do you think that would work if I do decide to go back? One more thing, he has said he will pay you what he was going to pay both of us together! That's so kind of him, isn't it?'

Sophie couldn't believe how things were turning out.

****

Sophie spent the next hour convincing her mum that of course she could manage the villa on her own, so all the worrying about it didn't need to happen. Sophie thought she actually owed Kennal a big thank you and kept her fingers crossed that the guests would go out to eat most nights so there would be little or no need for anyone else to get involved. But the most exciting thing about all of it? Sophie would get to live in the bungalow all by herself for the whole of the summer and autumn!

Once back at the villa, Madeline went into overdrive getting all the paperwork together for

Sophie – who arrived on what day at what time, when they would be leaving, each group's requirements when it came to what had to be in the kitchen before they arrived, etc. Why it all had to be sorted today Sophie didn't know as the filming wouldn't get started for a few weeks. Surely her mum would stay and have a bit of a holiday first? The one thing that Madeline and Sophie had both agreed on was that they would go to Del Duque that night for a meal and a switch off from everything. Sophie was looking forward to visiting the very popular town, which Ramon had claimed had the best restaurants.

After a couple of hours in the bungalow by herself relaxing, Sophie was showered and enjoying a glass of wine on the veranda while waiting for her mum to finish getting ready for dinner. Sophie had been avoiding finally turning her phone back on but she knew she had to do it eventually. Now was as good a time as any.

As expected, dozens of text messages flashed up on the screen – all from the same number. Without even looking at them she quickly deleted the lot, then did the same with the emails from the same person. There was one email from her neighbour, Greg, but Sophie knew she could read that one later because if anything was really wrong with her flat he would have left a voicemail. Phone turned back off, Sophie put it away and turned back to the view. With the future ahead looking brighter than ever, why waste time dwelling on the past?

****

The bus over to Del Duque didn't take long and to be honest they probably could have walked, which would likely have done them both good. As it was early in the year, the roads and the town were quite quiet, but they could both imagine the atmosphere come the heart of the summer when tourists would be abundant. After a walk around the town they found a little restaurant that was quite busy and looked to be full of locals. Assuming that meant the food must be good, they requested a table inside as the evening was still chilly. Sophie was shocked that Madeline was really quiet, almost nervous. Pushing her to reveal what was wrong, she confided that she wasn't sure she could still act after nearly thirty years away from it. This was a side of Madeline that Sophie had never seen before but she was glad that her mum was comfortable being open with her and talking about her uncertainty.

'I have the same feeling in my stomach I had when I was a young, sixteen-year-old actress just starting out,' Madeline confessed.

'I know, but I believe in you, Mum. You can do this – and you *should* do this! I want this to be such a success for you because you really deserve it.'

A young woman interrupted when she arrived to take their order and bring the wine. The food followed soon after and as mother and daughter both looked up they realised it was carried by someone they recognised – Luis!

'Good evening. How are you both? Have you settled in ok? Sorry, I won't ask you lots of questions – the food will get cold. Please enjoy your meal,' he said before rushing away.

'Sophie, if I'm not mistaken, that's the second time that young man has avoided talking to me,' Madeline observed, a confused look on her face.

Now that her mum mentioned it, she could be right. But the question of why would need to be asked later because they were both too hungry to do anything other than get stuck into eating. The food was lovely, the wine flowed – though perhaps a little too fast – and they both agreed that this was a special night, one that they would remember for a long time to come. Looking at the time later on and seeing how late it had gotten, they decided to get a taxi back to the villa as they weren't sure if the buses would still be running. Madeline asked for the bill, obviously hoping Luis would bring it so she could get into conversation with him, but it was another waiter who brought it over along with two complementary liquors. When they enquired about Luis, his colleague explained that he had left already as his shift was over.

Chapter 4

Sophie was shocked her mum hadn't used the dinner as an opportunity to bring up her avoiding her phone as she'd been expecting Madeline to spring more questions on her all night. In one way, Sophie was pleased for the reprieve, but in another she found she actually kind of wanted her to ask about it, as it would be nice to have someone else's perspective on things. But today was a whole new day and as well as continuing the discussion about the arrangements for the villa, Sophie knew she'd likely have opportunity to explain all about the person she was avoiding. Talking of Mark, Sophie was shocked that she was even considering talking about him to her mum as she'd never mentioned anything about her personal life to her before. But given the mess Sophie felt she had left behind, it was hard *not* to talk about it.

But no, it's his problem, not mine and now I'm here on the island of Tenerife, living and working at Villa Kennal, he's well and truly in the past, she thought to herself.

Opening the door with coffee in hand, there to greet her was the cat again. Sophie could tell this was going to be a daily thing, and if it was, perhaps she should put cat food on the shopping list? Not that the cat looked like he or she was hungry...

'Well, hello! I don't know your name so for now I will call you Mrmiss. I expect your life is quite fun, going from one villa to the next, being fed and fussed over, not a worry in the world and no ex-partners trying to reach you. The only thing you need to plan is where to lie in the sunshine. I promise you when I go shopping I will get you something – a little treat, some fish perhaps – but for now, I'm sorry to say I don't have anything. One thing I would love to know though is if you belong to that man up the lane. I'm sure I saw him again when we got out of the taxi last night.'

Looking at her watch Sophie saw it was nearly ten o'clock. Madeline would no doubt be up by now so perhaps she should go over to the villa and see if everything was ok? Looking over towards the villa Sophie noticed that the weather wasn't as nice today – the sky was very cloudy and it looked like there could be some rain. Normally she would Google the weather but that would mean switching her phone on and then there would be more messages from Mark to have to delete. Anyway, did it matter if it rained? There was plenty to be getting on with here at the villa.

Sophie also wanted to make a few changes in the bungalow as it was going to be her home for the next eight months. If she could find some boxes she could put away a few – well, actually quite a lot – of Kennal's personal possessions and make it feel more like her space, plus she might move the furniture around in the lounge/kitchen/dining area. She was hardly ever going to use the table so that could be pushed into a corner and then that would allow for the sofa to be angled a little, which would make the room look bigger. It was exciting, this whole adventure, which was something Sophie never thought it was going to be.

'Good morning, darling, what horrible weather – windy and it looks like it's going to rain. *Not* the weather I was expecting here on Tenerife, but saying that, it is very early in the year, so... I'm sorry I'm late coming over; I've been on the phone with Kennal. He's organised for the woman who he's hired to cook the evening meals when required, to pop in and see us tomorrow; her name is Cristina. And on that subject, you are definitely sure it's ok if I go back to England?'

'Yes, Mum. I'll be fine!'

'Ok, well, if you're sure? Oh! There is one other thing – he said he doesn't have a cat but when I described it he knew it as it pops in now and again. Apparently it is a she and she belongs to the man in the villa behind this one. Kennal said he is a little odd and not very friendly – the man, not the cat – and he is British. Also, the gardener that comes in each week is called Javier and you will have to pay him cash from the petty cash tin that Kennal has left in the kitchen cupboard.'

'Mum, just take a breath. I was thinking we could go and sit in the upstairs lounge in the villa. That way we can chat and have the lovely view at the same time and you can tell me everything Kennal said. Or, if you're hungry, I could nip out and get some food? It will only take me, say, an hour or so, then I will come straight over to the villa when I get back and we can catch up and sort out your arrangements for going back to England. Are you sure you don't want to stay a little longer?'

'No, darling, I need to have time at home to get my head around everything before rehearsals start. If I was here with you, I wouldn't be giving it my full attention and that's not fair to you. Now, I am feeling peckish so why don't you head out and we'll meet back in the villa in a bit?'

****

The plan agreed, Sophie headed off feeling good. Madeline was returning to England and Sophie would be running Villa Kennal. Her life was sorted for the next little while and with a woman on call to come in and cook if need be, all she'd need to worry about was keeping the place clean and tidy and helping the guests with reservations, groceries or directions when needed.

As Sophie went out through the gate, there was the man again, walking towards her. This time he was carrying shopping bags but as Sophie got nearer to him, he walked to the opposite side of the lane. It was so obvious he didn't want to say hello, let alone get into conversation, so she just smiled and said good morning. She did get a nod out of him in response, but that was all.

It was only a few minutes' walk to the supermarket but she was conscious to only buy as much as she could comfortably carry. There was no need for big bottles of water as there were loads already in the villa's store room, so she just needed enough food to feed them for today and perhaps tomorrow, plus some wine. Sophie smiled to herself. She felt good and this was now her life for the next eight months. How difficult could it be? Once the weather picked up and the guests started to arrive her life would be spent in between working and sitting on her veranda ... which reminded her, she needed to get some fish for the cat.

As she was coming out of the supermarket, she noticed someone she recognised getting off their scooter – it was Luis. She wished she had asked her mum what Kennal had to say about him so she could be prepared for their next meeting, but one thing was for sure, he wouldn't be rushing off today as she was going to corner him. Anyway, he did say that if they needed help with anything they should give him a call. *Think, Sophie, what excuse could there be for him to have to call at the villa so Mum can meet him properly? Something to do with maintenance, maybe?*

'Hi, Luis, how are you today? We were sorry you left the restaurant last night before we had time to chat. Would I be right to assume you're probably "in a hurry" again today?'

'Yes, I am, actually. Did you enjoy your meal and

are you settling in ok at the villa?'

Sophie could tell he didn't want to talk as he couldn't get on his bike quick enough and was fidgeting with the gears, obviously eager to take off.

'Yes, we had a lovely meal, thank you, and we are more than happy with everything at the villa ... apart from a couple of things I need your help with. But as you are rushing off again, they can wait until you have an hour or so to spare ... that's if you can find an hour in your extremely busy schedule? It doesn't have to be today, perhaps in a few days' time, if you have a slot in your diary?'

Sophie could see she had ruffled his feathers but couldn't understand why as he'd told her she should ask for help if she needed it. Given that he had never met her or her mum before she wondered if he might have a problem with Kennal, but then, he had been the one to hand over the keys to the place so they must be friends or at least know each other quite well.

'Look, I can see that you are a very busy chap. I have your phone number so I'll just text you and then, once you've had a chance to check your schedule, you can let me know when you're free. Sound good?'

'Perhaps I can help now. What's the problem?'

Sophie had to think of a problem for him to put right or sort out first so she thanked him but said it wasn't an emergency and then made her excuses and hurried off. There was something very intriguing about Luis and she wanted to find out from her mum what Kennal had to say about him.

Walking away, it crossed her mind that if she texted him she would have to leave her phone on to see his response. That meant if Mark called her phone it wouldn't go straight to voicemail but instead would ring incessantly. Perhaps she'd have to find another way to contact Luis...

She decided to worry about that tomorrow as today was about sorting her mum out and top of the list was eating the food she'd just bought as Sophie was starving.

As she was walking back up to the villa she heard someone say 'hello'. Turning around, she saw it was the taxi driver, Ramon. He asked her if they had settled in ok and Sophie said they had. She also explained how their plans had changed a bit and though she was still staying for the summer to look after the villa, her mum was going back to the UK.

'That will be nice for you – like a working holiday! I thought Kennal would have had Luis looking after it but then perhaps the stories are correct... Sorry! Ignore me, I was thinking aloud. You have my card and number if any of the guests need a taxi, also, remember that if you are over in La Caleta you should pop into my mum's shop. I don't need to tell you its name as you can't miss it – it's the one with all the colour in the window! Right, I must go. Have a lovely day, Sophie.'

Sophie waved goodbye to Ramon and as she carried on walking she thought about what he'd said. What was that all about Luis looking after Villa Kennal? Had she somehow taken his job? Was that why he'd been so rude and abrupt each time they'd met? She was determined to find out more about Luis because right now none of it was making any sense.

****

Back at the villa, she started to familiarise herself with the huge kitchen. Everything in the cupboard seemed very new, from utensils to crockery, and as there was a dishwasher, she hoped guests would use it so that there would be less work for her.

Having put bacon in the oven and buttered the

fresh bread she'd bought at the market, Sophie was looking forward to a perfect lunch of bacon sandwiches.

'Darling, I don't want to keep going on but are you sure you will be ok here by yourself?' Madeline asked as she walked into the kitchen.

'Yes, Mum, and you really don't need to keep worrying about it. Let me ask you this, do you want to go back into acting? And are you excited about this opportunity you've been given? If the answer to either question is yes then there is nothing else to discuss. Now, go upstairs and pull the chairs right up to the window so we can take in the view across Los Kalanchoe while we eat. I will bring lunch up for us just as soon as it's ready.'

****

It started to rain very heavily while they were enjoying their sandwiches so once they'd finished eating Sophie went down to the kitchen and made them each a cup of tea, bringing a couple of sweet pastries back up as well.

There was thankfully no more talk of whether she would be able to cope by herself but the one thing they did chat about was what Kennal had to say about Luis. Madeline explained that at the end of September the previous year he had to fly to America to do some filming for the pilot of his new TV programme. The villa still had guests staying until the middle of October so Kennal had paid Luis to look after the place as he had helped him out in the past and was a very good worker. The last guests all left on the tenth of the month and Kennal was due back on the eightieth and in between it was Luis's job to do a thorough clean and then shut the villa up for the winter by stripping all the bedding, defrosting the fridges and freezers, etc. It was all very straightforward but there was a slight hiccup. Kennal's work in America finished early so he got a flight back on the twelfth. He didn't let Luis know he was returning earlier than planned – not because he wanted to catch him out, of course, but because he just didn't think it was important. His bungalow hadn't been used since he left so as nothing had to be prepared for him there was really no need to give Luis a head's up. When he arrived back at nine in the evening, pulling up outside the villa, he went to unlock the gate and realised there was loud music coming from inside the complex.

Luis had invited friends for a party and the place was heaving. Not only that, he had let some of them stay in the bedrooms of the villa so the place was a right mess. Kennal was furious and fired him on the spot.

It all made sense to Sophie now. *This* was why Luis was so standoffish. Luis was likely mad at himself for messing up but he had no right to take his anger out on her and her mum just because they were doing the job he wanted to be doing. It was nothing to do with them – it was his problem and he had brought it on himself.

'Oh dear. I'm so glad I've found that out before I arrange for him to come and sort the problems. It also makes sense now what Ramon said.'

'Who is Ramon, darling, and what problems, Sophie? I wasn't aware of any.'

'Ramon was the taxi driver that picked us up from the airport and there aren't any problems at the moment but I will think of something. Luis needs to be taught a lesson for being rude to us.'

'So you have been in contact with the taxi driver? Darling, you haven't wasted any time! But I will say he's a lovely choice – polite and very good looking.'

'Mum, I'm here to work for the summer, not to

find a boyfriend! I just bumped into Ramon when I was coming back from the supermarket.'

'Well, let's see what the situation is at the end of the eight months...'

Sophie let her have the final word as there was no point continuing the conversation.

****

Pastries eaten and tea drunk, it was time to map out a plan for the next eight months. Sophie started by setting herself a routine and once that was done, she had time to rearrange the bungalow and to set up a little office area on the table in the corner. She also booked a flight back to the UK for Madeline, managing to get a cheap one for the next day. She felt bad her mum would be going so soon but she knew that once Madeline was back in London she would be able to get organised for the TV drama and that would help her to relax a little.

The afternoon had flown by and it was now nearly seven o'clock. The wine had been opened and Sophie was starting to prepare dinner for the two of them. The rain was still pouring down and as she stood at the hob cooking a stir fry it crossed her mind how lovely, fresh and modern the villa was, but also how she much preferred the bungalow. Everything was so much smaller and cosier and within a few days, once all Kennal's clutter had been packed away, it would look even more like her ideal home. She also thought it might be nice to buy some throws to cover up the settee and chairs, along with some new cushions, but that could wait until after everything was boxed up and taken to one of the store rooms. Thinking of that gave her an idea... It was probably a little unfair but ... no, it would be good to see what reaction she got.

'There you go, Mum, I hope it's ok. Let me pour

us another wine and then I will answer the questions you are no doubt dying to ask – no, sorry, that didn't sound right. I meant the questions you have the right to know the answers to,' Sophie said as she served up the stir fry.

'Well, darling, I have to say my head is in a complete spin. One, the acting job, and two, the villa, but more importantly, Sophie, is your situation – the one you have obviously run away from.'

Sophie started at the beginning and explained that it was four years ago that she first met Mark. He worked for the parent technology company that oversaw her own and they met from time to time at meetings. When that happened, they chatted and had a laugh, and she started to look forward to going to the meetings a lot more because it was a chance to see him. Then, one evening, about a dozen or so of them went for a drink after work to celebrate someone's birthday, which was nice. Everything was going well and when it was time to leave Mark offered to walk her to the bus stop. She had butterflies in her stomach – nervous and excited about being alone with him for the first time.

'It sounds so promising. What went wrong?' Madeline asked curiously.

'He was married. But of course I didn't know that back when he walked me to the bus stop, so when he kissed me I was, of course, thrilled. We saw each other off and on over the next few months but he could never stay the night at my flat because he lived with his mother – or so he said – and because she suffered with her nerves, our relationship had to be a secret. I foolishly believed him and the relationship went on for years, until I found out about his wife. He still wanted to keep seeing me on the side but how could I be with a man who was married to someone else? And though I knew I should hate him for lying to me I couldn't switch off from him as we still saw each other at work meetings at least once a month. I loved what I did, but having put my life on hold waiting for him to choose between me and his mother I couldn't face the prospect of facing him ever again. So, when my boss told me the company would be doing some downsizing, I volunteered to take redundancy in the place of someone else. My boss was shocked and offered me a promotion if I stayed but I just couldn't stay there if it meant having to keep Mark in my life. So I walked away from my career. What a waste I've made of my life.'

Sophie was surprised at how upset she felt finally telling her mum the truth, but then, this was the first time she had spoken about this to *anyone*. She hadn't told her friends the full story about Mark as they would have laughed at a boyfriend who claimed he had to spend so much time with his mum. Perhaps if she had talked to them or her mum she would have seen his lie for what it was much sooner, instead of thinking he was just a really devoted son and a genuinely good person.

'Sophie, I don't know what to say and I'm certainly not going to judge you. I'm so sorry you've never been able to talk to me about this before. So many years you've carried this burden all by yourself...'

'It's ok, there's nothing to be said. I loved him but he lied ... and he made me complicit in his deceit.'

'Look, I know it's late, darling, and we both need some sleep, but can I just ask one thing? How did things end exactly?'

'Very simply and very quick, actually. It was a Sunday and I had nipped to the shops for some food. Mark had said he was going to come around for some lunch later on, but then I had a text from him to say he was doing family things with his mother and he couldn't make it. This kind of last minute cancellation was nothing new – it happened all the time and I was used to it – so I got my shopping and walked through a little park that I don't normally go to on the way back to my flat. It was cold and I was in a hurry and that's when I saw him. He was kicking a ball with a little boy and there was a woman watching them, and I realised that it wasn't his mother I was competing with, but a wife and a child. I was a mistress. The other woman. A bit on the side. And it just hit me, what a dreadful thing I had been doing. I didn't need anyone to tell me how wrong it was and I'm still full of guilt.

'As I stood there, looking from a distance, he saw me. I reached into my bag and got my phone out and texted him just two words: *it's over*.'

'Oh, Sophie, I'm so very sorry. But you need to realise that you did nothing wrong. All you did was trust a man you were in love with one hundred per cent. But what does upset me is that you felt you couldn't tell me about this before now. I could have helped! I don't know how, but I really would have tried. But then I guess I know why you haven't – it's because I'm me, Madeline Mundey, the woman that's always in control, the woman that thinks she knows everything and that what she says is always right. But I needed to be your mum, not her, and so it's not you that should be feeling bad, but me. I'm so sorry. I should have been there for you when you needed me most.'

'No, Mum, you weren't to know any of this. How could you? I had a boyfriend that wanted me to keep our relationship secret from everyone and so I did. I can see now how much this need for secrecy has affected my relationships with my friends, but even more so with you. I'm so sorry.'

Chapter 5

It had been two days since Madeline had flown back to the UK and in those couple of days Sophie hadn't stopped. From first thing in the morning to last thing at night, she spent her time familiarising herself with the villa, making notes on every room and going through the cupboards of bed linen and towels to make sure each guest had ample. She did the same with the kitchen, making sure everything the guests might need to prepare a meal for themselves was there. She had also been in email contact with Kennal and they had arranged to speak on the phone in a few days' time. To prepare, she had got all the bookings and paperwork ready and would have it in front of her when they spoke to ensure she came across very professional, knowing exactly what she was doing.

The far more exciting task she'd completed was rearranging and decluttering the bungalow. She had been to one of the hardware cum clothes shops – actually it sold pretty much everything – and she had bought some cushions and throws. The place looked so different, and much bigger, and she was over the moon with the changes. She had mentioned the prospect of her changing things in the bungalow to Kennal in an email and asked if it would be possible to do and he had replied quickly, saying he didn't have a problem with it and telling her where she could get some boxes to put his things in.

One of the things she didn't mention to him was that she'd brought one of the spare sun loungers and a couple of chairs from the villa's pool deck up to her little veranda – one for her and one for the cat, who clearly didn't want to leave the veranda now that she was being regularly fed whenever she visited. Sophie had also fetched a couple of pots from the shed, which she hoped to find some plants to put in. The veranda really was her favourite place at Villa Kennal, although she did hope no one could hear her as she seemed to be spending a lot of time telling the cat her life story.

She had also had a meeting with Cristina about the cooking. She seemed a really nice girl, though not what Sophie had imagined as she was very glamorous and full of life. It would be perfect to have her help if the guests ever wanted to eat in, but Sophie couldn't help but wonder how Cristina already seemed to be familiar with the villa and the kitchen, as Kennal hadn't mentioned her having worked there before. She tried to get an answer out of her but every time Sophie brought the subject up, Cristina changed it and talked about the food. It did cross Sophie's mind that perhaps Cristina and Kennal were more than friends, but that wasn't a problem, or any of Sophie's business, really. As long as Sophie didn't have to cook, she was happy, and so they had agreed that Cristina would drop over a folder of sample menus. That way the guests could choose what they wanted to eat on specific nights and Cristina could prepare parts of the meals in advance.

With so much happening, the last few days had flown by, but later today would come the moment she had been waiting for. Sophie had spoken to Luis and he had said he could spare a couple of hours to help her with any issues at the villa. On the phone he'd kept asking her what she needed him to sort out but she didn't let on because she knew he wouldn't be happy to be called out just to help her move boxes into one of the store rooms as it was something she could do all by herself. But she wanted a chance to find out more about him and it wouldn't hurt if she could get back at him a little bit for being so rude and arrogant in their previous interactions. He would probably tell her to get lost and move the boxes herself but at least she'd have the satisfaction of knowing they were even.

But in the three hours before Luis's visit she needed to be getting on with a few other things that Kennal had asked her to do. One task was to contact the gardener, Javier, and arrange for him to come and trim some of the trees. She also had to arrange for the pool to be cleaned.

None of that was a problem, but it did mean she would need to switch her phone on and leave it on. Sophie knew she'd have to eventually – because she wanted her mum and Kennal to both be able to get hold of her – but it meant she would likely be bombarded with calls and texts from Mark. Unfortunately, she couldn't keep putting it off for ever.

Turning her phone on, it started ringing immediately. Her heart felt as though it had stopped but looking at the caller ID she was relieved to find it was her mum.

****

After half an hour not being able to get a word in edgewise, Sophie came off the call feeling good. Her mum was all sorted and ready for a hectic few months of filming, and she was excited to get started. Once again, Sophie was glad she'd talked her into taking the role.

About to put her phone down, Sophie saw there was a text from Luis to say he would be late and he could only spare her half an hour so she needed to prioritise what was important for him to do. He was really testing her patience now. Why did he have to be so rude? It wasn't her fault she was here managing the villa – if he hadn't messed up, he would be doing the job. She thought she should perhaps mention that to him, but worried it would be a little unnecessarily cruel.

As she went to make herself a little bit more presentable her phone went again and one glance at the screen told her this was the call she had been dreading. Should she ignore it or get it over with? She remembered three months ago, when she had last spoken to Mark. He had come up to her in the street, begging her not to end their relationship. Gosh, did she just use the word 'relationship'? That wasn't the right term for what they'd shared – it was an affair. Nothing more, nothing less. She was his bit on the side and seeing him with his wife and son she'd realised it should have been obvious all along. She was so embarrassed that she'd believed that silly story of his about needing to be there for his mother.

She waited until the call went to voicemail and after a moment of hesitation, she listened to the message. It was brief – Mark asking her to please call him back. She couldn't help admitting that she'd missed his voice, but deep down she knew it was best to get it over with so that her time here on Tenerife could really get going. But it would be on her terms. She would make the call and ask the questions.

Three ... two ... one... Here goes.

'Hi, Mark. Look, I don't want to talk to you. Please stop calling and texting.'

'But, Sophie, I need to... I want to explain.'

'Mark, if you don't let me speak, I will end the call. I'm not interested in ever discussing what happened between us. It was wrong and it should never have happened.'

'But please... Can we just meet up so I can explain?'

'No. I'm not in London anymore and won't be for quite some time. When I hang up, I will be blocking your number. I have been so stupid I've sacrificed my friends and my relationship with my mum because of you. That ends now. Goodbye.'

It was harder than Sophie had expected to speak to him. He'd sounded so upset but it wasn't just that; there was something else in his voice, a defeatist tone, like he had given up. But that wasn't her problem anymore, and she wasn't hiding from him anymore. She had put him in his place. The phone went again before she had time to block Mark's number but thankfully it wasn't him, it was her next door neighbour back in London, Greg, who was keeping an eye on her flat while she was away.

****

Coming off the phone to Greg twenty minutes later, Sophie gave a sigh. Apparently Mark had been around to the flat looking for her several times and each visit he looked worse – thin, unshaven, even dirty, and most of all upset. Greg said he had eventually even given in and let Mark come in for a chat and a coffee and he'd found out the whole story. Mark also told Greg he'd missed Sophie so much he'd confessed everything to Jane, his wife, and she had thrown him out of the family home as a result. He'd been staying on a friend's sofa ever since and was currently off work with depression. Greg said he felt sorry for him and Sophie had to admit she did too. Why did all of this have to follow her to Tenerife? In the end, it was a conversation she wished she hadn't had to have, but it was also nice to know someone was worried about her and wanted to check in.

Turning to face the window she could see Luis coming through the gate. The first thing she noticed was that he was looking quite scruffy in a very sexy way. After that phone call she wasn't in the mood for Luis and this silly game she was playing with him, but she would have to put on a smile and get on with it. Perhaps she wouldn't mention moving the boxes as she'd planned, as she could quite easily do that herself, and instead make something up to do with electrics or plumbing. Something quick, so she could get rid of him.

'Hi, Luis, thank you for coming. How are you today?' she asked as she strolled outside to meet him on the path.

'I've not come for a social visit, I'm just here to sort out the things that you aren't capable of. By the way, as I was coming through the gate I noticed that the place needs a good sweep and mop. It looks like it's not been done for days. Isn't that what you are paid to do?'

Sophie was gobsmacked and actually lost for words, but he would not be getting away with speaking to her like that. Because their paths would no doubt be crossing for many months to come, she needed to cut him down to size ... and there was no time like the present.

'What was it you wanted me to do that is so urgent?'

'And good morning to you as well. I see that your issues have only grown. I'm sorry, but-'

'What issues?'

'That chip on your shoulder, of course! Oh dear you are so very bitter, aren't you? But then, perhaps you should have thought of the repercussions of your actions before you tried to rip Kendal off. You don't want to be here right now and you can't stand me because I'm doing the job you wanted, so you know what? Have your way. Leave. I will sort my problems out by myself for now and I'm sure if I email Kennal he will have the name of someone else who can help in future. Goodbye, Luis.'

With that she turned and started to walk towards the villa. In her head she was counting to ten, wondering what number she would get to before he said something because she knew that the last thing he needed was her to contact Kennal about him being obstinate and refusing to help. He was in enough trouble with him as it was.

Seven ... eight ... nine...

'So you think you know all about it, then? You don't. It was a big misunderstanding but it's sorted now. There is no need to get anyone else in. I can help. What was it you wanted doing?'

'For a start, I need you to lose the attitude. I didn't take your job, you messed that up on your own, so your argument isn't with me or my mum, it's with Kennal, ok? And I'm not asking you to be my friend but I'm here for eight months and I've been told you are here to help if I need anything, so the least you can do is treat me nicely. I hope your childish behaviour is now behind us and we can start our working relationship over again?'

Luis nodded.

'Good. Now, I will go and get us a drink and then we can talk. Would you like beer or wine or something else?'

He said beer and she suggested they go and sit on the villa's terrace as there was no way he was coming with her up to the bungalow. As he turned towards the terrace and Sophie walked up to get the drinks, she realised she was shaking. Thankfully, it looked like she had won this one as he looked like he had been put in his place and had clearly been lost for words at her outburst.

Sophie took her time getting the drinks as she wanted him to think about what had just happened. She knew things could go either way now – either his pride would have been hurt and he would be angry, or he would be apologetic. She thought it was likely the latter as he would probably have walked out by now if it was the former.

'There you go, one beer. I brought a glass but I didn't know if you'd sooner drink from the bottle.'

'Thanks, a glass is fine, and I'm sorry. It was just that-'

'Sorry is enough. It's all forgotten and in the past now, never to be mentioned again. Tell me about yourself, how long have you been here in Los Kalanchoe?'

It took a little while before the atmosphere changed and they both relaxed but after a couple more drinks and a few hours spent chatting Sophie was pleased that they were getting on really well with each other. A few times, Sophie even saw him look at her with a huge smile that made her blush and feel a little uncomfortably warm, but she stupidly liked it.

Sophie had explained a bit about her life – being made redundant, her mum having to go back and film a television show – but the best bit was that she'd found out all about Luis. He was born here and apart from a couple of years spent working in Lanzarote, which he tried to brush over and clearly didn't want to talk about, he had lived here. It had been odd the way he refused to give her details about his time away, as if he wanted to forget those years, but she hadn't felt it was her place to press him, and all in all she was just glad that he was opening up at all. It gave her a chance to see the real him and not the bitter and twisted version she and her mum had first met.

'Sophie, you haven't said what it was you needed me to do. What's the reason I'm here?'

'Right, yes. I'm so sorry to have taken up your time, Luis. I know you said you didn't have long as you were busy. And didn't you have to be somewhere?'

'No, it's ok. When you went to get the drinks, I texted my friend and said I couldn't meet him, so I have all the time in the world.'

She had been starting to warm to him and now they had cleared the air he did give the impression he actually wanted to be here and to help out, but she needed to think quickly. What should she say? The truth? That she wanted to teach him a lesson and get him moving boxes when that was something she was more than capable of doing herself? No, that would upset the fragile truce they'd only just brokered, so she told him it could wait for another day and distracted him by asking about the area – places she would need to know about to recommend to guests – and asking if there was anything she would need to know about the villa in case of emergencies. He seemed to accept her assertion that the work could wait and happily filled her in on everything she'd asked. She made notes as he spoke, which she knew would be a big help to her later.

'I'm getting hungry, do you fancy something to eat? I haven't got a lot here – cheese, ham, bread, crisps – it's all very British, I'm afraid. Or perhaps another beer?'

'That all sounds fine by me,' Luis said with another one of his charming smiles.

Sophie didn't know what was happening between them but knew she was enjoying his company, and enjoying how he was looking at her as she got up to grab the food.

The moment was interrupted though by the sound of the gate opening and the arrival of Cristina. It looked like she had come to deliver the file of recipes for the guests to look through, but she stopped in her tracks when she saw Sophie and Luis together on the terrace.

'I've just remembered, Sophie, I have to be somewhere. Sorry, but I'm going to have to skip the food. Bye for now,' Luis said abruptly.

With that, he left, and as he passed Cristina

Sophie noticed there was a little tension between them, even though they didn't actually acknowledge each other. Now what was that all about?

Chapter 6

The first guests were scheduled to arrive in less than a week and Sophie was getting excited. Whether she would be saying that once they were here was another matter. She had gone through all their requirements and noted that they only wanted one meal cooked for them in the villa; it was to celebrate the grandfather's birthday, plus other holiday makers they knew would be coming to the party, so all in all there would be about thirty people. Cristina was ok with that as the rest of the time they were here they would be eating out every night.

With the food plans arranged, all Sophie had to do was focus on the cleaning.

For today though, she was off to do a shop and had arranged for Ramon to pick her up with all her purchases from the supermarket. But before all that she had to call Greg as he'd texted to say he needed to talk to her about her flat. She called his number and it went straight to voicemail but then her mind started to think the worst. What was wrong with the flat? What might have happened? Whatever it was, she was thankful that Greg lived next door and was able to alert her. She decided she would keep trying as she walked down to the shops.

Just as she was locking the gate behind her, she heard someone calling out. It was in English and turning around she could see the man from up the lane. He was looking behind bushes and under a parked car and he was calling the name 'Mable'. It quickly crossed Sophie's mind that he might be looking for Mrmiss.

'Hello, I hope you don't mind me asking, but are you looking for a cat? A black one?'

'Yes, I've not seen her for a few days. Normally, if she's been out, she always comes home at night.'

Sophie explained the situation and apologised for encouraging the cat to stay with her at the bungalow. She also introduced herself and told him she was on Tenerife looking after Villa Kennal for the summer. For some strange reason, the man didn't seem to really want to get into conversation, even when Sophie asked him if he wanted to go in and get the cat. He shook his head and said he was just happy to know the cat was ok. And then, without saying goodbye, he turned around and walked away. He hadn't even introduced himself, which was all a bit odd, but before Sophie could wonder on it, her phone went – it was Greg.

****

Half an hour later, having come off the phone to Greg, Sophie sat having a coffee in the bakery. What had she just done? Well, she knew what she had done – she had agreed to rent her flat out to Greg's sister. That was a good thing, as it would be bringing in a little income, and at least it wouldn't be empty, but the thing she wasn't sure about was that Greg's sister wanted to rent the flat for twelve months. So, the big question was: what would she do when the eight months here working at the villa were over? The obvious answer would be to move in with her mum, but the two of them under the same roof for all that time...? No, she couldn't worry about that now, she'd think about it down the road.

Looking at the time on her phone she saw she needed to get a move on as she had less than an hour to get the shopping done before Ramon was scheduled to meet her. Walking around the supermarket, she couldn't concentrate – her mind was back in England and she had rushed out without her shopping list. Thankfully she had a week before the visitors arrived and she could return to the supermarket before then. Once outside she realised she didn't really need Ramon to give her a lift as she only had two bags, but as she had booked him she might as well take the ride.

Once in the car, she explained about coming out without the list and having a call from the UK that put her off, though she didn't go into details. They both had a giggle about forgetting the list, as this was the most important part of her job so far, and she arranged with Ramon for a second supermarket pick-up in a couple of days.

'So will you manage ok running the place by yourself now your mum's not here? Cleaning, cooking and everything else that goes with it?'

'Yes, my mum was going to cook any meals that were required but Kennal's arranged for a lovely girl called Cristina to come and do that.'

'Do you mean *the* Cristina? I thought it was all over between her and Luis, but saying that, I've lost count of how many times they've split up and got back together again. Right, here we are, and I will see you again soon. Hopefully you will get everything you need then. Have a good afternoon!'

As she got out of the car a box of cat biscuits fell out of her bag onto the backseat and Ramon noticed and called to her so she didn't forget them.

'You've not been here that long and you have a cat already?'

'No, but a cat seems to have adopted me. It belongs to a man in a villa behind Kennal's. I met him this morning. He was a little strange but more than happy for me to take care of Mable.'

'That's Graham. Yes, I wouldn't say strange... Sad. Yes, that's the word – sad. It's such a shame how his life has turned out.'

Sophie paid Ramon the fare and headed into the villa. She wondered what he meant by 'sad'. She was also intrigued by what he'd had to say about

47

Cristina. So that's why Luis couldn't wait to leave the villa the other day – because by the look on his face they certainly weren't back together at the moment. It was all very interesting and she couldn't wait to find out more about the lovely Luis, who she was starting to warm to, but then, if he knew Cristina was going to be cooking at the villa, would that make him not want to be there?

She put away the little bit of shopping she had managed to get – at least half of it wasn't on the list when she checked – and just as she was locking the villa up and heading back to the bungalow, her phone beeped. It was an email from Kennal to say someone would be arriving in the morning for just three nights – probably a couple but he wasn't sure about that – and they would use the upstairs bedroom so he would advise locking the doors of all the downstairs bedrooms. If she had the slightest problem with them she was to phone him right away, and there was a PS saying that the name of the visitor was 'Emily' ... and she was Kennal's daughter.

How could Sophie contact him about his own daughter? Surely in three days she couldn't be that much of a problem? She sent a quick text to her mum to see if she knew anything about this Emily and a reply came right back saying, *not sure which daughter that is*. Well, that wasn't very helpful. What could she do now? Who would know more about the mysterious Emily? Ramon, perhaps?

No, there was only one thing for it – she would have to ask Luis.

Given that he'd worked at the villa before he'd likely be able to fill her in on Emily, but she found she was nervous to call him. This time last week it would have been a problem, but since those few hours the other day were so lovely, perhaps he felt the same and would be happy to help her? After all, he'd cancelled the meeting with his friend and he

48

had said he would have something to eat with her. Who knows where the evening would have gone if Cristina hadn't arrived.

Right, she was going to call him.

When the phone rang through to voicemail she left him a message.

'Hi, Luis, I was just wondering if you were free for a meal before the first official guests arrive next week? Oh, by the way, I've someone staying tomorrow for a couple of nights and I wondered if you might know them. Give me a call back when you have a minute.'

It didn't take long to get an answer as he phoned right back, very curious to know who was staying. As Kennal hadn't said it was a secret she told him it was Emily. At first, Luis didn't say much and then he told her that the villa would be filthy by the time Emily left, and she would probably have a boyfriend with her – though which one he wasn't sure as there were several. He also took her up on the offer of a meal and said he would be there that night at eight o'clock.

****

Sophie spent the rest of the afternoon and early evening giving the villa a good dusting and making up the upstairs bed. In the morning she would sweep and mop outdoors. She smiled to herself at how this was actual work now. Things had to be done at a given time as this was what she was being paid for and she was getting used to the schedule of tasks. Surprisingly, these last couple of days she had been feeling like she belonged here and was getting the impression that life was going to be ok for the summer.

It got to six thirty and she headed back up to the bungalow.

'Are you waiting for me, Mable? So, tell me about Graham. Why he is sad and why isn't he bothered you are staying here and not with him? Surely you can see he is not happy and needs a little love?'

After a quick shower she threw some chicken and vegetables in a casserole pot. Hopefully Luis wasn't a vegetarian. The beer was cooling in the fridge and a little bit of music added ambiance. She was looking forward to the evening and finding out all about Emily and, if she pushed her luck, what the situation was between him and Cristina as well.

****

'Let me get this right, Emily lives on the other side of the island, in Santa Cruz, and comes here to stay with her boyfriend, and Kennal puts up with her leaving the place a mess?' Sophie asked once they'd sat down to eat and Luis had filled her in about Kennal's daughter.

'Yes, and by the way, this chicken is beautiful. Do you mind if I finish off what's in the dish? The cat is looking at it as if she should be having some as well...'

'No, I don't mind, I've had enough, thanks. And as for Mable, she's got biscuits if she's hungry. You go ahead though. You certainly like your food, but then I suppose you are used to nice meals with Cristina being such a good cook...?'

Sophie could see she had caught him off guard with the Cristina comment but he carried on eating, obviously thinking of what to say, so she continued their conversation about Emily. Now she knew all about her, Sophie couldn't wait to meet her. Once Luis had finished eating, she took everything back into the bungalow and brought him out another beer and a glass of wine for herself.

'I think it best I explain, just in case the story you've been told isn't the right one. Cristina is the reason you are here overseeing the villa instead of me. It was her dumping me that led to me having the party here at the villa and getting caught out by Kennal. I was upset and wasn't thinking straight; one friend popped in for a drink and before too long there were loads of us, loud music and lots of alcohol. And the rest is history, as they say.'

Sophie was interested to hear that Luis and Cristina's break-up had led to his ill-advised party but what she really wanted to know was if he was well and truly not with Cristina anymore, or if they were just on one of the breaks Ramon had said they frequently took. If that was the case, well, at least she would know where she stood with him.

'Yes, but that's the end of the story, Luis, how about the beginning? How did you get together? Were you a couple for a long time? Come on, I'm intrigued!'

Sophie had him in a corner. He couldn't just sit there and say nothing, so once he'd poured the beer into the glass he took a deep breath and started. 'I met her when I was working in Lanzarote about eight or nine years ago. To start with, we had a lot of fun together, both working long, hard hours in hotels and restaurants, but we also played hard as well. It was a great summer of non-stop partying but then I came back to Los Kalanchoe for a month to see my family and when I got back she had moved on to someone new. And that was that.'

'But it couldn't have been the end of things as you are both back here now.'

'You're right. It wasn't the end as we eventually got back together and even lived with one another for a few years, until she got bored again. That's when I came back here for good. The end of the affair, as they say.'

Sophie was confused. Why was Cristina here if they weren't together anymore? Had she followed him back in a bid to reunite? And if they aren't together now, why has she stayed? Sophie wanted to ask but she felt she was already grilling him and if the roles were reversed, would she want him to be asking questions about Mark? No, of course not.

'Go on, Sophie, I can tell you are itching to ask why she's here if we're no longer together, and the answer to that is that, apparently, she can't live with me and she can't live without me. At least, that's the answer she's been giving me for the last two years. Now, that's my story of being in Kalanchoe, what's yours? You must have a job and a home in England and surely you couldn't just drop everything and come here for the summer. Has something happened that you needed to get away from?'

'What do you mean?'

'Nothing really, I just sense the reason you've come to Tenerife for the summer is because you're running away from something or someone. Am I right?'

'No, I'm not running away from anything. I was made redundant and my mum was coming here so when she invited me along it was the obvious thing to do. It's good to have the break between jobs and today I've rented my flat out to the sister of a friend so I'm all set to stay here and focus on my work at the villa. In short, this is a nice and very welcome change of scenery.'

'Well if that's the case then I'm pleased for you. I was thinking that perhaps you had split up with a boyfriend and just needed to get away.'

Sophie was feeling uncomfortable and beginning to think she wanted to tell him the truth, but no, she wasn't ready to discuss Mark with anybody new. She started to clear the plates away and was about to offer Luis some dessert when he stood up and thanked her for the meal, saying it was time he should be leaving. Before she could say anything else, he was gone. It certainly wasn't the end of the evening she had been hoping for.

Chapter 7

'Good morning, Mable, what are you doing here? I thought you would be down living it up at Villa Kennal with the new lady and not here waiting for grumpy old Graham, but then, I do feed you so that might have something to do with it. I'm sorry, little cat, I know you aren't just here for the food but to be company for me. It's hard to believe that it's been two years – yes, two years! – since you entered my life the same day that my beloved Robert left it. Oh Mable, where have those two years gone? I feel the same today as I did when he died – lost, lonely and scared – and that can be summed up in one word: numb. And I know I say to you every day "what should I do?" but I still don't know the answer, and come to that, I really don't care. I hate this horrible morning feeling. It's as though I'm just waiting for eleven o'clock tonight to come around so I can go back to bed and sleep again. How long can I carry on like this?'

****

As Sophie opened the door to the veranda there was no Mable to greet her. This was unusual as she was normally always there waiting to be fed and yesterday Sophie had even gone to the trouble of buying her fresh fish. Right, enough of the cat, she had to get organised. Kennal's daughter would be arriving soon and she wanted to give a good first impression, even though Luis had said Emily wouldn't notice anything. The first thing Sophie did was lock all the downstairs bedrooms. She also emptied the big cupboard of all the spare towels and bedding, leaving just half a dozen towels, and put a bottle of wine and some beers in the fridge, along with some big bottles of water. Once all that was done, she started on the outside, sweeping, mopping and tidying. The morning flowed by and before long it was lunch time. She had expected Emily earlier but that wasn't a problem as the least amount of time she was here, the better.

****

Come three o'clock, Sophie was on the veranda of her bungalow and from where she sat, she could see through a gap in the bushes and trees if someone came through the gate. Afternoon turned to evening and she was starting to wonder if she should email Kennal to say his daughter hadn't arrived yet, when all of a sudden there was a lot of noise the other side of the wall of the villa complex and then the gate opened. She made her way down to greet her guests and she wasn't really surprised by what she saw because Luis had sort of warned her what to expect.

'Hi! You must be Emily. It's nice to meet you.'

'Is the villa open? If not, can you open it now?'

'The villa is unlocked so why don't you make your way up and I'll follow with the bags?'

Emily turned without a thank you and she and her guest wandered along the path towards the house.

This was going to be worse than she had thought. Not only did Emily have an attitude, she and her boyfriend were also very drunk. As Sophie watched them both stagger up the path to the front of the villa she got the impression the bloke hadn't been here before. Now she knew why Kennal had said to call him if there was trouble. But that was something she was determined not to do. She could handle this situation herself.

Sophie gave them a couple of minutes before following them so that she wouldn't have to make conversation with them. As she got closer she could hear music. The one bag they'd brought was as light as a feather in hand. Obviously they don't intend changing their clothes very often in the few days they were going to be here. She stood at the patio door and knocked. There was no reply so finally, after a minute, she shouted, 'I've left your bag on the kitchen work surface.' She was turning to leave when Emily appeared further along the corridor.

'Sorry, I've left your bag over there. Have a nice stay and shout if you need anything.'

'Actually I do. If you get a piece of paper you can write everything down.'

There was no 'please' or 'thank you' but Sophie decided to play Emily's little game. She knew there was a pad and pens in one of the kitchen drawers but she took her time getting them. By then, the scruffy lad had appeared and so they both started shouting out food shopping they needed – all of it junk food and booze. Sophie wrote it all down and didn't ask any questions. She hoped she'd be able to get a hold of Ramon to pick her up as it would be quite heavy.

'Right, if that's everything? Give me an hour and I will be back. Oh, I nearly forgot, have you the money for me?'

'No, you pay for it and I will give it to you later. Or don't you trust me?'

'It's not that I don't trust you, it's that I don't have the money.'

'Take it out of the money my dad's left for bills and bits and pieces.'

Sophie felt like saying no but was it worth it? They were both looking for an argument and she wasn't going to let that happen seeing as they were both drunk. She would just have to take it out of the float money and talk to Kennal about it later.

'One more thing before you go. Could you be

quick? I'm hungry.'

She ignored Emily's snide comment and went back up to the bungalow to get her bag and purse. A quick call to Ramon and they arranged that he would pick her up shortly and then wait for her outside the store.

****

'Hi, Sophie. What a way to start – having her here as your first guest,' Ramon said as she hopped into the back of his taxi. 'But I wouldn't worry. If she's rude, just ignore her. I've lost count of how many times Kennal has apologised to me for her behaviour. Anyway, you won't see that much of them, I would think, what with the way they were carrying on in the back of my taxi earlier.'

He went on to explain they were all used to Emily's visits and the trouble she left behind. He also mentioned that he hadn't recognised this boyfriend.

Once at the store, Sophie quickly did the shopping and back at the villa Ramon helped her carry everything in through the gate and up to the door. Sophie was just thanking him when Emily appeared.

'About time! I was beginning to think you had gone to Los Cristianos for it. Just put everything away in the fridge but leave out four of the beers. Oh, I didn't see you there, Ramon. You just can't take those big brown eyes off me, can you?'

'No, you are right, Emily, I was definitely looking at you ... and I was thinking, what the hell have you done with yourself? You've become a fine example of how *not* to grow up. See you later, Sophie, and good luck with this pair while they're here.'

Sophie wanted to laugh but she daren't. She

didn't even look in ether of their directions, she just carried on putting the shopping away. Ramon left and Emily muttered something about him just being jealous as she had turned him down years ago. Sophie thought to herself it had probably been the other way around, if truth be known. When Emily picked up the beers and headed up the stairs it was Sophie's cue to leave. Fingers crossed she wouldn't see her again, only the mess that she would undoubtedly leave behind.

Back at the bungalow the music from the villa was even louder. Sophie looked at the time and as it was only eight-fifteen she decided to head down to the town and get a pizza. Hopefully by the time she got back they would both be asleep and the music turned off.

****

Sophie was sitting in one of the little restaurants with a large glass of wine and waiting for her pizza to be cooked when in came Cristina. She waved and asked if she could join Sophie, jokingly asking if she was out avoiding Emily. Sophie smiled and thought it funny how everyone seemed to know the trouble she was when she came visiting. She also couldn't help but feel sorry for Kennal. And yet, why didn't he do anything to put a stop to his daughter's antics?

'Have you had one of these pizzas before? They are the best! I've tried to copy the way they make them but mine are useless. So, tell me, how are you settling in?'

'Yes, I must say I've never had such good pizza – this is fast becoming my second home! I'm settling in fine, thanks. I heard you're also newer to the area and you've not lived here that many years? Luis was telling me you worked together in Lanzarote a few years ago. That must have been fun.'

'Yes, we were a lot younger then and were very silly – there were definitely too many parties – but we had a good time. It's just sad we had to grow up and even sadder we couldn't get old together... But that's another story. Tell me about you, Sophie; no husband or boyfriend?'

Sophie briefly told Cristina about splitting up with Mark but she left out the bit about him being married, just saying that the relationship had been going nowhere.

'That's sad. Perhaps while you're here he will miss you and when it's time to go back things will be different.'

Sophie smiled but didn't answer. They ate their pizza, drank more wine and just generally chatted, and though there were questions Sophie would have loved to ask Cristina about Luis, the opportunity didn't come up.

It was a lovely couple of hours but eventually it was time to say goodnight. They both agreed it would be nice to do it again sometime and perhaps even go dancing one night. Cristina told her there were a few little clubs in Playa de las Américas where a lot of the locals went when they'd finished their work in the bars and restaurants and just wanted to let their hair down.

'I would really like that, Cristina, thank you. Right, I'd best get back and see if the villa is still standing. Goodness knows what they've been up to.'

'Knowing Emily, I think we know exactly what's she's been doing. Thankfully she brought a man with her this time so all the wives in town can breathe a sigh of relief she's not after their husbands.'

'Surely she's not that bad?'

'You wait and see. When she arrives by herself it's like a tiger prowling the streets. Lock up your man, Emily's arrived!'

Chapter 8

It was early – and another morning without Mable appearing – and while she sat drinking her first coffee of the day, Sophie laughed. Perhaps now she had poured her life story out to the cat she had moved on to someone else. Such a shame as the fish she had been and bought would likely go to waste. She wouldn't be doing that again!

Thinking back to what Cristina had said the night before, it sounded like Emily was a bit of a goer. Sophie smiled to herself. What had she got herself into coming here to work? The first job of the day was to put a note under the villa door politely asking if Emily needed the rooms cleaned or any shopping done, then she'd do a sweep and mop around the patios. As she was finishing off her coffee her phone beeped with a text from Cristina saying what a lovely evening they'd had. It crossed Sophie's mind what Luis might think of them becoming friends ... followed by a little thought wondering if Cristina was possibly using her to get to Luis. One thing was for certain, it was too many questions for so early in the morning!

****

Two hours later, a note had been put under Emily's door, all the outside areas had been swept and mopped – a task which was getting quicker every time she did it as it was now a part of her daily routine – and Sophie was back up at the bungalow, making herself some toast, when she thought she could hear someone outside. By the time she'd turned around there – just walking in like she owned the place, with no knock or hello – was Emily.

'I haven't any sugar, do you have some? If not, can you go and get it?'

'Yes, I'm sure I have some, just give me a minute and I will see... There you go. Was there anything else you needed?'

'You think you're clever, don't you, just like all the other women my dad has got involved with. But at the end of the day, when it comes down to it, I'm his daughter and I can get rid of you just like all the others. You know why? Because blood is thicker than water and he thinks more of me than anyone else in the world. And if he dies, everything is left to me, so don't get your hopes up that this will all be yours one day. Oh, and there's one more little thing, did you not wonder why you haven't been invited to go with him to America when all the other girlfriends have always travelled with him? Oh, I know, perhaps it's because you aren't the only one!'

With that she picked up the sugar and left. Sophie didn't know what to say but one thing was for sure, Emily had gotten the completely wrong end of the stick. She had never met Kennal and didn't even know what he looked like! It was all very funny – if also a bit perplexing – and if that was what Emily wanted to think, it was easier to just let her.

Sat eating her toast, Sophie Googled 'Kennal Scott' and found he'd actually had small parts in a few major films she recognised. She couldn't find any references to him living here on Tenerife though – he had evidently kept that a secret. There were a number of photos of him with women in the search results but they were all at premiers or Hollywood events, nothing personal. She was miles away, focused on her phone, when she heard her gate open again. What did Emily want now?

Looking up she saw it wasn't Emily but an elderly chap. How did he get in through the main gate? It was meant to be locked! She jumped up from her chair and asked him what he wanted.

'Hello, sorry, I didn't mean to scare you. I'm Javier the gardener. I was told by Mr Kennal to ask for Madeline and she would give me my instructions?'

'Madeleine's not here but I'm Sophie, her daughter, and I will be looking after Villa Kennal for the season. Would you like to take a seat? I can get you a coffee and we can chat through what Kennal would like you to be doing.'

'A coffee would be nice, thank you.'

While the kettle was boiling, Sophie went and got her notes on what jobs Javier was expected to do around the grounds of the villa. Cleaning was all well and good but she knew nothing about gardening and was glad she'd have his professional help.

'There you go, Javier. Now, I have to be honest with you, I know nothing about gardens and certainly don't have a clue about plants in a foreign country, but Kennal has left some instructions so I think the best thing for me to do is read them out to you. Sound good?'

Sophie went through the list and at the end Javier said it sounded like a normal summer season for him and they agreed on him coming to do the work two mornings a week.

'I think we are going to get on just fine, Sophie. I have to admit I was worried that it might have been Luis I was working for... Oh! Don't get me wrong, he's a lovely lad ... as long as that girlfriend of his isn't around because then he gets all stressed and snappy.'

'I've met Luis. He seems very nice and he's been so helpful since I've arrived. And I don't think he has a girlfriend at the moment, not that it would be a problem if he did...'

Sophie felt uncomfortable after saying that and

she could tell by Javier's smile he was reading more into her words than she'd meant him too. She quickly steered the conversation back to the garden.

'I think we are sorted, Sophie. I'm going to look forward to working together and I hope I can be as helpful as Luis while you are working here at the villa for the season. I'll be off now; see you next week.'

Once Javier had gone, Sophie worried she had made a fool of herself with that talk of Luis, but it was too late to do anything about it now. The big question was what she was going to do with herself for the day because she sure wasn't going to be hanging around here to be talked to like that again by Emily. Besides, the note she had put under the door had her phone number on so if Emily needed her she only had to ring.

****

After a quick shower it crossed Sophie's mind that she could catch the bus to Los Cristianos for some exploring. But before that she was going to drop the fish that she had bought for Mable around to Graham, so that it didn't go to waste. She was hoping this might also break the ice between them but something told her making friends with her neighbour wouldn't be a straightforward task.

After a few minutes of knocking on the gate without any answer, she was just about to leave when she heard a noise the other side of the house. She wanted to call out but she didn't want to use Graham's name because she wasn't supposed to know it. Oh, blow it, she tried the handle of the gate and it opened.

'Hello? Is anyone home? It's Sophie from the villa next door. I've brought some fish for Mable.'

Graham appeared around the side of the house

63

looking startled and frightened. Sophie apologised profusely for making him jump and explained that Mable hadn't appeared for a few days so she thought she'd drop the fish around. Graham mumbled a 'thank you' and then just stared. Sophie knew it was time to leave so she waved her goodbye and said she hoped Mable enjoyed the fish.

Walking down to the square to catch the bus, Sophie remembered how Ramon had said Graham was sad and it appeared to be true. But what was it that was making him sad and lonely? And was there anything she could do to help?

She found the bus stop and after the short ride to Los Cristianos she found she wasn't in the mood for a visit to the shops so she walked down to the sea front instead. Before long though, the wind was getting up so she decided to abort her journey.

Walking back towards the town the wind was now behind her, which was a lot easier to manage. She could imagine it would be very busy here in the height of summer and no doubt the atmosphere would be lovely with all the restaurant and little bars open. Sophie was getting hungry and decided it was time to find somewhere to eat. As she made her way up to the main part of the town she could see a few restaurants with locals sat around chatting, and if they were good enough for the locals, they were bound to be good enough for her.

The first restaurant she passed was busy and quite noisy but then a few buildings later she found another one. It wasn't as big and there were still quite a few people inside, but they seemed a lot older and more mellow. This would do nicely. She sat at a little table just inside the door and a nice Spanish girl came over to take Sophie's order. She asked for a glass of red wine but looking at the menu Sophie was overwhelmed by the choices.

'I'm not sure what I fancy. Could you suggest

something?'

The waitress laughed and said she knew just the thing. She told Sophie it would be a surprise but she would really enjoy it. While she was waiting, she checked her phone, grateful to find no missed calls – meaning Emily must be fending for herself – and no emails.

The food arrived then, a huge bowl with steam coming off it, and as for the smell ... it was divine.

'There you are, enjoy! And if you don't, I won't charge you. I suspect you will though, and that you'll be back time and time again.'

Sophie ordered another wine and dove in. It was very tomato-based with succulent chicken that melted in her mouth. The waitress was right – she would definitely be back! Dipping the freshly baked bread into the sauce, she thought that it was one of those meals you just didn't want to finish.

'I see you enjoyed it. I knew you would; everyone does,' the waitress said with a smile when she returned to retrieve Sophie's plate.

'It was beautiful! What's it called, please?'

'You will laugh because it has a very original name: Tenerife chicken stew. Apparently it's been made in this region for hundreds of years. I was brought up on it and I still never get tired of it. Can I get you anything else?'

Sophie was so full she couldn't eat anything else so she asked for the bill, paid and then decided to have a little walk around. Los Cristianos was joined to Playa de las Américas, with the big shopping centres and the designer shops, so she decided to have a look before catching the bus back. A lot of the tourist shops were busy and the clothes shops had such lovely window displays. The price tags were expensive but Sophie was content to browse.

Looking at her watch she saw it was nearly six fifteen. Where had the day gone? She started to make her way back towards the bus stop and was just heading down one of the side streets when a scooter pulled up beside her. It was Luis and he had someone on the back.

'Hi, Sophie, what brings you here? Escaping the Wrath of Emily? I don't blame you. By the way, this is Tony; he's a friend of mine.'

'Hello! I suppose you're right, I am keeping out of her way. It's also good to have a day out somewhere different and it's so lovely here. I will definitely come back again.'

'You're English! So am I. Whereabouts do you come from?' Tony asked.

'London, well, on the outskirts. How about you?'

'Nottingham, originally, but I've lived all over the place really and now I'm working here in Tenerife.'

Sophie couldn't help but notice that Luis had gone very quiet, and eager to take her leave, she told them she was off to catch the bus. Just before they drove away Tony asked her out for a drink. Surprised, Sophie found herself agreeing – what could it hurt to meet more people while she's here – but the look on Luis's face suggested he wasn't happy with her.

The bus was nearly back to Los Kalanchoe when a text come through from Luis. All it said was: *I wouldn't go for a drink with Tony if I was you.* Sophie realised someone was a little jealous but what had she done wrong? She certainly hadn't encouraged Tony and anyway it wasn't Tony she wanted to go for a drink with. Couldn't Luis see that? As she stepped off the bus and headed back to the villa, she said to herself, *oh Sophie, you are in for a fun summer.*

Chapter 9

Sophie hadn't replied to Luis's text yesterday and she wasn't going to take his advice. She was definitely going to go for a drink with Tony as she wanted to make friends while she was here in Tenerife, but she had no intention of ending up as a notch on his bed post. But enough of that, for now she had other important things to sort out – for one, the mess she had come back to after her day out. With glasses, bottles, plates and rubbish everywhere it had looked like there had been a party going on. Thankfully, Emily would be gone tomorrow and then Sophie had three days to get ready for the first proper guests. If she was honest, she was a little nervous about that. Ok, it looked like it would be very straightforward as, apart from a bit of shopping they had requested, they didn't need any cooking done other than the birthday party, which Cristina was all organised and ready for. The thing she was concerned about was sharing the place with strangers. Yes, she was out the way in the bungalow, but it would still be different than it was now, when she could come and go as she pleased.

Sophie was nearly finished with her morning cleaning and thankfully there was still no sign of Emily or the boyfriend yet. She couldn't get over how two people could make so much mess, and then a thought crossed her mind – what would happen if some of the other guests were like this? Kennal had no control over who he rented the villa out to.

Sophie was just finishing the mopping on one of the terraces when out the corner of her eye she noticed someone coming out of the villa. As much as she wanted to ignore them, she felt it was only polite to say good morning – actually, it was nearly afternoon – but as she was about to speak he turned and walked down towards the gate. She was surprised to see it wasn't Emily's boyfriend and she hoped he hadn't slept in one of the other bedrooms, but then, he couldn't have because she had locked them all. He must have slept on one of the sofas, but did that mean there would be others? How many more people were in there?

As much as she would love to go out for the day and be out of Emily's way in case they had another party, she thought she'd best stay and keep an eye on the place. After all, that was part of her job.

Back at the bungalow she made a sandwich and a coffee and went and sat in her happy place – her veranda. Still no visit from Mable and that was something she was missing as she had got into the habit of talking things over with the cat and without that outlet, the thoughts only went around and around in her head.

She was sitting watching for any more comings and goings through the bushes when her phone beeped. It was an email from Kennal to say the four week booking for August had cancelled due to a death in the family and if she heard of anyone wanting to stay she should let him know. Also, he might be a while getting back to her as he was tied up with the filming.

She felt as though she should email him back and tell him not to worry, she would find guests to stay those weeks, but how would she do that? And was it her job to be taking control like that? The one thing she did know was she needed to fill every spare date as the last thing she wanted was Emily coming back for even one day. She decided to bite the bullet and put an email together, which seemed to take ages. Having pressed 'send' she wondered if she'd done the right thing. Would Kennal think she was taking over? More importantly, was she capable of coming through on her promise?

Surprisingly it was only a few minutes later that he messaged back.

Hi Sophie,

Thank you so much! You can't know how much of a help it would be for me if you take full control of everything with the villa. The demands on me here in America seem to increase by the day so it would be a major problem off my mind. But of course, if you do have any issues you can't resolve, don't hesitate to contact me.

To make things easier, I think it's best if I give you my password for the villa website so you will be able to control the bookings and respond to any enquiries that come in. I'm also sending across the villa's bank account details so you can access it as needed for bills, float money, etc.

The email went on with all the account numbers and passwords plus a list of contacts. Kennal ended by saying that as she was doing all of this in addition to the work they'd previously agreed, he would pay her another two hundred euros a month.

She had to read that bit a few times! It was hard to believe that she'd gone from cleaning a few rooms a day and answering to her mum to now being in sole control of Villa Kennal and making more money than originally agreed. It was scary but it was also exciting. The first thing she needed to do was turn her laptop on and sign into the website. She had looked at it before but only briefly and, to be honest, she did think it was a bit dated. But that was none of her business, what she needed to see was the villa calendar to check if Kennal had taken the cancelled booking off and if he'd had any new enquires about bookings.

Sophie was just about to go back into the bungalow when she heard her little gate go. She was so glad it squeaked as it was like an early warning system and she guessed it would only be one person:

Emily. She was right and she was ready to kill her with kindness.

'Hi, Emily, is there anything I can help you with?'

'Yes, the villa needs cleaning from top to bottom and I need some shopping but first, where were you yesterday? I came looking for you as I needed things doing.'

'I did leave you my phone number in a note.'

'You think you are so clever but I can see right through you. My dad might not be able to but once he's back from the States your days will be numbered, mark my words.'

Having finished her little speech, she gave Sophie her instructions and first on the list was shopping. Thankfully she didn't need much so Sophie wouldn't need to get a taxi. After that, Emily wanted the place cleaned, which was good in one way as at least Sophie would be able to see what state the inside of the villa was in.

The downside to all of this was that she wouldn't be able to get on the laptop to sort out any bookings, but she would have all evening for that.

Having gathered her things, she was on her way down to the gate when she spotted Emily sat on the terrace looking at her phone. Sophie was tempted to shout up 'have a nice day', but she didn't want to push her too far.

****

Once down in the town, she saw the restaurants were starting to open, along with more of the tourist gift shops. The season was getting ready to kick off and with that would come the hot weather, which was something she was looking forward to so much.

By the time she got back to the villa there was no sign of Emily. Taking a deep breath, Sophie stepped

70

inside the villa and to her surprise the place looked ok. The lounge hadn't been used as the cushions were as she had left them, and even the kitchen – apart from some dishes and glasses – looked ok. She put all the shopping in the fridge then went back to get all the plates and glasses. She also needed to check the other bedrooms hadn't been used. She was pretty sure they hadn't, but if the stranger hadn't slept in the lounge, where else could he have slept? It was all very odd.

Dishwasher loaded and counter wiped, Sophie was just about to start sweeping and mopping when Emily appeared by herself.

'You can clean the bedroom now while I sit down here. The bed will need changing as well.'

'Should I not wait until your friend comes down?'

There was no reply so Sophie headed up the stairs and on her way she checked the other bedroom doors. Thankfully they were still locked and a quick look in the TV room showed her nothing had been touched in there either. She hoped the boyfriend would be in the lounge and not the bedroom so she could get in and out quickly, but he wasn't. He also wasn't on the little balcony overlooking the pool. Looking back towards the bedroom, she saw that the door was open and the room was a mess. She poked her head around the bathroom door but he wasn't there either ... and then the penny dropped. How could she have been so stupid? The boyfriend must have left and the lad Sophie saw leaving earlier today must have stayed the night with Emily.

****

It took nearly two hours to clean the upstairs. Sophie couldn't believe two people could make so much mess ... no, actually it was three people. The annoying thing about it was the fact she would have to do it all again when Emily left the next day. When she went back downstairs Emily was still sat outside so she gave the ground floor a good sweep and mop. As she was leaving, she went to ask if there was anything else Emily needed but she didn't get the chance as Emily walked silently by her and back up the stairs.

****

Back in the bungalow, after a quick shower, Sophie sat down to enjoy a glass of wine and a bag of crisps – which she had well and truly earned – and opened her laptop. As she remembered, the website was basic and quite dated, but there was also a link to a Facebook page. Thankfully, there were some up-to-date photos on the feed, which were a million times better than the website ones, and it would be quite easy to switch them around and update the site. But first she needed to check the diary page. Yes, Kennal had updated it and the four weeks in August were showing as 'available'. As Kennal's passwords were all very similar she thought it worth checking to see if she could get into the Facebook account to advertise the weeks that were free. She added it to her to-do list and then checked the villa's inbox, seeing that there were a couple of emails asking about availability next year and one saying that if there was a cancellation in September they'd love to book in.

****

Sophie suddenly realised she was sitting in the dark. As she put the light on, she glanced at the clock and saw she had been at the table for over five hours.

Her stomach was starting to rumble but she had achieved so much. The Facebook post had had lots of positive reactions and she had given the website an overall revamp. It now looked new and fresh with stunning photos of the villa and the wider town. She had also added a couple from Costa Adeje and Los Cristianos, making it clear just how much was in the vicinity of the villa. Switching the laptop off she remembered that the bins would be emptied early in the morning and she hadn't put them the other side of the gate yet. She decided she would do that before she cooked herself some pasta.

****

Bins deposited on the kerb, Sophie walked back up the path and couldn't help but look up towards the villa. Emily was sat outside, a glass in hand and a bottle of wine on the table beside her. Sophie waved but didn't get even a look back even though she knew Emily must have seen her. Sophie found she felt sorry for her. Ok, she was rude and probably very spoiled, but she was also obviously a sad, troubled soul. Should she walk over to her? No, she would only have her head bitten off. Better to go back to the bungalow and make some food after a very odd day.

****

She was just about to eat when her phone rang. Looking at it, she could see it was Luis calling. Did she want to speak to him? Yes, of course she wanted to.

'Hi, Luis, how are you?'
'I've just noticed Kennal's website has changed.'
'Yes, I've updated it. Is that a problem?'
'But why you?'

73

'Because Kennal has asked me to take over everything to do with the villa and that includes all the social media.'

'I can't believe he has handed everything over to you when you're only here for eight months. I'm not happy about it, especially as it's all because of one silly mistake – a misunderstanding! How long am I going to have to keep paying for it?'

He ended the call before Sophie could tell him she was only doing what she had been asked to do.

Chapter 10

Today was the day! Sophie was looking forward to Emily leaving and fingers crossed – as it looked like she had been in the villa by herself last night – it shouldn't be too messy. One thing she wanted to do before Emily left, however, was explain why she was here and to make it clear she wasn't Kennal's new girlfriend. It was clear Emily was a mixed-up kid and Sophie didn't want any misconceptions she might have about the nature of Sophie and Kennal's relationship to add to whatever was screwing her up. The only problem was, would she leave without saying goodbye, before Sophie had the chance?

Sophie's phone beeped with an email inquiring about availability for one of the August weeks. Apparently the guest had stayed last year and enjoyed it so much they wanted to return. She emailed back and confirmed, then had a sweep around the villa's patios to see if there was any sign of Emily. Her phone went again and this time it was a text from Tony asking if she fancied going for a drink tonight. She didn't need to be asked twice but a drink was all he was getting. She had just replied when the patio doors opened and there with a mug in her hand was Emily. No time like the present! It was time to get it over with.

'Good morning, Emily, can I get you anything?'

Emily gave Sophie a look and mumbled something she didn't understand. Perhaps she shouldn't bother and just let the little madam think what she likes? But no, if she did know the truth, she might be a little nicer, which would make life a lot easier if she came to stay again.

'I'm sorry, Emily, I can tell you aren't in the mood to talk and I understand that, but there is something you need to know and I think it's important.'

Emily shrugged her shoulders as if to say 'ok, get on with it' but she didn't answer. Sophie started at the beginning, explaining how Kennal had asked her mum to come and run the place for the summer and Madeline had then invited her along as she'd been made redundant. She made it quite clear that she had never even met Kennal so any idea of their being in a relationship was ludicrous. Emily shrugged her shoulders again and when she stayed silent, Sophie took that as her cue to walk away.

'I hope you've had a nice stay and I look forward to you coming back again. Have a safe journey.'

****

Back in the bungalow, Sophie went to get the file for the first guests, confirming that it would be ten adults – four couples and two single people. For their arrival they had requested the basics – tea, coffee, sugar, lots of bottled water, a few bottles of wine and two cases of beer – and the notes said their flight would be a late one so they wouldn't be here until around eleven o'clock at night. It crossed Sophie's mind that she might add some cheese, bread and crisps to their groceries, just in case they were hungry when they got in.

She heard her gate go and knew it could only be Emily as the main gate in was locked from the inside.

'Hi, are you off?'

'Yes, here's the keys. Thanks.'

Sophie sensed something different in Emily's tone, it wasn't as aggressive and the last thing she had expected was a thank you. She took the keys off her and then she was gone.

Now it was time to go and see what state she had left the villa in...

Shock, horror, oh my goodness! Emily had left it spotless. Even the mug she'd had her coffee in that morning was washed up. Going up the stairs, Sophie found the lounge was tidy and Emily had striped the bed and put the dirty linen and towels in a neat pile. What was this? One thing was for sure, it wouldn't have been like this if she hadn't had that conversation with her earlier.

Now, what jobs to do? First, a quick call to Ramon to arrange for him to pick her up at the supermarket tomorrow, and then she could start making up the downstairs bedrooms.

****

After a very successful day, the villa was ready for the guests apart from a wipe around and a mop a few hours before they arrived, and Sophie had met up with Tony for their drink.

'So, how long have you been here in Tenerife, Sophie, and why here?'

Sophie told Tony the story of how she'd ended up at the villa but all the time she was talking she could tell he was only pretending to be interested. So when the bar started getting busy and he suggested they go somewhere quieter, she was about to say no when Cristina walked in and Tony made an excuse to go to the toilet.

'Hi, Sophie, how are you?'

'I've had better evenings out,' Sophie said, rolling her eyes.

They laughed and Cristina said she was off to meet some friends in a bar in Del Duque and was just waiting for a taxi. She invited Sophie to come along but cautioned that Tony wouldn't be welcome as he had upset quite a few of the girls who would be there.

'That would be great but first I need to dump him. Just give me a minute.'

'So, are you ready to make a move somewhere nice and quiet? I know just the place,' Tony said as he arrived back at the table.

'Tony, I need to put my cards on the table because I don't want to waste your time. You and I are not going to ever end up in bed together.'

'So you don't fancy me then? I'm sure if you got to know me a little better you might-'

'Might what? Sleep with you? No, I can assure you that won't be happening. Now, let me pay you for the drink you bought me. I would hate you to think your investment didn't pay off.'

Sophie didn't wait for an answer, dropping money on the table and standing to go over to Cristina, who had heard everything. They both laughed all the way out of the bar.

It was now getting on for ten o'clock and Cristina explained as it was still early in the season the bar they were heading for wouldn't be too crazy.

It was busier than she'd expected and Sophie recognised a few faces she had seen around Los Kalanchoe. The music was good as they went to the bar for drinks and Cristina introduced her to lots of people. There was no way she would remember all of their names but it was all very relaxed and everyone was nice.

****

Walking back from the bar after getting them another drink a while later, she spotted Luis in the corner with a long face and went over to join him.

'Hi! Why the sad face? It might never happen.'

'What do you mean?'

'You look sad and the season's not even started

78

yet.'

'That's it though, it *has* happened – you've got my job unless you mess up and Kennal begs me to go back and look after the villa. And we both know that's not going to happen, don't we?'

'You never know, Luis, I might not be any good at it. Perhaps I'm not cut out for the holiday industry.'

'There's no way you will fail, Sophie, you will succeed because you can accomplish anything you set your mind to. You are a good person, and more than that, you're special. Enjoy your evening.'

Sophie walked back over to Cristina thinking that she didn't like seeing Luis like this, but what could she say or do? The job at the villa was hers and she was loving it, so much so that if the opportunity to come back next year and carry on running it came up, she would jump at it.

No, she couldn't help how Luis was feeling. She had no control over that.

Chapter 11

'Thank you so much, Sophie, you have made our holiday very special and we're already looking forward to coming back again next year. We will look forward to seeing you then.'

'Thank you! I'm glad you all have had a good time but I don't think it will be me you see as I'm only looking after the villa for this season.'

'The owner would be mad not to employ you again and I will tell him that when I write my holiday review! You make this place very special and it really wouldn't be the same without you. Goodbye now, and thank you again.'

As Sophie waved off her first guests after what appeared to have been a perfect stay, she couldn't help feeling warmed by their kind words and she really hoped that she would be here next year to see them again. But as it stood, come October she would be at the end of this adventure. But enough of all this thinking, she had just over six hours to get the place ready for the next group of guests.

Thankfully, the family that had just said goodbye had left the villa pretty much exactly as they had found it. Hopefully this was how the rest of the summer would go.

The first two weeks of guests was officially out of the way, with the bonus that Mable had reappeared – and yes, she wanted feeding and a cushion on the chair. Sophie was glad she had someone to talk to again, even though it was just a cat. She only wished she could answer her questions about why Graham was so sad. Mable would no doubt know everything.

She had also had Javier in a few times and the work he'd done had really improved the garden. Things had been cut back and everything was looking healthier. She had made him the odd cup of coffee during his visits and on one occasion had given him some pastries. They had sat for a short while to eat them and he had explained how his late wife had been English. She had visited the island on holiday and they had fallen in love and so she stayed in Los Kalanchoe. Both had worked hard and had a lovely life until, sadly, she died four years ago. Sophie liked Javier and felt honoured that he was comfortable enough to open up to her the way he had.

In short, it had been a really good two weeks and she had set up a good routine and was getting so much quicker with the cleaning and the turnaround, so everything was soon ready for the new guests to arrive. Hopefully they would be just like the ones that had left earlier and she would have another good couple of weeks ahead.

She heard a mini bus pull up outside and then there was the sound of a lot of happy voices. She opened the gate and her first impression was that the next two weeks might not be as nice and easy as the last two.

Here goes. Put the smile on, Sophie.

'Welcome to Villa Kennal! I hope you've had a good journey and if you'll follow me, I'll show you up to the villa.'

****

Kicking her shoes off two hours later, Sophie poured a large glass of wine and then plonked herself in her chair on the veranda. She could not believe how two groups could be so different. The last few weeks the family were sweet and appreciative, but this lot? First, she had to carry all the bags and cases to each of their rooms even though they were all in their thirties and were quite capable of doing it themselves. Then she had to move the outside

81

furniture to different areas as directed and had to run around delivering more towels to everyone while being bombarded with questions – why wasn't there this or that? Could she go fetch more of X, Y, Z? Where was the...? And the noise. Did they really have to have the music so loud? And to top it off? They decided they wanted meals cooked for them at the villa on multiple nights even though they hadn't prebooked them, which meant she would have to hope Cristina was available and give her a hand with the serving and clean-up late into the night. Oh, she was definitely in for a completely different experience with this group. Only thirteen days to go...

****

What a night. Sophie hadn't managed to get to sleep until about three in the morning with all the noise that was coming from the villa, and now the hard work would start with clearing up after the night before. No doubt there would be rubbish and glasses everywhere. Seeing it was nearly eight o'clock she decided she would start on the patios and terraces. Getting her cleaning things together, she downed a much-needed coffee and headed over to the villa.

As she'd suspected, it was a mess, but surprisingly there was someone up and she was already starting to clear up the glasses.

'Good morning. You can leave that. I'm here to do the cleaning.'

'Hi. You really shouldn't have to face all this alone. I'll give you a hand. By the way I'm Jill, and I'm so sorry, I really am.'

'Please don't worry, I can do it. You're on holiday, why not go into the villa and make yourself a drink and let me get this sorted?'

Jill smiled and kept apologising but eventually

she went off to get herself a drink as suggested. Sophie collected all the glasses and plates and then started on the rubbish. Once that was done, she swept, mopped and tidied the furniture. It was now gone ten and no one else was up other than Jill, who sat reading her book by the pool. Sophie went and said she would come back when everyone was up to clean the bedrooms and do any other jobs that needed doing.

'I really am sorry. I'm hoping last night was a one-off – the first night and everything – but somehow I think every night might be like that. Can I tell you something? But you must promise me not to repeat it.'

Sophie nodded and Jill explained that the holiday was all being paid for by Rich and his wife, Mandy, and neither she nor her husband, Keith, wanted to come. The same was true of the other couple, Rob and Becky, but none of them could get out of it. Rich had come into some money and as all the blokes were best friends from school he wanted to treat them. Though they saw each other occasionally back in England for parties and meals out, that was only a few hours at a time, and this was twenty-four-seven for two weeks. She was worried it was going to be a nightmare.

'Sophie, there's worse to come if Mandy has too much to drink and starts... Sorry, I've said too much.'

Just as Sophie had thought, the next two weeks were not going to be straightforward. But for now, until everyone was up, she couldn't do any more at the villa so she went back to the bungalow until she could hear a few more people up and about. She made a quick call to Cristina to explain about the cooking and to mention what type of guests they were but she was laid back about it and said she had come across groups like this before and their bark was normally worse than their bite. But Sophie wasn't so sure. The other thing that crossed her mind was that she must go next door to Graham and apologise for all the noise last night.

It was now one o'clock in the afternoon and she could hear lots of laughter and chatting so she made her way back down to the villa. As she went through the little gate she counted seven people at the table and as she was walking towards the patio doors she heard someone shout over, 'Here, darling, can you get us some beers?' She ignored him and proceeded inside the villa, finding the loud women from last night and thinking it must be Mandy as she looked like she was in charge.

'Hi, I was just wondering if it was ok to start on cleaning the bedrooms?'

'Yes, but first my husband wants some beers and we've run out. Come to think of it, I will give you a shopping list of what we need and after you've been shopping then you can clean up before cooking us some food.'

Deep breathe, Sophie, time to explain the rules.

'I'm sorry but I need twenty-four hours' notice for any shopping requests and any cooked meals need to be approved and paid for in advance. I also need access to the rooms now in order to complete the cleaning by three p.m., as per the villa's terms of use,' Sophie explained calmly.

'So you're telling me you're not going to get the shopping or cook for us? But we're paying for this villa and you, young lady, come with it.'

'Oh, I'm sorry. Perhaps I've made a mistake and you have a different arrangement than all the other guests? I'll just nip and get the booking details that you agreed with the owner. Just give me a minute.'

Sophie went up to the bungalow and got all the information out. Give Kennal his due, he was very thorough with the booking contracts and he'd left no stone unturned.

'Here you go,' she said, offering the information packet to Mandy once she was back in the villa. 'This is the booking form you filled out online and this is the copy the owner printed off. And this is the list of the extras you can book prior to arrival. As you can see, apart from the welcoming pack, and a couple of dinners, you haven't ordered anything else.'

'Rich, come here. The skivey hostess says she's not going shopping as we've not booked it in advance.'

'Sorry, the name's Sophie, not "skivey".'

'Don't you be cocky with me, young lady.'

Sophie noticed a few of the other guests looked embarrassed as Rich took her to one side.

'Sorry about that, is there any way you could help us out with the shopping rather than cleaning the bedrooms today? Also, would you be able to contact the person who cooks the meals to see if there's any chance she could cook tonight?' he asked.

He was a bit smarmy but very apologetic and so Sophie agreed.

****

Half an hour later a huge shopping list had been written and Cristina had agreed to come down and cook a barbeque that evening. Rich went and got his wallet, which was jammed packed with euro notes, and cash in hand, Sophie went out to meet Ramon, who had agreed to come and pick her up to go to the supermarket.

'Thank you, Sophie, you are a star,' Rich said as she was leaving. 'I really appreciate this.'

'It's ok, just one thing before I go – your mother said she needed some sun cream. What factor should I get?'

'Sorry, my mother?'

Sophie pointed to Mandy, and Rich – aware she knew Mandy was his wife and not his mother – smiled and gave her a wink.

'I think she might have met her match with you. I can see we are going to get on just fine for the next couple of weeks.'

****

The rest of the day went ok. Cristiana had arrived for the barbeque full of confidence and also dressed to impress, and it was clear that Mandy and one of the other women weren't too keen on all the attention their husbands were paying to their cook. Cristina played up to the attention and Sophie thought that if it was left up to Mandy, the group would be eating out most nights for the rest of their stay.

'You really knew how to handle them, Cristina; I'm so impressed! Do you have time for a drink before you go? We could go up to the bungalow,' Sophie said as they finished cleaning up the kitchen after the meal.

'That would be nice, Sophie. I'm in no hurry as it's only ten thirty and I'm not working tomorrow.'

Sophie lit the candles on her little veranda and fetched a bottle of wine. The noise from the villa wasn't too bad – certainly nothing like the night before – but that could have been because two of the couples were going to walk into the town and see if they could find some entertainment in one of the bars.

'This is really nice. I must say I can't believe what you have done with the bungalow, it's completely different to the way Kennal usually has it. You must be feeling more settled now?'

'Yes, I am, thanks, but I might not be saying that after two weeks of this lot. I'll probably be packing my bag to go home!'

'Home to what though, Sophie? You said you were made redundant so you would have to get a job, and it's not like you've mentioned going back to someone. Would there be anyone there welcoming you home?'

'Yes, there would, but he's not what I want now. Perhaps a few months ago, but definitely not anymore.'

The floodgates opened, Sophie told her the whole Mark saga from the beginning to the end.

'Telling that story now feels strange. It's as if I'm talking about someone else and not myself,' Sophie said once she'd given Cristina all the details.

'Is that good or bad? Is it making you happy or sad?'

'I don't really know. I guess sad for all those wasted years, but happy because I now know that's not what I want. I can't believe now I've stepped out of it how obsessed I was with him. I dreamed for so many years that Mark and I would eventually be together in a nice house with a couple of kids. Life would be so perfect. And do you know, that's the last thing on my mind now.'

'Oh dear, you need to be careful, you might end up like me – the complete other end of the scale, just going from one party to the next, no responsibly, no steady relationship, just carefree and single, not a worry or care in the world.'

'You say that now but give it a couple of years and you and Luis will be settled down, wanting to start a family.'

'No, you're definitely wrong there. We will never end up together. We were together for all the wrong reasons and I told him that for years. He'll definitely make someone a good husband and father one day, but it won't be me. But saying that, between you and me, I'm not sure I could cope seeing him with someone else. I think that's because I know he's a good bloke and would do anything to please me. Right, enough of this chat! I need the loo and shall we open another bottle of wine?'

Cristina went off to the toilet and Sophie thought that whoever got involved with Luis would have to be careful because at the first opportunity he would probably end up going back to Cristina.

Chapter 12

It was getting to the end of Rich and Mandy's holiday with just two days to go and surprisingly the time had flown by. It had been far easier than Sophie had expected and though she had done lots of shopping, she'd only needed to clean the bedrooms every other day, which was a plus. The other thing that had helped was the fact that they had eaten out most nights and when they got back, they went to their rooms rather than continuing the party. She had also noticed that during the day the couples had started doing their own things, with some going to the beach and others hanging by the pool. It was as though they were all getting fed up with each other.

One of the things that Sophie had spent the whole time doing during their stay at the villa was trying to chase up the next group of guests who were coming. They had only paid a partial deposit and there was no address on the paperwork, just an email and phone number that no one ever responded to or answered. She was getting so concerned about it that she had emailed Kennal to ask if he had another way to contact them. He said he couldn't remember taking the booking so all they could do was wait for the group to arrive so Sophie could take some sort of payment off them before she let them into the villa. And if that became a problem, she needed to call him right away, day or night.

But that was a problem that could wait, especially as today promised to be a good day. Rich and the rest of the group had been up and out of the villa early as they were going on a boozy boat trip and wouldn't be back until late in the evening. Sophie couldn't believe her luck! It was only ten thirty in the morning and all her cleaning was done.

The place was in complete silence and she was ready for a day by the pool with her book. It had been nearly a month since she had been able to use the pool but seeing there was no fear of anyone disturbing her, she was going to make the most of it. But first, she wanted to try the phone number again for the mystery group and this time she was going to try a different angle when she left the message on the answering machine. Secretly, in her head, she was hoping they wouldn't turn up and then she could have the pool to herself for the next two weeks.

'Hi, this is a message for Mrs Smith. It's Sophie again from Villa Kennal in Tenerife. As I've said in all the other messages I've left, we have a booking for you for two days' time and as you have only paid a partial deposit and not confirmed your stay we have to assume you have changed your minds and won't be coming. As such, we will be reopening the property for alternative bookings. Thank you and have a good day.'

Now that should do it! Being honest, she wished that was how she had handled it in the first place.

As she gathered her things to go down to the pool her phone rang. She wasn't too surprised to see that it was the number she had been contacting for the mystery group of guests.

'Yes, this is Villa Kennal.'

'This is Mrs Smith. You left me a message and of course I will be arriving as planned in two days' time. I have booked it and a booking is a booking.'

'Yes, I understand a booking is a booking, but as I mentioned in the many emails and voicemails I've left for you, we do require payment up front and a list of names for all the guests that are staying. As you have not provided either, I'm afraid we can't hold the booking for you.'

'Well you can tell Kennal I will have much to say

to him about the terrible service his employees are delivering. Who are you by the way? Are you are you related to Kennal?'

'I don't understand why that would be relevant, Mrs Smith. Now, should I expect you to arrive as planned in two days' time? If so, do you have a credit card handy so we can take care of the deposit now?'

The response was a terse 'I will be there' and then the line went dead.

What was all that about? Sophie wondered if she should contact Kennal about the strange Mrs Smith but didn't want to come across as incapable of coping with difficult guests. No, she would wait until they arrived, though perhaps it would be good if she had Luis here for a bit of moral support.

Talk of the devil...

Luis walked through the villa's gate and waved hello.

'I was just thinking of you. Would you like a coffee? I might need a favour...'

As Sophie made them both a coffee she explained about the booking and the conversation she'd just had, and Luis agreed to pop down in case the group got argumentative when they arrived.

'Cristina told me your current guests have also been a problem. You should have phoned me; I would have come down and sorted them out.'

'No, they've been ok overall, just initially a little too much of the high spirits, I think. We're getting along ok now, thankfully. But saying that, I will definitely be glad when they leave... Who knows, maybe I'll even start to miss them once the next lot arrive! But enough of that, let's talk about something else – you, for instance. Why are you and Cristina not together? You should be.'

He laughed and disagreed, saying he wasn't denying that they'd had good times together, but

91

that was in the past when they were young and partying and had more shared interests.

'It got boring though, and that's why I thought this place would be good for me. But as you know, I messed it up.'

'But this wouldn't have been permanent, only when Kennal wasn't here. Anyway, there's always next year, and the year after, and so on. Who's to say Kennal doesn't make it big in America and needs someone here permanently? You know where you went wrong so you just need to prove to him you can do it right.'

'So you aren't coming back again next year then? I think you're doing really well and you always look like you're enjoying it, plus you've settled into the area and made friends.'

She laughed and explained her in charge at the villa was all down to her mum having had to go back to the UK. If her acting work didn't continue she would jump at coming here next year to take on the job. 'I don't think it would work, the two of us here together, and we definitely wouldn't be able to live together in the bungalow as we'd end up arguing all the time. Oh! Look at the time. Do you fancy something to eat? Maybe a sandwich? No, I've no bread... I was going to go shopping later but I can nip out and get us something now, if you're interested?'

'Why don't we go out for lunch? If you don't mind getting on the back of my bike we could drive over to Playa Paraíso. You said you have all day spare and it will do you good to get away from the villa for a bit.'

'Do you know, that would be nice, but on one condition: I treat you to lunch. Well, not me technically, but Rich. The amount of tips he's given me to keep me happy and not upset his wife...' She laughed. 'Just give me a sec to get ready.'

Sophie went to change and lock everything up. It had been years since she had been on the back of a bike but the one thing she did remember was that you have to be very close to the person you were holding onto...

****

The road out of Los Kalanchoe was busy but once they got nearer to Playa Paraíso things quietened down and Luis found a place to park under a shady tree.

'Food first and then a walk, I think. Is that ok with you?'

Sophie thought that would be fine though she wasn't that hungry. It was strange, Luis being in control; today felt different than the other times they had hung out, but she liked it.

The restaurant was more like a café and she was just about to look at the menu when Luis interrupted her and told the waitress that they'd have two large steak sandwiches. He also ordered himself a Fanta Orange and Sophie said she'd have the same. When she gave him a look after the waitress had walked away, he said that if he'd let her choose what to eat she likely would never have gone for the sandwich but it was what the place did best. Sophie was about to argue but her phone rang, and when she saw the name she worried there might be a problem.

'Hi, Greg, is everything ok? ... Yes I'm missing you too. Why don't you take some time off and come over to Tenerife? It will be fun – I can show you the sites and we can party... Look, I need to go but I'll catch up with you soon. And promise me you'll try to come and visit!'

The food arrived and Luis was right, the sandwiches – which were like door stops – were beautiful. The steak just melted in your mouth and thinking of mouths, Luis seemed to have kept his closed since her phone conversation. Was that because she had invited Greg to visit? She was tempted to just let Luis sulk but that would spoil the rest of their day together and she was enjoying herself.

'That was my neighbour, Greg, who's keeping an eye on my flat for me. He might be coming to visit while I'm working here.'

The look on Luis's face hadn't changed – if anything, it had got worse. Was he … jealous? However did he put up with being with Cristina? If she was anything like as flirty as she was now back then, he must have been on the edge all the time.

'It will be nice to see Greg. He's fun and I'm sure we'll have some great nights out together while he's here. And there's really no need for that sad face, Greg and I are just friends. Neighbours, nothing else.'

'I don't know what you mean by "sad face".'

'You know exactly what I mean and so I'm not going to waste my time explaining. Now, get the bill and I will pay it and then we can go for a nice walk and see how many handsome men I can flirt with. That was a joke, by the way, you are my date for today and you have my full attention.'

'Your date? What do you mean by that? We've just come out for something to eat and a walk, that's not a date.'

'Now you've disappointed me, Luis.'

He blushed as he realised she was taking the mickey out of him. Sophie paid the bill and carried on teasing him, asking him to be her tourist guide and to lead the way. Eventually he relaxed again and joined in with all her jokes, and even started to play them on her, making up silly stories as they walked by buildings and boats. It was nice and they both were enjoying themselves. After a while they turned back towards where they'd started and Sophie suggested they go for a drink in one of the bars overlooking the sea wall. She had a glass of wine but as he was driving he said he wasn't going to chance it, so just had a Coke. It had been a lovely few hours and neither was in a hurry to get back to Los Kalanchoe.

'I've enjoyed myself, thank you, Luis. It's lovely to get away from the villa and let my hair down.'

'Yes, I've enjoyed myself too. It's been a long time since I've laughed so much.'

'Me too! A very long time. Look, I think I should tell you a few things about my life back in England. I've already told Cristina so there's no reason to keep it secret anymore.'

Sophie briefly went over the Mark story and as she did so she realised it was now easier to talk about it. She was finally getting over Mark and she told Luis as much.

'You say that now, Sophie, but what will happen when you go back to England when the summer is over? Won't you be tempted to reconnect with him? You would have both had a break from each other and his life might have changed, making it possible for you to be together. What if he's not with his wife anymore? Would that make a difference to you?'

'No, Luis, it wouldn't.'

Chapter 13

Just one more day and Rich and his friends would be leaving and thank goodness. But Sophie's priority today was Mable. She had been at Sophie's without leaving for days and was eating more but there was something else Sophie had noticed; she was putting on weight and something told her it wasn't just the food. It looked like she was expecting kittens and as that was something she would not be able to cope with here at the villa, she would have to go and tell Graham. Her only fear was what if he wasn't interested? What would she do with a pregnant cat?

As she pulled the gate behind her after giving up on trying to get Mable to follow her up to Graham's villa, Sophie could see Rich and Mandy heading to the pool. She'd have to start the whole process again tomorrow with different guests but any worry about that would have to wait. For now, it was Mable's welfare she was off to sort out.

She knocked on Graham's gate but just like last time there was no reply so she tried the handle, which was unlocked.

'Hi, hello, is anyone at home?' she called as she moved along the path.

This time she went a little further and as she passed one of the windows of the villa she could see the room was full of boxes piled on top of each other from floor to ceiling. Perhaps he was in the process of moving? Looking the other way, she saw the garden was a right mess that looked like it hadn't been touched for years. Then, all of a sudden and as if from nowhere, Graham appeared.

'Hi, I'm sorry to bother you but I have a problem ... well, actually, I think we both have a problem. It's Mable, I think she's pregnant as she seems to be putting on weight and her routine has changed.'

'How exciting! Kittens on the way!'

Sophie was taken aback by his enthusiastic response. This was a completely different Graham to the one she'd met before; he was smiling, happy, friendly...

'Yes, I'm afraid there's no way I can have Mable and the kittens down at Villa Kennal because with the holiday makers I won't have the time to look after them and so would be worrying all the time.'

'I understand completely. By the way I'm Graham. Now, we need to get her to come back here and then I will keep her inside. I've had lots of cats over the years so I've seen this before and as Mable found me rather than the other way around, I feel I owe her.'

This was Sophie's opportunity to find out more about him but all the time he'd been talking he'd also been stepping towards her, causing her to step back along the path almost to the gate. There was no way she was going to see inside his home today as it seemed he didn't even want her in the garden!

'Look, Graham, why not come back with me to the villa? You can see Mable, and we can have a coffee and talk over what we need to do next.'

He agreed but Sophie sensed that was only because he didn't want her to see around his home. What was Graham hiding?

****

Back in her bungalow, Sophie went to make them a coffee and Graham went to fuss over Mable, who was looking very confused to see them together.

'I'm afraid I don't have any biscuits because I don't trust myself not to eat them all in one go,' Sophie offered apologetically.

'That's ok, I'm not a lover of sweet things anyway. Now, Mable, what are we going to do about you, and more to the point, how have you got yourself into this situation? I've always been worried this would happen and really, it's my fault. I should have found a vet and had you spayed when you first turned up on my doorstep.'

'I think a visit to the vets now might be a good idea. Has she been with you long?'

'Yes, it will be two years on the 8th of March.'

'Oh, I wish I could remember dates that easily! I would have struggled with how many years, let alone the exact date.'

Sophie could immediately see she had said the wrong thing as Graham had that look on his face again. He looked so sad so she quickly changed the subject and talked about Villa Kennal to give him time to recover himself. It seemed to work and Graham started talking again.

As it was getting on for lunchtime Sophie asked if he fancied a sandwich. She was expecting him to say no but shockingly he said yes. While she went off to make them lunch, she could see he was taking everything in.

'Your little bungalow is lovely. Far cosier than these big villas.'

'Yes, even though Villa Kennal is modern and very chic, I much prefer it up here, tucked away. As it's lunch time, shall we have a glass of wine? Red or white?'

'Oh I don't know if I should. I haven't had an alcoholic drink for a long time – since the day Mable turned up, actually... Oh, go on then, I'll have whatever you're having.'

'White it is then. Could you take the plates out onto the veranda for me? I'll get the wine and a treat for Mable. I always feel guilty sat there eating if I don't give her something.'

'I'm the same,' Graham admitted sheepishly.

****

Over the next hour the sandwiches and crisps were eaten and the wine topped up a few times. Mable had eaten her tuna treats and Sophie was thinking what to ask next but before she had a chance, Graham jumped in.

'You must find me odd, Sophie, and you would be right. I'm not the person I was before coming here – it's circumstances that have made me like this. And the reason I can remember when I last drank and first saw Mable was because that was the day my partner died.'

'Oh dear, I'm so very sorry. Please, you don't need to explain, it's none of my business.'

But he evidently wanted to explain and as he started Sophie got the impression he had needed the liquid courage provided by the wine.

'My partner and I moved to Tenerife after selling our little village shop to a retail chain. We'd had it for ages and worked seven days a week for far too many years, with no days off, let alone holidays, and as our home was above the shop we had to find somewhere to live. We rented a little house for six months and then came here on holiday and we both instantly knew it would be a nice place to retire to. Travelling to and fro for a few months, we finally found our villa and moved over here permanently. Our possessions came a week or so after us and we were both so excited – it was the start of a new life, a real adventure. Then, one day soon after that, after we'd been for a walk and had lunch in one of the local restaurants, Robert said he didn't feel very well and went to have a lie down on the bed. And, well ... he didn't wake up. He had a heart attack.'

'Oh, Graham, I'm so sorry. I don't know what to say.'

'Mable turned up that same day and we've been

together ever since. That's ... that's the first time I've talked about it to anyone. I always knew I would have to and wondered what it would feel like... It's strange, now someone else – well, you – know the situation.'

'Can I ask, do you have any relations?'

'No, Robert and I don't have any family beyond a few distant relatives, so it's been just me and Mable these last few years.'

Sophie wanted to give him a huge hug as she knew that he needed someone to help him get through this, but perhaps that wasn't the right thing to do at this precise moment. Instead, she thought it best to change the subject. She didn't want to dismiss what he had told her, of course, but she wanted to give him time to process the fact that he'd finally shared his pain with someone. Thankfully, Mable decided just then to jump off the chair and demand to be fussed over, which helpfully bought the conversation back to the cat and the impending arrival of her kittens.

'I've had a thought, why don't I see if one of the people I've met here knows where we can get a cat carrying box, and find out which vets to go to? That way we can take her to be checked out and then we can take her back to yours. I know, I'll call Ramon the taxi driver. He'll know how we should do it.'

'That's a good idea. Ramon has always been kind to me, helping me by doing some food shopping and taking me to Playa de las Américas and back to sort registering Robert's death.'

Sophie quickly called Ramon who did indeed know where to borrow a cat basket. He also gave her the phone number for the vets and they got lucky as when Sophie called she was told the vet could see them at five o'clock that same day. Sophie and Graham agreed to meet back outside Villa Kennal at four forty-five, when Ramon would pick them up to take them and Mable to the appointment.

'Thank you for all of this, Sophie. It was a lovely lunch and I really appreciate you listening. I think it's done me good to talk about things and hopefully I don't come across as being that strange old man that lives up the lane anymore.'

****

As Sophie walked back from showing Graham out, she could see Rich and the rest of the guests around the pool. All were very quiet – the rowdiness of their first night having long gone – and somehow she thought this would be the last holiday they would all be having together. She had three hours before going to the vets, so she spent the time working on the Villa Kennal website, checking bookings and updating the calendar. But she found her mind was wandering. Although Graham had explained about his partner dying, there seemed to be a lot more to his story ... but Sophie couldn't put her finger on what it might be. There were still secrets to be discovered when it came to Graham... She smiled to herself at the thought, realising that she used to have secrets like Graham, but not anymore. She had told them to her mum, and Cristina and Luis, and each time she'd talked about Mark she'd felt different – lighter, somehow. And the best thing? She felt the distance between her and Mark was getting bigger all the time, and that was a good thing.

****

'Thank you so much, Ramon, it was very kind of you to wait for us while we were in the vets,' Graham said as they piled out of the taxi after the appointment.

'Yes, thanks! Now, Graham, let me carry the box into yours; it will be heavy,' Sophie offered.

'Oh no, dear, I can manage. Thank you both, goodbye for now!'

With the way Graham hurried off it was clear there was no way he was letting Sophie through that gate. But then Ramon said he needed to get the cat box back. Could this be an opportunity to have a look by volunteering to go and get it? No, if Graham didn't want anyone to go in, she should respect his wishes.

Ramon was back with the cat box in what felt like literally seconds and asked if she had got over Emily's visit.

'I have, but I'm also very keen to fill all the vacant dates in Villa Kennal's diary so she doesn't come back!'

Ramon laughed. 'Some of Kennal's other family members are very nice, but it's been years since I've seen anyone other than Emily at the villa.'

'Interesting. Right, thanks again, Ramon, for today. Like Graham said, it was very kind of you.'

'Sophie, can I ask you something? I'm just a little curious and I know it's none of my business, but ... do you know why Graham has never unpacked his belongings? And why he doesn't have any furniture apart from the garden furniture, which is indoors? Also he wears the same clothes every time I pick him up with his shopping. I've tried to make conversation and create an opening to see if he's ok, but he doesn't want to talk. It's all very sad.'

'I've noticed something is off as well. I think I'm going to do some digging and see if I can't find out what's going on with him.'

'That's a good idea. Let me know if you need any help.'

'I will. Thanks again, Ramon.'

Chapter 14

Though happy to be saying goodbye to Rich and his friends, Sophie was dreading having to clean the whole villa before the next guests arrived. Thankfully, the leaving group had an early flight so they would be up and out by seven o'clock, giving her plenty of time to prep the villa for the next guests' arrival later in the day. It was nearly six and she was raring to get stuck in, partly to get the work done but also partly as a means of taking her mind off of what Ramon had said yesterday. She had to agree that Graham's life was very odd and she worried that the only thing that had happened since his partner died was Mable coming into his life. It was as if the world was standing still for him and nothing mattered now that Robert was gone. How sad that was.

She also couldn't help thinking about Ramon saying Kennal had 'other family'. What did he mean by that? Were there other children – please, no more Emilys! – or did he mean ex-wives?

Between Graham and Kennal there was certainly more than enough to keep her intrigued!

All of a sudden, she heard her little gate go. Someone was coming up to the bungalow and a quick glance out of the window told her it was Rich. Thankfully, he was by himself and there was no sign of Mandy.

'Hi, Sophie. I didn't think we should leave without saying goodbye and wishing you well. We've had a great time and I just hope the rest of the summer's guests are a lot easier than we've been!'

'You've been no bother, Rich, and I'm glad to hear you've all had a lovely holiday.'

'Thank you, we have. Even Mandy, not that she would admit to it... But no, it's been fun. The minibus to pick us up should be here any minute so before I go, here's a little something for you,' he said, handing over a sealed envelope.

'Oh! You shouldn't have, but thank you.'

It was nice of him to leave an additional tip but she placed the envelope on her little coffee table as it seemed the wrong thing to open it in front of him. Following him back to the villa to say goodbye to the rest of the guests, she found them all heading down to the main gate. They shouted 'goodbye' and 'thank you' – also a few apologies, which Sophie brushed off, saying they had nothing to apologise for. She really just wanted them to depart so she could go into the villa and see what state they'd left it in.

Unsurprisingly, Mandy didn't say goodbye or thank her and no doubt she didn't have a clue about the tip her husband had left. A few more steps and they would be gone... But then Mandy turned around. 'I think I've left my best flip-flops down by the pool. Go and get them for me.'

Sophie just smiled. If Mandy thought she was having the last word, she was mistaken. Off Sophie went and of course there were no flip-flops, but there was a book. Hopefully by the time she got back with it she would have a full audience.

'No, sorry, Mandy,' she said as she walked through the villa's gate. 'There were no flip-flops, but if I find them, I will post them to you. I did find a book though. I think it belongs to your son.'

'My son? What do you mean? He's not my son, you rude girl! He's my husband!'

She was fuming not only because of what Sophie had said but also because she hadn't had the last word. Sophie could see all the others smirking to themselves and before Mandy could say anything else Rich ushered her out of the gate, turning around to Sophie and giving her a wink.

Walking back up to the villa, Sophie was

laughing and feeling very proud of herself. It was worth all the hassle they had caused just to see that look on Mandy's face. Once inside, she was quite shocked at how far from terrible it was. No doubt that was all down to the other couples.

****

Six hours later and the place was spick and span. Everything had been cleaned to within an inch of its life, the beds were made, the complimentary wine, water, milk and biscuits were in place and so all she had to do now was wait for the guests to arrive. Locking the villa behind her – because until she had payment from this next group they weren't going in – she checked the airport arrivals on her phone to confirm the plane would be on time. Then she sent a text to Luis to let him know so he could be here when they arrived. She hated asking him but she was nervous they might try to force their way in.

She had a few hours to kill so she had a shower and grabbed something to eat. Sitting on the veranda she realised she was missing having Mable for company and that thought brought her back to thinking about Graham, and if there was a way of helping him.

As her gate made its little warning noise and Luis came into view, she smiled.

'Thank you for this. I'm so sorry you've had to come though,' she said in greeting.

'It's not a problem. I think it's happened before when Kennal had twice as many people turn up than there was booked. By the way, what did you say they were called, and do you know how many of them there will be?'

'The person I've spoken to is a Mrs Smith – which is the same as the name on the booking – but that likely won't be her real name, and I don't know how many of them there will be. I've just checked my phone and the plane lands in about ten minutes so we have a couple of hours before they get here. As you're here early, do you fancy a beer while we wait?'

Luis said yes and as there was no one else there Sophie suggested they go and sit by the pool to enjoy the last of the sunshine. Sophie was pleased she'd had time to shower and get changed as it was important to make a good impression on the holiday makers, but she was also glad because of the way it was making Luis look at her. Yet still, in the back of her head, was Cristina. Sophie knew her friend would have a problem with any girl liking Luis, especially her.

As they waited they chatted about the villa, Graham and the cat, and when Cristina's name came up he said he was surprised she hadn't moved away yet.

'Perhaps that's because you're still here,' Sophie suggested.

'No, she doesn't want me – I'm too boring. Look, enough of her, can I say something? I know we didn't start off on the right foot but that's my fault – both for messing up with Kennal in the first place and for taking my frustration out on you – but now we seem to be enjoying each other's company and, well ... how about we have a night out sometime?'

'I'd like that. So ... are you officially inviting me out on another date?'

Luis was blushing and Sophie wished she hadn't said the word 'date' as that put pressure on the evening for both of them. It also stopped the conversation dead. Thankfully, they were saved by the sound of a car pulling up and doors opening, followed by muffled voices.

'This sounds like them. I have to admit I'm a little nervous.'

'Come on, everything will be fine. If they haven't got money to pay, well, they aren't coming in and that is it.'

Sophie knew she had to go first and introduce herself – Luis was really only meant to be there in case she needed back-up – but as they walked down to meet the guests her heart was racing. Opening the gate, she could see the taxi driver and two women she didn't know. Stepping outside to speak to them at the gate, she watched as the taxi driver got into his car and the older women walked towards her. She was a very smartly dressed and glamorous fifty-something and the other woman – who was a lot younger; a daughter, perhaps? – stood behind her.

'Hello. Welcome to Villa Kennal! Now, this is a little awkward, but before I can let you in the owner has insisted that I need to take payment for the booking.'

What happened next was something she never could have expected and certainly never even crossed her mind as a possibility.

'My my, little Luis is not so little anymore... Look, Casey, whoever would have thought it?'

'Hello Mrs—' Luis mumbled from behind Sophie.

'Just call me Velma, you always used to,' the older woman interrupted him. 'Now, are you going to let us come in and see what he's done with the place? And Sophie? One phone call to Kennal and I think you will find that I will not, in fact, be paying for this holiday. You see, Casey is his daughter ... and I am his ex-wife.'

Sophie paled. If Emily had been a nightmare, what would his ex-wife – and a second daughter – be like?

'By the way, he didn't know we were coming. Could you let him know?'

Chapter 15

Sophie was up early as she was determined to get out of the complex before Velma and Casey were up. Well, that's if Casey ended up coming back last night after her evening out with Luis. But first she tried reaching her mum again. She needed to find out if Madeline knew anything about this pair. Aside from a lot of swearing, Kennal had been very close-lipped about them, telling Sophie to just leave them to it and confirming that there would be no charge for the accommodation.

'At last, Mum! I left messages for you all last night. Why didn't you call me back? It could have been life and death for all you knew!'

'I'm sorry, darling, I turned my phone off when we were filming and forgot to switch it back on. Now, what is so urgent? Your message said you want to know if I knew the guests who had just turned up?'

'Yes, Mum, it's Kennal's ex-wife and another daughter and I wanted to know if you knew-'

'Velma. Yes, I know Mrs Glamorous And Very High Maintenance. Have you told Kennal she's there? I bet he's glad he's in America!'

'So you do know her?'

'Yes, I think she was wife number two ... or was it three? I'm sorry to say this, darling, but somehow I don't think she will want to leave in a hurry. Now Kennal has hit the big time again she will want to see what's in it for her. I wish I could be more help but I really should go as I need to get ready. I'm expected on set in a couple of hours.'

Sophie wished her mum luck and coming off the call she found it wasn't Velma that she was interested in, it was Casey. Once Velma had swanned into the villa Casey had been all hugs and kisses for Luis, her childhood friend and, well ... they were both a lot older now and from what Sophie saw last night it seemed like they might be interested in moving from playing together in the school yard to playing together in the bedroom...

****

An hour later, with beach bag in hand, she was ready to head off and wouldn't be coming back until late in the evening. Spotting Velma and Casey down by the pool as she made her way to the gate, she wondered if she should wave or just pretend she hadn't seen them, then it was too late as Velma called her over. She had to be polite but she would make it clear she was in a hurry to be somewhere.

'Good morning, have you and your daughter settled in ok? Do you have everything you need? Kennal said it was best to leave you to get on with things for your stay so I won't be in to the villa to clean while you're here.'

'Yes, I bet he did. "No extras for Velma" were probably his very words. Tell me, how do you fit into this little set-up? Are you the latest girlfriend, or perhaps the last one and he has a new one in America?'

'Neither. I've never met Kennal. I'm simply here to work for the summer and apparently I now have two weeks off – fully paid – so if you will excuse me? Have a lovely holiday. Goodbye.'

The look on Velma's face was a picture but there was no way Sophie would be forced into conversation with that woman again. She couldn't imagine what Kennal had seen in her.

Deciding to stop in and see Graham before she went to the beach, Sophie walked up the lane and knocked on his gate. This time, he was there within seconds.

'Hi, Sophie, have you come to find out how Mable's getting on? She's fine apart from the fact I'm not letting her out of my sight. But saying that, she seems quite content not to wander off ... but perhaps she's tricking me into a false sense of security.' He laughed lightly.

'Oh that's so good to hear. Would it be ok if I came in and said hello to her? Also, does she need anything?'

'Perhaps another time as I'm actually just on my way out. I'm going for a little walk and I thought I would have some lunch down in the town.'

Yet again there was no way he was letting her in.

'That sounds lovely, may I join you? I had to get out of the villa today and can explain why over lunch.'

'Of course! I'm more than happy to have the company.'

As they headed down to the square she couldn't help thinking this was a positive development. Perhaps she could use this opportunity to question Graham about his mysterious life.

Coming to a bench overlooking the little church, Sophie thought that if she was very open and honest about her life, Graham would perhaps do the same. She would start by telling him the whole story of how she'd ended up at Villa Kennal, and everything that had happened so far, right up to Velma and Kennal's daughter arriving.

'So, where do you fancy going for some lunch, Graham? You choose as you've been here longer than me. Where's the best place?'

'Oh, no, I just go to the same couple of restaurants. Have you found anywhere you like? You could introduce me to somewhere different.'

'Well, my favourite places so far are over in Del Duque. Would you like to catch the bus with me? Do you have the time?'

'Yes, and that would be nice. I've not been there for years – not since before Robert and I moved here. We stayed there on holiday in a lovely hotel with beautiful sea views.'

'Great! I know of a fantastic restaurant that serves a specialty chicken dish that is absolutely delicious. The recipe is decades old!'

Once on the bus the conversation was all about the sights they were passing and general chit chat but all the time Sophie was wondering how she could get Graham to open up. It was actually making her feel a bit uncomfortable because she really wanted to help him but she also didn't want to put Graham in an awkward situation.

When they got off the bus the first thing they did was go and look over the sea wall. With all the boats bobbing gently in the water it looked amazing.

'This is what sold the area to Robert and me – this view. It's making all those memories of our very first visit come flooding back. It's lovely here in the daytime but it doesn't have the atmosphere of the evenings, or the smells. I remember walking around the lanes and passing the little restaurants with all the beautiful aromas coming from them. Do you mind if we sit down for a few minutes? I'm feeling a little wobbly.'

'Of course! There's a bench over there, look. You sit and I'll go and get us some bottled water.'

Sophie walked with him to the seat in the shade and then went to find a shop for the water. Oh dear, was coming here a step too far for Graham? There was obviously a reason he hadn't been since Robert died: too many memories. Perhaps today wasn't the right time to be asking any questions after all. Drinks bought, she headed back and handed one over.

'Thank you, my dear, it is very warm, isn't it? Now, tell me more about this restaurant that you've recommended.'

'Well, it's nothing fancy and if you'd like to go somewhere different that's absolutely ok with me, but when I first went in, I felt instantly at home.'

'That sounds perfect. Please lead the way.'

Sophie could see that during those few minutes alone on the bench he had got himself together, but she was still worried about him. Was this how he was living his life here in Tenerife, by blocking everything out and avoiding anything that brought up memories of Robert? But that wasn't living, it was just existing... She realised that was likely why his villa and garden were like they were. Graham was going from one day to the next without purpose, feeling as if nothing mattered. It made her want to cry.

'Here we are,' she announced as they approached the restaurant. 'It's quieter than the last time I was here, but that's probably because of the time – it isn't really lunch or dinner time, is it? Can you smell the chicken? Oh, even if you weren't hungry, that aroma would make you want to eat! There's a table over there under the canopy that will shade us from the sun. Shall we?'

Once settled they gave the waitress their orders and then sunk into a companionable silence as they waited for their food.

'I hope you're hungry,' Graham said as the heaped plates were set before them.

'I certainly am! This is so lovely, isn't it? It could even become a habit seeing as I don't have any work to do at the villa until Velma and Casey have gone in a couple of weeks' time.'

They got stuck in and chatted about the area and the people walking by. It was as though Graham had really switched off and let himself relax, which Sophie felt good about.

'We'll be rolling back to Los Kalanchoe after all

this food! Do you fancy another carafe of wine? I think we will need it to wash everything down.'

****

Nearly two hours later the food had gone and they were finishing off the last drops of wine. Sophie had done most of the talking, telling Graham everything from the fact her mum was an actress, to the ins and outs of her relationship with Mark. Her life was now an open book and secretly she was hoping he would feel comfortable to be as open and honest with her as she'd been with him.

'Shall we make a move? And this is my treat, by the way. The food and the wine have been beautiful. If you'd like to, and if you have time, we could go for a little walk around the lanes and shops? Not that I need to buy anything...' Graham said, trailing off.

'Thank you for the offer but I should be the one to pay as it was me that invited you up here. Also, you might not need any shopping, but that doesn't mean you can't still treat yourself to something!'

That was evidently the wrong thing to say and Sophie watched in horror as Graham's face changed, going from hopeful and happy to sad and almost distant. Quickly changing the subject, Sophie asked for the bill and bundled Graham off to discover what else apart from lovely restaurants this town had to offer. Neither of them could believe how fast the time had gone; it was now going on for six thirty but they agreed there was no need to rush back. All Graham had waiting for him would be a grumpy Mable. She had been shut indoors for her own sake but once the kittens had been born, she would be free to wander from villa to villa again. Graham had mentioned the atmosphere here at night and how lovely it was to look across into the other bays with all the twinkling lights when it got dark, but Sophie was wary about staying until then as that might bring back too many memories of his time here with Robert. She was about to suggest they catch the bus home when Graham turned to her.

'It's getting busy. Would you like a coffee before we go? Or maybe a gin and tonic to finish the evening off. I think I need it; it's about time I come clean to you about my life here in Tenerife,' Graham said softly.

Sophie nodded and they wandered over to a café bar in one of the little lanes. Two gin and tonics were ordered and before Graham said anything Sophie explained he didn't need to talk about anything he didn't feel comfortable talking about, but he said perhaps it was time he did.

'You see, both Robert and I had so many dreams when we arrived here. We had arranged to have our villa decorated. We had looked at furniture pictures and spent hours planning the garden's design ... and then he died. It was all of a sudden and without any warning, and all the dreams went with him. I'm sure you've figured out that my life has stood still since that day. I've done nothing and that's because why should I? There's no one to share it with so what is the point anymore? My days are filled with waiting for the day to end so I can go back to bed and try to sleep.'

'I'm so sorry, Graham. Life can be very cruel, but surely-'

'I know what you're going to say. "Surely Robert wouldn't have wanted you to live like this." Of course he wouldn't, but I get into a kind of fog and it never occurs to me to unpack our belongings or take steps forward with the villa – even my clothes are still in suitcases and boxes! I just live – or should I say exist – in the same clothes because I have nothing to get dressed up for.

'But in a strange way I'm content with my lot.

I'm not hurting anyone and I have Mable to get out of bed for every day, and soon, a few kittens.'

'I don't know what to say. How have you felt today? Have you enjoyed yourself? It's been something very different for you.'

'Oh yes, I've loved it. It's been very special.'

'Graham, you could have lots of days like today and as you've seen it wouldn't take much effort. Also, I think Robert would be really happy that you've had a day out.'

There was a silence for a while as Graham pondered what she'd said. Sophie wasn't going to push him to do anything that made him feel uncomfortable, but she also wanted him to start to realise that when someone dies, no matter how sad the situation, life still had to go on, even if it was only eventually, and after a few stuttering starts.

'He would be more than happy. He would also be so mad at me for the way I've lived my life since he died. I can actually hear him now going off on one because I've been wasting my time for so long. You're right, Sophie, Robert would want me to start having fun again.'

Chapter 16

'Good morning, Mable! Yes, you can go out, but only into the garden where I can keep an eye on you. There will be *no* visiting any other villas until after those kittens are born, do you hear me? But before you go out, I need to say something ... well, I should have said something a few days ago, not that you'll understand me. The day I went out with Sophie I talked about Robert and I just know I've opened up a can of worms. For a start, she is probably going to encourage me to do things more often. Oh, I liked our day out, don't get me wrong, but that was a one-off and I don't know if I'm ready to do other things. You aren't listening to me, are you, Mable? Go on then, I've opened the door for you, but as I said, don't wander off.'

Graham made a tea and took it outside so he could keep an eye on Mable. His head was full of jumbled thoughts, some of which he had been blocking out for the last few years, like the acknowledgement that the garden in front of him was a mess. How had he ever let it get into the state it was? Robert would be annoyed and that thought hurt but nowhere near as much as the hurt he had in his heart for Robert's loss. Why had life been so cruel? Why hadn't he been the one to die first? Robert would have coped a lot better if it was him here by himself.

Graham pushed the thoughts out of his head. Now, if he could only avoid Sophie, he could get back to how he was before she arrived.

****

It had been a few days since Sophie's day out with Graham and their conversations had been playing on her mind. She needed to check on him and make sure he was ok but first she needed to answer the flurry of emails from Kennal wanting to know what Velma was up to. The truth was, she didn't know. Sophie had been avoiding her and Casey as though they were playing an unspoken game of hide and seek. While they were around the pool or on the patios Sophie went out. When they went out to eat then she would sit on her veranda, hurrying back into her bungalow when she heard them coming through the main gate. But now, after saying she should leave them to it, Kennal wanted her to try and find out why they were here. Sadly, and very annoyingly, it meant she would have to get into conversation with a least one of them.

Just as she was planning her day, in came Javier. After a quick hello and a review of what his jobs were for the day, she mentioned there were two guests currently staying in the villa – a mother and daughter. And then it crossed her mind that perhaps he knew Velma from when she'd been married to Kennal.

'You might actually know the guest, Javier – it's one of Kennal's ex-wives.'

'Please tell me it's not the one who thinks she is a beauty queen. She was the only one of Kennal's lady friends I didn't get on with. I think she's called Velma?'

'That's the one and I can understand why you'd say "beauty queen". She's very glamorous.'

'Yes, and if you ask a few of the men in Los Kalanchoe, they will say the same, but I know better. Do I take my orders from her while she's here?'

'No way. She's a guest on holiday and you don't need to do anything she tells you to do. The sooner she goes, the better, as far as I'm concerned.'

To create an opportunity to speak with one of the two guests and get some answers for Kennal,

Sophie decided she would sweep and mop around the pool and the patios. Looking through the bushes she could see they weren't outside yet so she walked over to the villa to get started. She wasn't sure what she was going to ask them if they did get into conversation but as long as she had something to feed back to Kennal, that was all that mattered.

It was surprising how dirty the pool area had gotten in the few days since she'd stopped doing it regularly, but thankfully it appeared there was no rubbish from Velma or Casey. As she was sweeping she glanced up at the villa to find the doors were still closed. It looked like neither was up yet. After going to fill her mop bucket she saw the gate open on her way back to the pool. It was Luis, the last person she needed to see today. She couldn't let him see she was jealous of him and Casey spending time together; she had to make out everything was normal as much as she wanted to tell him where to go.

'Hi, Luis, how are you? Was it me you were looking for, or *Casey*?'

Well, there went her resolve to keep her feelings to herself...

'Both, actually. I've come to pick Casey up as we're going out for the day on my bike, and I also wanted to sort out a night when you and I can have our date.'

Sophie was fuming and rubbed the mop so hard across the ground that she nearly snapped the handle. Here he was going on a date with Casey and he had the audacity to try and arrange a time to go out with her too? What type of person did he think she was? Did he honestly expect that she would just stupidly wait around for him?

As she turned her back on him the villa door opened and there was Casey, dressed to the nines with beach bag in hand. There was no way Sophie

118

was going to get in a conversation now so she walked to the far end of the pool, hoping they would head right out. Only once she'd heard the gate close and Luis's bike start up did she turn around. As she still had nothing to report back to Kennal, she'd need to make conversation with Velma at some point. As if in answer to her prayers, Velma walked out of the villa just then and plonked herself down on the top patio. Sophie gave her a little wave and finished off the pool area by wiping down the sun beds and the handle down into the pool. She was just going to empty her bucket and get some clean water when she noticed Velma was heading down towards her.

'Good morning. Thank you for that. I thought you had some time off?'

'Hi, I have, but if I leave this more than a few days it's a nightmare so it's best to keep on top of it. Are you having a nice holiday? The weather's been good for you.'

'Yes, it's been an interesting few days. When we were out to dinner last night Luis happened to mention your mother is Madeline Mundey. Now you being here makes sense. Madeline was the lucky one as she got away. Sadly, I fell for the charm and became one of the many Mrs Kennals. Both your mum and Kennal seem to be having a little bit of an upswing in fame in their later years, which must be nice for both of them ... but not so much fun for you, what with being left to clean this place for the summer. I'd argue you got the short straw, just as I have. But if he thinks he can just sweep me away again he is very much mistaken. It's time for Velma to have her day and not be pushed into a box and forgotten about.'

'Oh, it's not too bad,' she said, once Velma had finished slagging Kennal off and saying 'at least you can't really mess up with cleaning'.

'It's lovely, actually, a couple of hours cleaning and then I walk the half an hour to the beach and while away the rest of the day. And I'm paid well for doing it. How could I complain? By the way, this must be a nice change for you – to have open space instead of being stuck in a flat. It must feel like paradise to you, Velma, even though it's – unfortunately – just for a couple of weeks. Yes, I do appreciate having what I've got.'

Kennal had asked her to find things out but he didn't say Sophie had to be nice to Velma.

'So, you have a sharp tongue just like your mother, and I see Kennal has filled you in on my life as well. That can only mean one thing – he wants to know what I'm up to being here and no doubt he's sent you to find out for him. Is this a game to you, Sophie?'

'I haven't time for games; I have a life to lead here in the beautiful Tenerife sunshine. I'm young, free, single... The world is my oyster! You must remember those days, surely? Right, I best be off. Have a lovely day!'

Sophie didn't know where any of that had come from – and she hadn't come away with any information for Kennal – but she was proud of herself for standing up to Velma. The only thing was, did she really believe what she had just said? Was the world her oyster or was she just a holiday cleaner? One thing was for sure, she had to show Velma she was having the time of her life even though she wasn't. So, an afternoon on the beach it had to be.

****

After a quick shower she sent an email to Kennal to tell him she hadn't found anything out, and then headed off to the bakery. Today she had earned not one, not two, but *three* of the biggest pastries they had for sale.

She was just walking to her favourite part of the beach when coming towards her she spotted Ramon.

'Hi, Ramon, how are you? A lovely day, isn't it? I'm off to the beach as I've some time off.'

'Time off? But didn't you just have guests arrive the other day?' Ramon asked, confused.

'I did but you will never guess what's happened – the visitors are Kennal's family!'

'Emily has returned?'

'No, not Emily, one of Kennal's ex-wives and another daughter.'

'Casey is here? Really? It's years since I've seen her... I mean... I'm sorry, I need to go... I have a fare to pick up.'

He didn't even give Sophie time to say goodbye before he was gone but she didn't have time to ponder on his odd behaviour because Cristina had appeared from around a corner and was heading towards her. What were the odds?

'Hi, Cristina, another gorgeous day in Tenerife, isn't it? How lucky we are to live in such a lovely place.'

'Sophie! You are just the person I was hoping to see. Do you know what's going on with Luis and this girl from England? They seem to be spending a lot of time together, going out during the day and eating in restaurants every night. Are they a couple? I thought it was you he was interested in.'

Sophie wanted to say so did she, but instead she just explained that from what she gathered they had sort of grown up together. And though she wanted to ask why it would be a problem if they had got together, she knew it was because Cristina didn't want to be with Luis, but she also didn't want anyone else to have him.

'I'm sorry. I must sound like a bitter old

woman.'

'No, you don't sound old or bitter, but have you thought that perhaps what you really want is Luis? Why don't you both give it another go? There's obviously an attraction and a tension between you still.'

'No, he's gorgeous but he's boring – or, at least, he was, until this woman came into the picture. I need someone who wants to travel the world, but saying that, I guess if I'd wanted to I could now be living it up in America on a film set. It would be the lifestyle I wanted, but not the man I would want to be there with. You see, Sophie, I had a short fling with Kennal.'

Sophie was speechless.

'Please don't repeat that. No one knows, not even Luis, as it only lasted a couple of weeks last year. I would have loved being part of everything Kennal's involved with in the US – the glitz, the glamour, the excitement of the Hollywood set and the chance for travel – but he just wasn't the one for me.'

Chapter 17

The more Sophie thought about Kennal, the more she was glad her mum had never been involved with him. But perhaps she had been, because from what it looked like he just went from one woman to the next. And as for Cristina... She really didn't deserve Luis. Actually, thinking about it, perhaps she and Kennal should get together again. They seemed well suited and it would also stop them messing up anyone else's life!

After the confrontation with Velma yesterday, Sophie decided she'd better keep busy today. Cleaning equipment at the ready, she headed off to sweep all the paths around the villa. Looking down towards the pool, she could see three people on the loungers – Luis was there. She hadn't heard him come through the gate ... did that mean he stayed the night? Oh, she didn't want to think that! No, she wanted to believe that he and Casey were just two old friends, who hadn't seen each other for years, who were spending time together catching up. Perhaps she should leave the cleaning until another day... No, blow it, she hadn't done anything wrong so why should she be the one hiding?

Go on, Sophie, head in the air and the same confidence that you had yesterday.

She decided to start by sweeping up by the villa. It was the farthest point away from the three of them and it was quite easy to keep her back to them.

She felt it the moment she'd been spotted and wondered who would be the first to speak to her. She didn't have to wait long. Velma appeared beside her, on her way into the villa with a tray of plates and mugs.

'Hello,' she said, surprisingly politely.

'Good morning,' Sophie said, and thought they'd

leave it at that. But apparently Velma was out for the kill.

'You think you are so smug, don't you, young lady? Well, I will tell you this, you might not be Kennal's girlfriend, but he will still use you and then, when he's had enough, he'll get rid of you. And then where will you be?'

Sophie shrugged. 'Probably back in the UK, working. Oh, but saying that, I seem to have made a few contacts here in Tenerife... I could probably stay and work a few seasons because that's what you can do when you are young and free with no responsibility.'

Velma huffed and walked on into the villa, and Sophie continued sweeping the paths. She'd thought it would feel good to hold her own with the older woman but she actually felt bad about snapping at Velma. This wasn't her at all. She had never been a nasty person and didn't want to start being one now, so she resolved to email Kennal once she was done with the cleaning to tell him she hadn't found anything and would not be doing any more snooping. What she really wanted to say though, was that he might get what he was looking for if he just asked her himself. After all, Velma had been his wife and was still the mother to Kennal's daughter. Sophie was just the cleaning woman.

Once she had finished the cleaning, she got herself ready to head off out. The last thing she wanted was to get into conversation with Velma or Luis, and besides, she wanted to pop up and see Graham and find out how Mable was. Perhaps now she'd had that chat with Graham and he'd started opening up, he might let her into the villa?

****

After popping down to pick up a few pastries from

the bakery, Sophie knocked on Graham's gate. There was no answer and she wasn't able to open it as it was locked. Sophie was just about to give up when she heard Graham call out.

'Oh, I'm sorry, Sophie, I've been keeping it locked so no one can accidentally leave it open, as I don't want Mable getting out. She's feeling a little cabin feverish but the last thing I need is for her to wander off and have the kittens somewhere that's not safe.'

'Of course! I've brought a few pastries and thought you might like an update on the visitors at Villa Kennal.'

'Yes to both, please, and I think it's about time I let you through the gate. I warn you though, the garden is not a pretty sight.'

Graham was right, the garden *was* a mess, but surely that was something exciting – a blank canvas to build from. Sophie handed him the bag of pastries and took him up on the offer of a beverage. She could see Mable basking in the sunshine on the patio so went over for a fuss. The cat had been getting bigger by the day and gave Sophie a look that seemed to shout, 'why are you disturbing me?'

'There you go, one coffee. I've also bought a couple of plates to put the pastries on. By the way, I must thank you again for the lovely day over in Del Duque. I really enjoyed myself so much; it was very special.'

'I did as well! Now, let me tell you what's been happening in the villa...'

Sophie explained how she was a bit concerned she was getting pulled into Kennal and Velma's differences and had emailed him to say that.

'I've spoken to him half a dozen times since I've lived here and he's always been very pleasant. There is one thing though... It annoys me that he always has sunglasses on, whatever the weather, and I can

125

never see his eyes. Oh, and also a baseball cap. It's as if he's constantly in hiding, but now I guess, being an actor, he does it because he doesn't want to be recognised...

'I have something to tell you as well, Sophie. It's not that exciting, really, and very normal for most people, but I've unpacked a few boxes of kitchen things – plates, glasses, cutlery – and do you know, it wasn't that hard once I got started? And it's all thanks to you and our day out.'

'Oh, Graham, I'm so pleased! I've been worried about you and have spent hours wondering how I can help. Don't feel you need to rush to get everything done though. Take your time and if one day you aren't in the mood, it really doesn't matter as there will always be other days.'

'That's good advice. I think the kitchen was the easy bit to start with as most of the things go in cupboards so, technically, they're still packed away, in a way.'

He was right, unpacking boxes was a great start, but Sophie could tell this garden would need professional help.

****

As she said goodbye and closed the gate behind her some time later, she thought about what a huge step forward it was for Graham to unpack boxes after two years of not even looking in them. It was a promising start and she would be here to help and encourage him all the way.

As she walked down the lane she could see Luis coming out of Villa Kennal. He was just about to get on his bike when he noticed her – the last thing she wanted to happen. No matter, she wouldn't let him see how miffed she was with him about all the time he was spending with Casey.

'Hi, Luis, are you having a nice time with your friends? The weather is lovely for their visit,' she said, an edge to her words.

'Why all the hostility, Sophie? From what I've seen, you've been completely rude and offhand with Casey and Velma. That's not really the right attitude to have when you're supposed to be creating a warm and welcoming atmosphere for guests at the villa.'

'You what? One, I've not said more than two words to Casey, and as for Velma ... well, I think you'll find *she* is the one with the attitude, not me. And also, I'm employed by Kennal and his exact words to me when he found out his ex-wife had turned up here were, and I quote: "Sophie, you are doing a wonderful job running Villa Kennal. It's the first time I've ever been able to completely switch off from it all. Please take the two weeks off while Velma is there. You've earned it." Now, was there anything else you had to say, Luis, because I'm in a hurry?'

He got on his bike and drove off without saying another word. Sophie felt bad about her outburst but how dare he talk to her like that. Who did he think he was? But enough of him and Villa Kennal, she was off to have a day on the beach.

****

Graham locked the gate behind Sophie as he didn't want Mable to get out and if Sophie was going to be popping in and out more frequently, he just needed those few extra seconds the locked gate would grant him to compose himself before she came in. Why? Because all of this business about unpacking boxes was an act. Oh, he hadn't lied to her; a few kitchen things had come out of boxes and gone into drawers, and though their day out was lovely that was because it didn't happen inside the villa. No, here

127

there were too many memories of conversations he and Robert had had about their future together, planning what they were going to do in and around the property, and now that was never going to happen. And he didn't think he could ever move on from that.

'So, Mable, until Sophie leaves at the end of the season, I'm going to have to put on an act and let her think I'm moving on with my life. Not like you. No, before long you'll have brand new kittens to look after and a whole new adventure will start. Somehow, though, I think you are going to be a good mum.'

****

Sophie liked the walk to the beach even though it took a good half an hour. Los Kalanchoe being inland made it that little bit different and made it feel more of a town than a holiday resort. It also put off a lot of holiday makers so when she walked around, the locals recognised her and said hello. Oh, there was the odd person who would ask if she was staying in the film star's villa, but she made it quite clear that she was looking after it, not vacationing in it. The last thing she needed was everyone thinking she was destined to be the next Mrs Kennal!

She was nearly at the beach when her phone rang.

'Hi, Greg, is everything ok? Is your sister enjoying living in the flat?'

'Hi, Sophie! Yes, she loves it and that's actually why I'm phoning. The company she moved here to work for have asked her if she would stay for two years instead of just the twelve months, as they have a project they want her to head up, and so she asked me to call you and see if you might be open to letting her sublet the flat for the whole of her stay.'

Sophie didn't need to give it any thought; she instantly said yes. After saying goodbye and coming off the phone, however, she asked herself what she'd just done. But then, maybe she could stay here in Tenerife? Could that even be possible? One thing was for sure, without a home to go back to in the UK, she had some thinking to do!

Chapter 18

Sophie still hadn't really processed the fact she had agreed with Greg yesterday to allow his sister to sublet her flat. Would Kennal want to keep her on after the agreed eight months? Luis certainly wouldn't like that as she'd told him several times she wouldn't be here next year and Kennal might ask him back... But enough of those thoughts for now, she had work to do.

She got through a little bit of paperwork and emails and then headed off, eager to get out of the complex before Velma and Casey were up. She had no clue what she was going to do with herself for the day but a coffee down in the square would be the perfect start, and if she took her beach things with her she wouldn't have to come back if she suddenly decided she fancied a day of lying in the sun. She was nearly in the centre of Los Kalanchoe when she saw Luis on his scooter. She knew he had seen her too but there was no wave, let alone stopping for a chat. He was obviously still annoyed that she had upset Velma.

She had just sat down and ordered a coffee when her phone rang. Looking at the screen she saw it was Graham, which could mean only one thing – the kittens must have been born!

'Hi, Graham, how many are there? Are they gorgeous?'

'No kittens yet, I'm afraid.'

'Oh, sorry, I thought that must be why you were ringing.'

'No, I'm phoning because Mable has got out without me seeing and I thought the first place she might head was to your bungalow.'

'Good point. What a madam she is, climbing walls in her condition. I bet she thinks she's going to be fed twice. I expect she'll be curled up on one of my chairs – or, if she could speak, what she'd probably call *her* chair. I'm just having a coffee in the town but I'll get it to go and head back. I'll pick her up and see you within the hour.'

Walking back to the villa it wasn't Mable who was on Sophie's mind, but Velma. She was bound to be up now and ready to have a go after yesterday's put down. Could Sophie get through the gate without being noticed? There was no one by the pool or on the terrace, but as she got nearer to her little gate she could hear voices ... well, one voice. Why was Casey up by her bungalow? This was something she didn't need.

'Hi, Casey, can I help you? Was there something you needed?'

'Oh, no, I just heard the cat and I came to investigate. Is it my dad's cat?'

'No, she belongs to one of the neighbours and as you can see, she has taken a liking to a male cat. There are kittens due any day now.'

'How wonderful! I always wanted a cat or a dog but my mum wouldn't let me and now I live by myself in a rented flat it doesn't seem fair to have either when I'm out to work all day. Also, the landlord probably wouldn't allow it.'

'Yes, I know what you mean; I'm the same. Well, I was, but I'm not at the moment, obviously, because I'm here working for your dad. I'm surprised you weren't tempted to go and visit him in America. All the glitz and glam of Hollywood ... I'm sure it would have been a lot of fun.'

'No, it wouldn't have been possible because, well ... because I haven't seen my dad for quite a few years. I'll get out your way now. Hope everything is ok with the cat and her kittens.'

'I'm actually just about to make a coffee, would you like one?'

131

Of course Sophie was lying, she had only come back to pick up Mable and take her back to Graham's, but it seemed like Casey might need someone to talk to right now.

Unsurprisingly, Casey said yes, and so Sophie went inside to put the kettle on. She hadn't expected Casey to follow her into the bungalow so she couldn't help but jump a bit when Casey suddenly spoke from behind her.

'When I was last here this was still just an old shack. He's done a great job doing it up. I love all the colours in the furnishings. It's not a bit like the style he used to prefer.'

'I have to own up, Casey, the throws and cushions are mine. I felt that if I was going to be here for a few months, it needed a little bit of colour and to feel more like me. I'm sorry, I hadn't realised you've not been here for several years. I thought this would be your permanent holiday destination of choice.'

'No, sadly it's a little complicated. Up until I was eighteen, I came here a lot, but after my mum and dad split up certain things happened and ... well, let's just say it was best I didn't come.'

'That's so sad. There you go,' she said, handing over a coffee mug. 'If you want to take a seat on the veranda I'll just get a cushion for Mable and come join you.'

There were so many questions Sophie wanted to ask her but where to start without coming across as nosey? And, of course, the big question was: why are they here now when Kennal is in America? But maybe that was the answer – they were here precisely *because* he wasn't.

'So, you're here now. How does it feel to be back? Hopefully you and your mum are having a good time, and it must be nice for you to catch up with Luis.'

'Yes, but all he talks about is you, Sophie. Not in a bad way,' she hastened to add when she saw the look of shock on Sophie's face. 'He's very keen on you but he knows you aren't interested in him. Sorry, I didn't mean to embarrass you, I'll change the subject. No doubt you want to ask me a million questions so I'll tell you that I haven't seen my dad for years because my mum made me choose between them. She said I couldn't have both her and my dad in my life, it had to be one or the other. And the only reason we're here now is because Mum read about Dad working on a TV series in America and wanted to check up on the place while he's away.'

'I'm so sorry, Casey. You shouldn't have been forced to choose between your parents. If you don't mind me saying, your mum does seem...'

'... controlling, is the word you're looking for. She's also bitter. She had a good life here with my dad but once their relationship ran its course, he moved on. I only wish she could too. Don't get me wrong, she doesn't want him, per se, just the lifestyle she used to have with him. On that note, I best get back over to the villa before she sees I'm missing. But before I go, can I ask you about Ramon?'

This took Sophie by surprise.

'Of course, what do you want to know?'

'Is he doing ok? And his mum, is her shop doing well?'

'Yes to both. He's a really nice guy and he's been such a help since I arrived. He's also ... he's also single, just in case you were wondering?'

Casey blushed and Sophie knew they'd gotten to the question Casey had really been wanting to ask.

'Thank you, Sophie. When you next see Ramon, would you say hello from me?'

'I'd be happy to.'

Casey blushed even deeper and made a hasty retreat.

Sophie didn't know what to say or think about Casey's revelations. Velma was obviously a very sad and bitter woman, but the conversation had also brought up more questions about Kennal. Why hadn't he kept in contact with Casey? Could he really just walk away from his daughter as if Casey didn't exist?

'Mable, I know you're comfortable on that cushion but we have to go back to Graham's now as the last thing I need is kittens running around here.'

Mable gave Sophie a look and before Sophie had time to pick her up she started to head down to the main gate. Hurrying to follow, Sophie watched as Mable exited the complex and walked up the lane towards Graham's.

Arriving at his gate, Sophie called out, 'We're here, Graham, and I have something to thank Mable for – because of her I found out more about Velma and Casey! How are you today?'

Graham was prepared for that question and he knew it was time to put on the act that let Sophie think he was starting to move on with his life. He had been around long enough to know you should let people hear what they wanted.

He suggested a coffee but Sophie declined, explaining she had just had one with Casey.

'I had planned to stay away from the villa to avoid Velma but I'm not sure what to do with the day. Would you like me to help with the boxes? Or I could do some gardening, not that I would know what to do, but I know a man who could help. His name is Javier and he comes to look after the gardens at the villa.'

Graham panicked. The last thing he wanted was to look in the boxes or dig into the garden. Thinking quickly, he suggested they have an early lunch, which Sophie jumped at.

'You sit here in the sun with Mable while I make

us some sandwiches. Red or white wine?'

'White, please,' Sophie replied.

She knew he had suggested lunch because he didn't want to do any work on the villa and needed to change the subject. Was he actually making progress, as he'd said, or was he merely putting on an act for her benefit?

Mable had followed him into the villa so Sophie decided to investigate the garden, which looked a huge mess. She could just about make out a path and it was actually quite easy to follow it as everything was crisp and dry ... or completely dead. She doubted it had been watered since Robert died. Coming to a stop part way down the path she could just make out the indent of a swimming pool on the lawn, and then a bit further on she could see the wall separating Graham's land from Kennal's. That must be where Mable gets over to jump down to her bungalow. Sitting on the little wall and looking back at Graham's garden she came to the conclusion that it wasn't as bad as she'd initially thought. It just looked worse than it was because of all the dead shrubbery. Once that was cleared away, and the pool cleaned, Graham would have the makings of a lovely garden. As she was starting to walk back she saw Graham coming outside with a tray – lunch was ready, but was *she* ready to lead the way in helping him get his life together? Yes, she was. They had a connection now and if he didn't want her help, on some level, he would never have let her into his life in the first place.

As they ate their lunch Sophie told him about Greg's sister wanting to rent her flat for two years and then all about Casey and Velma. She also had to ask his opinion on what Casey had said about Luis talking about her all the time, and find out if he knew anything about whatever was – or wasn't – happening between Ramon and Casey. By the time

135

lunch and chatting was over, the bottle of wine was empty and it was late afternoon. The flow of conversation had stopped briefly, and Sophie decided to take her shot.

'Graham, can I ask you something? Wouldn't you like to be sat here looking at something nice rather than all those dead weeds? It wouldn't take a lot to sort it out, to be honest – a good rake and let the air get to the ground. I'm sure Javier would help, if you thought it was too big a task to take on alone. I'm sorry if I'm over-stepping but I just feel you would feel a lot better and more yourself if you were-'

'Living a life instead of just existing. I know, and you're right, Sophie, but as I've told you before, I don't know how or even if I want to.'

As Graham burst into tears, Sophie felt terrible that she had driven him to it. All she'd wanted to do was help. Not sure what she should do, she stood up and went across to him, bending down and putting her arms around him. The tears turned to sobs and he was shaking so much but she just held on to him and didn't say a word, letting him get every bit of pent-up emotion out.

It was a good twenty minutes before he was able to compose himself and then they both sat in silence. The last thing Sophie was going to do was force him to talk about it. He had to do it in his own time and in his own way. She had pushed him far enough.

'I'm so sorry, Sophie, I really don't know where all that came from. Well, I do, don't I? It's been building up inside me for the past two years and it all came out in one. It's been so difficult not having had anyone to share Robert's death with. I remember when both Robert's and my parents died, we talked about them all the time with each other and that helped. When one of us was down, we'd

136

each help to pick the other up and that's how we managed our grief. But here ... I've had no one and so the grief has just grown, getting ever bigger and more overwhelming. It's a constant darkness that has stopped any light getting to my brain. I know I sound silly and a lot more, but I loved him so much and to have him taken away so suddenly...'

It went quiet again and Sophie wasn't sure if she should say anything. She wanted to help but how and what should she say?

'I shouldn't have put you in this position, Sophie, you have enough on your plate with the many wives of Kennal; you don't need my problems as well.'

The phrase 'the many wives of Kennal' made them both laugh, cracking the fragile atmosphere and making them each feel a bit lighter.

'I wonder how many more will turn up?' Sophie giggled.

'Perhaps you should ask him how many he's actually had,' Graham offered. 'Come on, let's open another bottle of wine – I think we both need it. And also ... would you like to have a look around my collection of boxes? There's no furniture to look at but there are boxes and boxes, and I think I need to warn you, there might be more tears as well...'

'I'm prepared for both,' Sophie said with an encouraging smile.

They went in through the patio doors to a huge lounge but it wasn't the boxes that shocked Sophie, it was the two garden chairs. It was so sad that this had been his only furniture for the last two years – for one, they couldn't be all that comfortable. She knew she didn't need to make a comment though – they spoke for themselves – and this little look around the villa needed to be positive if it was to be the starting point of Graham moving on with his life.

'The kitchen is the best room in the villa but –

no surprise – up against the back wall I have more boxes. I hardly know where to start... Look, you go and look around the rest of the place and I'll open another bottle of wine and see you back outside.'

Sophie felt uncomfortable walking around Graham's home by herself so she was quick, not dwelling in any room more than a few seconds. That's really all that was needed though as there wasn't a lot to look at apart from boxes spread out over three bedrooms as well as the lounge. As she walked back out onto the terrace she knew she needed to be positive about a very odd and sad situation.

'I love the bathroom, Graham, it looks new like the kitchen. Is it?'

'Yes, both the bathroom and the kitchen were done up just a few months before we bought the place – a real selling point to Robert and me as it meant we wouldn't need to get builders in for major work. We were looking forward to doing the decorating ourselves and we'd actually ordered the paint before he died. It's all in the out building now ... I couldn't face doing it all alone. Oh, I must seem stupid to you.'

'I promise you don't. I think we're actually both very similar. Your life has stood still in the years since you lost Robert, in the same way mine stood still while I waited for Mark to choose me. But, thankfully, I've moved on, and you can too. Instead of embracing the sadness that comes with your grief, you could be celebrating Robert's life and the time you had together. One way to do that is to talk about him, and I, for one, would be delighted to listen, the same way you've so kindly listened to all my drama. I want to help you and repay you for what you've done for me because we both deserve a new beginning.'

Chapter 19

Sophie's phone alarm went off. It was time to get up but she would definitely need coffee to kick start her day. She was drained from yesterday with Graham as there had been so many emotions for both of them. It didn't help that they had both drunk too much as well, but she was hoping that their time together had helped him and he was ready to start moving forward.

She was going to go up to his villa and start to put their plan into action later on, but first she had Villa Kennal to sort, including a sweep and mop around the pool area ... hopefully before Velma and Casey appeared. A quick look at her phone while eating breakfast showed a couple of emails from upcoming guests with shopping lists, which were all straightforward, and then she noticed she'd missed a text from Kennal late last night, saying, *the problem is sorted*. Sophie guessed by the word 'problem' he meant Velma and though she wasn't sure how she'd been 'sorted', it was still something nice to wake up to.

****

An hour later, the cleaning around the pool had been completed without seeing either of the villa guests, and Sophie was looking at the booking diary. She updated all the information and sent an email off to Cristina to let her know what days she was required to cook for the next group of guests. She was just getting her things together to go and check on Graham when she heard the main gate opening. She assumed it would be Casey heading down to the shops, but then her little gate opened and there stood Luis. She didn't have time for him if all he wanted to do was tell her again how rude she had been to Velma.

'Hi, Luis, can I help you?'

'I was wondering if you have a minute to spare me? I have something important I need to say.'

Sophie nodded, not sure where he was going with this.

'I need to apologise. I've now seen for myself how rude Velma is and I've realised that I didn't really take much notice of her when I was younger so I've never really seen that side of her and I'm sorry for-'

'Luis, it's ok. Apology accepted. They'll be gone in a few days and we can get back to normal ... whatever normal is.'

'That's the other thing. I'm not sure Velma will go. She misses living here in the Tenerife sunshine. Also, she thinks she's been treated badly by Kennal even though it was quite a few years ago and I'm pretty sure they both said and did things they now regret.'

Sophie decided not to say she'd had a text from Kennal last night telling her he had 'sorted the problem' as she didn't want Luis to say anything to Casey. She needed him to go so she could get off to Graham's, but Luis wasn't moving. What did he want? This was awkward and uncomfortable. She had to say something.

'I really have to go. I'm expected up at Graham's in five minutes; I'm helping him sort his villa out.'

The look on Luis's face changed, making it obvious that he didn't realise who Graham was. Sophie explained it was the man that lived in the bungalow behind Villa Kennal.

'You mean the cat man? He's an odd one. Are you sure you're safe going in there by yourself? Would you like me to come with you?'

'No, it's fine, and he's not odd, he's just getting

over the loss of someone and he likes to keep himself to himself. Anyway, as I said, I need to be getting off. Are you having a day with Casey?'

'No, I'm off to work, but do you think once this Velma problem is over with and she's gone we could perhaps go out for a meal or a drink? My treat, of course, to apologise for my bad behaviour.'

Sophie said she'd think about it, stretching over to pick up her bag and phone. Thankfully, Luis finally took the hint and they walked down to the main gate together. They said goodbye and there was no denying that the smile he gave her made Sophie feel good.

****

'Good morning, Graham, any kittens yet?'

'No, but I don't think it will be much longer; Mable's getting very restless. By the way, how is your head? Mine's a little sore. We drank quite a lot yesterday, more than I have for many years, but saying that, I have woken up feeling more positive than I have since ... well, since Robert died. Thank you for that.'

'You don't need to thank me, all I did was listen! Now, we need a plan of action. Where is the list we wrote yesterday? I'm sure in no time we'll be ticking jobs off it.'

'Yes, but first a coffee, I think.'

As Graham went off to make the coffee Sophie looked at the list of jobs. The first thing that needed sorting was the boxes, which would undoubtedly be one of the hardest jobs for Graham. But maybe it didn't need to be...

'I've had a brain wave, Graham! You have three bedrooms and as you only need one, why don't we stack all the boxes in the other two rooms and close the doors? That way they will be out the way – and more importantly, out of sight – which will allow us to get on with the second job on the list: paint your bedroom and the lounge. Time for the terracotta to go and nice crisp white walls to appear!' Sophie paused as another thought hit her.

'Oh, but saying that, you really won't want to be sleeping in a room that's just been painted. Do you think we can get most of the boxes in one room if we stack them floor to ceiling?'

'That might work. I like this idea, and I promise you I will start to go through them at some point. I can't put it off for ever.'

****

After the coffee they picked the bigger of the two spare bedrooms and started piling the boxes inside it. It took most of the morning, not because the boxes were heavy, but because they wanted to make sure they could fit them all in and so had to place them strategically. Thankfully, with a bit of trial and error, it worked and the lounge and two bedrooms were now clear and ready for painting.

'I love the tiled floors here in the lounge and once the walls are painted it's going to look so much brighter. I suspect it won't take too much time to get the painting done.'

'I know, and that makes me feel worse as this is something I could quite easily have done months ago ... or even years ago.'

'Enough of that talk! That's behind you now and I'm sure once you've got the villa decorated and looking good you will feel a lot better. Why don't you lead me to this shed with all the paint in it because once that's all done then the exciting bit starts – shopping for furniture!'

As Sophie moved to tick 'move boxes' off the to-do list, her phone rang with a call from Madeline.

'Hi, Mum.'

'How you are, darling? Has Velma left yet?'

'Yes, I'm fine. And no, Velma and Casey are still here but Kennal says he's got it sorted, not that I know what that means... You're phoning early. Is everything ok? How's the filming going?'

'I've just heard that I'm going to have two weeks off from filming so I've decided to come and stay with you!'

'What? Here to Tenerife? Umm, I'm kind of in the middle of something. Can I call you later today, say, around nine tonight, so we can talk this through properly?'

'Ok, darling, have a nice day and we'll speak later.'

'Is everything ok?' Graham asked as she put her phone back in her bag.

'Yes and no. It was my mum. She has a few weeks off from filming soon and she wants to come here. It's the last thing I need – a villa full of guests and having to share the little bungalow with her, also, she will undoubtedly swan in and tell me all the things I'm doing wrong with the place. But enough of that for now. Let's find the paint.'

****

Six hours later the lounge was looking very white and while they both agreed it was stark, they also agreed that the soft furnishing would soften everything and bring some much needed warmth to the room. As they'd painted they'd talked about possibilities for the furniture – should it be one sofa and two chairs, or two sofas and no chairs? Where would they go? Would they face each other or be in an L shape? Which wall would be the feature wall and would a dining table fit better in this space or that space? It was now getting late and they were both hungry so they wandered into the kitchen, where Mable had settled as it was out of the way of all the painting.

'That's more than enough progress for one day. How about we walk down to the square and get something to eat? I'm hungry and as you've worked twice as hard as me you must be as well,' Graham said.

Sophie agreed and they decided to each take a quick shower to wash off the paint and then meet up outside Villa Kennal in forty-five minutes. Sophie hoped there would be no sign of Velma when she went back to get ready.

****

They ended up in one of the little local restaurants and agreed to keep it to just the one bottle of wine between them this time.

'How am I ever going to be able to thank you, Sophie? I can't believe how my life has changed since you arrived. It's not the moving the boxes or the painting so much as it's what's going on in my head. Things don't seem so bleak now and I never want to go back to that place. Can I tell you something? I was thinking before you arrived this morning that some of my inability to move forward with the villa transformation was because Robert made all the decisions in our relationship. Don't get me wrong, I was happy with that because he always had great ideas, but in all those years we were together I never really had to think for myself. I'm ready now for that to change, though I do worry that choosing the furniture will be more difficult. Yes, we had to paint the rooms, but Robert had already picked out the colour and ordered it, so it wasn't as difficult as starting from scratch.'

'It might be, but the great thing is that you don't

need to rush into everything all at once. Take each day as it comes and if some days you don't feel like doing anything, well ... don't. As I mentioned, it might be useful to get some outside help with the garden so you don't have to take on the house and garden at the same time. Would you like me to ask Javier to pop around and have a look?'

Before Graham could answer, Sophie's phone rang.

'Sorry, it's probably my mum again...'

The number wasn't one she recognised so she decided to ignore it, but as it rang three more times in quick succession, she realised she'd better take it.

'Hello?' Sophie asked cautiously.

'Sophie! Hi, it's Casey. Mum asked me to call because we've had a major problem at the villa and we need you to come right away.'

Before she could ask what the major problem was, the line went dead.

Thankfully, Graham and Sophie had finished eating already so they paid the bill and headed back towards the villa. They said goodnight at the gate and Graham wished her well with the problem as he headed up the path to his villa. Going through the gate Sophie could see three people up on the terrace. She recognised Velma and Casey but the other person had their back to her. As she got closer they turned around ... and Sophie's stomach dropped.

Emily was back.

Chapter 20

Sophie was in two minds about whether she dared to go out on her veranda this morning. Perhaps it was best to have her coffee in the bungalow as the last thing she needed was more shouting from Velma asking why Emily was there – a question Sophie could answer quite easily: because Kennal had sent her, hopeful that would make Velma leave. How embarrassing it was last night, both Emily and Casey just stood there, not saying a word, while Velma went all guns blaring at Sophie, until she told her to phone her ex-husband and ask him about Emily's arrival. That had shut her up! She'd stormed back into the villa and then the oddest thing happened – Sophie, Emily and Casey all said 'sorry' at the exact same time. It was an awkward moment and nothing else was said before all three of them walked in different directions. Today, Sophie was going to leave the three of them to sort out their differences while she took herself off to see Graham and hopefully get some more painting done. But before that, she had to do what she hadn't done last night: call her mum about her visit.

'Hi, Mum, sorry I didn't get a chance to call you back yesterday. How's the filming going and what dates are you thinking of coming?'

'There you go again, question after question. I know how you need to know everything but I'm afraid I can't talk now. I'll phone you back in a few days.'

Sophie was startled to realise her mother had hung up without even a 'goodbye'. What was all that about? Surely she knew the dates when she'd be coming?

Well, as long as she doesn't just turn up like everyone else seems to do here, everything will be

146

ok, Sophie thought to herself.

****

'Good morning, any kittens?' Sophie asked. She was starting to feel like a broken record.

'Nothing yet. How are you doing? I can't wait to hear what the problem was at the villa last night!'

'Problem is not the word for it, it was definitely more of a drama,' Sophie said, rolling her eyes.

Graham went to make them a coffee while Sophie checked out the walls in the lounge. It was as she thought; they would all need another coat of paint. She had been hoping they wouldn't so that she and Graham could move on to the next thing on the list, but you could see the terracotta colour coming through on some bits. One more coat of paint would hopefully sort it.

They went out on to the terrace with their coffee and Sophie told Graham all about the goings on at the villa, which they both laughed about. It sounded just like a soap opera.

'Talking of soap operas, I had my mum on the phone today and she was acting very oddly. All I did was ask her if she knew when she was coming to visit and she was right down my throat, saying I was asking her a million questions. She actually sounded a little stressed... I'm sure it's nothing. Now, enough of the drama, let's get going and fingers crossed the lounge will be finished by lunch time and we can move on to finishing up your bedroom.'

'I'm looking forward to the end result and that's quite a shock as up to a few days ago the last thing I would have ever wanted was to be doing this. Is that your phone that just beeped?'

Sophie had a look and found a text from Kennal, asking how things were going. She was done being the one in the middle of all of this so sent a quick reply with just three words: *Velma's not happy.*

****

The walls in the lounge took longer than they'd hoped and it was three o'clock before they had a chance to break for lunch. At least one room was finished though, and the biggest one at that.

While Graham went to make them cheese sandwiches and a cup of tea, Sophie checked her phone. There were no messages from the villa, which was good, just a text from Cristina asking if she wanted a have a night out.

'There you go, one sandwich and some crisps. By the way, Sophie, where do you think I should get the furniture from? I know it can be ordered online but I would like to actually see things first – you know, sit on the chairs and sofas – but as far as I know, there's nothing here in Kalanchoe, and maybe not even over in las Américas.'

'I don't know really, but I think I know someone who might be able to help – Cristina. She's actually just texted me so I'll ask her in my reply.'

Text sent, they moved Graham's bed into the other bedroom along with a few more boxes that were in the bedroom closet. Sophie got the impression these contained the clothes he wore from day to day. To think he'd gone two years with no wardrobe and not even a bedside table... She was thankful, once again, that he was now moving forward.

****

The bedroom was so much easier to paint as it was just four walls with a door and a window, and by seven that evening they had managed two coats. One more tomorrow would have it finished.

'Shall I cook us something to eat?' Graham offered.

'That's very kind but I'd best get back to the villa and make sure it's still there. I do have time to sit and have a glass of wine in the late sunshine before I go though – a treat for the day's work we've both done.

'I have some furniture news from Cristina,' Sophie shared once they were settled. 'How would you like a day out shopping? She's offered to take us to some sort of big retail park near the airport as she said it should have everything we need.'

Sophie watched Graham's face light up and of course the answer was a big yes, which was good as Cristina had suggested they go first thing in the morning.

****

As she walked through the villa's main gate, Sophie hoped no one would be on the terrace and she would be able to slowly creep up to the bungalow unnoticed. She was in luck! Although the patio doors were open, there was no sign of anyone. Once in the bungalow she had a quick shower before sitting on the veranda with a glass of wine. She would cook some pasta and have an early night but for now she was content just flicking through the villa emails. She was glad to see there was nothing that couldn't wait for a day or two. Just as she was about to head inside to start dinner, she heard her little gate squeak.

Oh no, not Casey. Or even worse, Velma.

She was surprised to see it was neither.

'Hi, Emily, is everything ok?'

'Not really. I don't know what I'm doing here. Well, I mean, I know I'm here to try and get rid of Velma and Casey, but my dad hasn't said *how* I'm

149

supposed to do that.'

'It's a tricky one. I think Velma's on a mission to stay and apart from your dad actually being here to kick her out himself, I'm not sure how it's going to happen. Would you like a glass of wine and we can chat through some ideas?'

At her nod, Sophie fetched a glass for Emily and brought the bottle out to top up both glasses. She also grabbed a bowl of nuts, thinking what was nuts was that this was a completely different Emily to the one she'd first met.

'There you go. Can I ask, have either Velma or Casey talked to you about their plans?'

'No, but I think if Velma wasn't around Casey would open up to me because when we were younger, we really got on well. We've drifted apart since then, which is a shame as we have so much in common – particularly a father that moves from one relationship to another and leaves his children behind. That sounds bad, sorry. He's been a good dad and I've never gone without as he's always provided for me. It's just ... he's changed. When I was younger, he always had time for me but he doesn't anymore. I know he's never really approved of the way I carry on and I can't blame him – I was a rebel, and I suppose I still am – but these days I only do it because that's what people expect from me, which is stupid, really, as back in Santa Cruz I live a quiet life. Ok, there are boyfriends, but it's like there are two Emilys – one there and another one here...

'Sophie, I need to apologise to you for the way I was when I last came to the villa. I don't have any excuse for being so horrible to you. The thing is, over the years I have met so many of my dad's girlfriends. Some I really liked and got on well with, but then I would go away and come back months later to find them gone, which upset me and meant I had to get to know another one, all while knowing she would probably disappear from my life too.'

'You don't need to apologise, Emily, it's all forgotten. And as for you being two different people, I love that idea I and I wouldn't mind being more like that myself. Sadly, there's only one me, and she's boring and foolish. But that's a story for another time. For now, we need to figure out how we're going to get rid of Velma because if she doesn't go, I'll have a major problem to deal with. There are guests scheduled to arrive on the day she should be leaving.'

'It's not our problem, really. I know you're here looking after the place for my dad, but Velma's argument is with him, not us, and so he should be the one to sort it out. And that's what I'm going to tell him.'

'Sounds like a good plan to me. I was just about to cook some pasta; would you like some?'

'If it's not too much trouble, I'd love that, thank you.'

Sophie topped up their glasses and went inside to start cooking. Emily followed her in.

'Were you not temped to go stay with Kennal in America while he's filming?' Sophie asked.

'No, the thought of the fake Hollywood life didn't appeal – one minute everyone's your friend, the next they're stabbing you in the back. I had enough of that with my mother and all her friends. She was – well, still is – an actress here in Spain. I grew up around them all and it's part of why I loved coming here and escaping it. Once I was old enough, I was able to get my own place and live my own life. It's all very boring, really, but it's real, and I like that. I'm also not having to put up with all my mum's dramas,' she added, rolling her eyes.

'Sounds like we have something in common. My mum's also an actress ... well, she was back in the day. She stopped just before I was born and has only just gone back to it. It's got me wondering if I'm the reason she never went back to it before. Although, I have to say that I've seen a different side to her since she started filming again, and when I talk to her on the phone, she isn't the confident and in control woman I've always known. Anyway, I'm sure she's fine. Shall we eat?' Sophie asked as she dished up the pasta, glad to change the subject. 'I'm afraid it's just plain old carbonara.'

'Carbonara sounds perfect,' Emily said with a smile.

They went back out onto the veranda and chatted about life in general as they ate their pasta. Emily explained that she worked freelance for a big PR company and a lot of her days were spent on the computer working from her apartment, hence why she could come here so easily and so often. For her part, Sophie opened up about being made redundant and how that had led to her being here at the villa for the summer.

'So your dad, Sophie, what does he do?'

'I've never met him. He and Mum split up before I was born.'

'I'm so sorry to hear that. Do you miss him?'

'I don't think you can miss something you never had,' she said thoughtfully.

That stopped the conversation dead for a while but eventually they talked about the villa and how hard Kennal had worked getting it to the standard it was now. Sophie cleared their bowls and found Emily deep in thought when she got back.

'Could I ask you something? You said you've never met your dad and ... well, your mum's an actress, like mine, and we are quite similar ages, give or take a few years. You don't think ... we could be sisters, do you? Is it possible Kennal is father to both of us?'

Sophie felt her legs giving way and just managed

to catch the edge of the chair.

'I'm so sorry,' Emily said, seeing her distress. 'Forget what I've just said. I'm sure it's not true.'

'No, you're right. It could be true. But I've never in all my life heard my mum mention your dad's name before we got this job. Do you think that's why he asked her to come? Is that why I'm here? Was this all planned by my mum and Kennal? How stupid of me not to question any of this!'

'I'm so sorry to have said what I have and to have upset you. I think I best go and please don't overthink this and worry. In fact, why not just call your mum now and ask her? You never know, that might be the opening she's been waiting for,' Emily said with a sympathetic shrug.

Chapter 21

Sophie hadn't slept at all after what Emily had said even though she was convinced there was no way they were actually sisters. No, that wasn't right. There was a niggle of uncertainty about the whole situation that still lingered and the only way it would go away was if she asked her mum to tell her the truth. Was it possible that after all these years of not having a father in her life, Madeline would have brought her here to Tenerife for the summer to meet him? She couldn't deny that she'd thought it strange from the beginning that Kennal had asked Madeline to run the place for him, but no, if he'd known about her, she would have met him long before now. Despite the differences he may have had with their mothers, he had generally been a good father to Emily and Casey. It made her certain he wouldn't have put up with not seeing Sophie or being a part of her life if he'd known she existed. No, she was one hundred per cent sure he wasn't her father – well, perhaps ninety-nine per cent...

You need to think it through, Sophie. Take the emotion that's kept you awake all night out of the situation and think practically.

Sophie knew she had to put everything to the back of her mind for now as today was all about Graham and shopping for furniture.

She was just getting herself ready when she heard her little gate go.

'Hi, Sophie,' Casey called out as she approached the bungalow. 'I have to be quick as my mum's in the shower – and please don't tell her I've told you – but we are leaving the day that was planned so there's no need to worry anymore. I wanted to make sure you knew as she might still give you the impression she's staying on, but she knows I have to get back to work and she wouldn't mess that up for me. She'd never admit it but she also wouldn't want to be here without me.'

'Thank you, that's a huge relief! Umm, while you're here ... I was chatting to Emily last night and she was telling me all about the happy times you used to have together as children. Those memories clearly mean a lot to her, and though I know Velma wouldn't like it, don't you think it would be nice if you two could be friends again? I get the impression Emily misses having you in her life.'

'I miss her too. Thank you for sharing that with me. I'd better go now but I really am sorry for what you've been put through by having us here.'

'It's already forgotten,' Sophie said with a kind smile.

Casey nodded and turned to leave, but just as quickly turned back. 'I forgot to ask, did you get a chance to mention to Ramon that I asked how he was?'

'I'm sorry, I haven't seen him since we spoke, but I promise I will.'

Casey smiled her thanks as she left.

****

With sensible shoes on for a day that was likely to be filled with lots of walking, Sophie headed over to Graham's.

'Morning, have the kittens arrived yet?' she asked for what felt like the umpteenth time.

'No, Mable's holding on to them a little longer. I was actually just about to text you. I'm not feeling that good today so I wondered if we could put off our shopping trip?'

Sophie was confused and couldn't help but notice he'd made the request without looking at her. She quickly realised this was an excuse – he was having second thoughts, and maybe not just about the shopping, but also about moving on with his life. To be honest, she'd thought this might happen at some point while they were decorating. Now the moment was here, she had to think quickly because Cristina would be here soon and the last thing she wanted to do was force him into doing something he didn't want to do. A little encouragement was obviously going to be needed if she hoped to turn the situation around.

'If you aren't up to it that's totally fine. What if we still have a day out though? I know Cristina loves her clothes and is always up for a spot of shopping, and you will be the perfect person to tell us if things look good or not. Now, go get yourself ready, we're off to the boutiques of Tenerife as soon as she arrives.'

With that she walked over to fuss over Mable, denying Graham the opportunity to protest. Oh, she wasn't daft, she knew he could probably see through her little plan – half a dozen clothes shops and then, just by chance, a furniture shop would appear – but if that was what it took to help him, that's what they would do. She sent a quick text to Cristina to tell her the change of plan, but to look surprised when she arrived.

By the time Graham came back from getting ready he seemed to have perked up a little, and when Cristina arrived soon after, they headed off.

****

The journey was lovely and Cristina pointed things out along the way. Sophie insisted on sitting in the back to ensure Graham was involved in the conversation and as they got closer to the shops, both Sophie and Cristina put on a little act saying how excited they were to be going clothes shopping.

Of course Graham knew their game but what a lovely thing these two women were doing for him. He certainly didn't deserve it and the least he could do was look like he was enjoying himself so he played along. Eventually they arrived at a huge retail park and parked the car.

'Right, I don't know about you two, but I need a coffee and something to eat. There are all sorts of restaurants and cafés scattered around, do you have a preference?' Cristina asked.

Sophie and Graham were happy to go wherever she suggested, as long as there was strong coffee, and the place Cristina chose was lovely, with delicious cheese croissants to eat. Sophie could see Graham was pushing his food around the plate and not joining in with their conversation and at that point she realised furniture shopping was definitely not going to happen today. It didn't feel right to push him into anything he didn't want to do, even if they likely wouldn't get an opportunity like this again as there were no big furniture outlets anywhere near where they lived.

After paying the bill and nipping to the toilet, Sophie and Cristina emerged to find Graham sat on a bench outside, looking upset. She realised she had made a big mistake; they never should have come all this way when Graham had said he wasn't up to it. Sophie had to say something.

'I was just thinking, Graham, why don't you stay here in the sunshine while we look around the clothes shops? You can people watch and enjoy this lovely weather until we pop back in an hour or so. How does that sound?'

'I'm really sorry to both of you. You've gone to all this trouble to help me out and though yesterday I was all for finding things for the villa, waking up today I feel I'm back at square one. My head is telling me I'm daft and silly but my heart is saying how much I miss Robert and telling me I'm not ready to move on. How can just going to look at furniture be so hard? It's not normal to feel this way.'

'Of course it's normal. You've just never had to do it before by yourself as you've always done it as a couple.'

For a few moments the three of them sat in silence with their thoughts, before Graham eventually said, 'Right, the initial plan was to drive all this way to buy furniture and I think that's what we should do. Lead the way, ladies, because if I don't do it today, I don't think I ever will.'

****

It was very late and they were nearly back at Los Kalanchoe. Graham had slept most of the journey and Sophie and Cristina had had a whispered conversation, both so happy for him. He had eventually really gotten into the furniture shopping, testing different pieces and comparing measurements. Having bought several pieces for his villa, they'd shared a lovely meal before heading home, Sophie pleased that what had initially looked like it was going to be a disappointing and disastrous day, had turned out to be so successful.

'Wakey wakey, Graham, we're home and you have a very cross Mable to face. She's been shut in for ages so won't be happy.'

'You're right, though it might not be just Mable. You never know, there could be some kittens! Thank you so much for today, both of you, I know it wasn't easy to start with but hopefully it was a happy ending.'

'Of course it was! Now come, let's get in and see Mable. Have you got your key? Thanks again, Cristina, we couldn't have done it without you,' she added as they waved Cristina off.

Letting them into the villa, Graham called out, 'I'm home, Mable, and I have some lovely fish in the fridge for you that will make up for leaving you alone for so long— Oh! Sophie, look, I'm sure... Yes, it's... There ... in the corner on those blankets... She's had the kittens! Who is a good girl? I'm sorry I left you by yourself all day.'

'I think that's probably what she was waiting for – to be by herself so she could just get on with it. If you can entice her into the kitchen I'll take a look in the blanket and see what we have.'

Mable was happy to follow Graham – food always came first for her – and Sophie took the chance to have a quick look. There were three very little kittens, which looked nothing like kittens at the moment and were probably just a few hours old.

****

Half an hour later, Mable was asleep in the pile of blankets. She probably realised she would need as much rest as possible because once those kittens grew a little and started running around she would have her hands full ... well, in her case, *paws* full.

'I'm completely worn out but I finally have furniture on the way and I have you to thank for that. Now that my life is sorted though, we need to start sorting yours!'

'What do you mean?'

'You're here in Tenerife for the season with no idea what you're going to do when it's time to leave. Luis fancies you and I get the impression you like him too but nothing seems to be happening. How come? And soon your mother is going to turn up and – in your words – try to take over running Villa Kennal, which I must add you are doing an excellent job of. In short, it's time you started to think about

159

what you want to do with your life, and start making steps to achieve it.'

Chapter 22

What Graham said was right – she needed to think about her life and where it was going. What would happen when the villa job was over and she needed to go home? She now no longer had a home to go to as Greg's sister was living in it. She also had no job waiting for her, and this job had shown her that she might not be cut out for a typical nine to five. She'd really come to love the freedom – popping here and there, stopping for a coffee whenever she wanted – and if she was honest, it didn't feel like work most of the time.

The only thing she did know for sure was that she wasn't letting her mum get involved with anything when she came to stay. That was a start and she would just have to avoid any conversation about her future until she'd figured out the rest. Now, enough of all this thinking and self-doubt. She had one more day of Velma, and just like she had for the whole of the two weeks since they'd arrived, Sophie was going to keep out of her way and head off to the beach for a quiet day by herself.

Just as she was getting her bag sorted, her phone rang.

'Hi, Mum, how are you? Is the filming going ok? And have you got a date for your visit yet?'

'I'm tired and, well ... I'm not sure I'm cut out for it. In the old days we rehearsed for days – the same scene over and over again – but now you learn the script on your own – not even with the actors who are in the scene with you! – and there are no rehearsals. You just have to turn up and get it right the first time, and if you don't, people aren't happy.'

'Oh dear, it all sounds horrible.'

'It is, darling, but I have to keep going – contracts are signed and all of that! The reason I'm

161

phoning is to apologise for not pinning down my holiday yet. They keep changing the filming dates – and the script, come to that. I have to go as there's a car coming to pick me up soon, but I will call you the moment I have a date.'

Sophie had never heard her mum like this before – she was normally always in control. She'd sounded so down and most alarmingly, she didn't even ask how everything was going at the villa. That was a first! Usually she liked to give the impression she was running Villa Kennal from London.

Now more than ever, Sophie needed a day away from everything to just completely switch off.

****

An hour later, laid out on her towel and listening to the little waves, Sophie was feeling much lighter and happier. This was paradise and something she would definitely miss when she returned to the UK. She shoved that thought to the back of her mind. Today was about switching off and she would start with a dip in the beautiful blue sea.

Floating around on her back in a circle she realised this really was her happy place. After a while she got out and walked back up to where her towel was but as she neared it she noticed two people further along the beach – it was Emily and Casey together, and no Velma in sight. It was so nice to see and she gave them a quick wave.

'Hi, Sophie! Come and join us. We have a day – well, a few hours – away from my mum,' Casey said with a laugh.

Sophie could make an excuse that she was now leaving and then walk along and find another bit of beach, but perhaps half an hour or so spent chit chatting wouldn't be so bad.

As she settled next to them on the sand they

162

chatted about the beach and the town and how lovely their dad had made the villa. Sophie asked what Velma was getting up to and Casey explained that her mum had gone to the hairdressers and was also getting her nails done. That was the reason they could spend some time together.

'So tell me about your dad. You both seem to have lots of happy memories from growing up with him, but what's he like now? I've heard bits and bobs about him but what's he really like?'

'Well, as you've probably gathered, he doesn't like to not have a woman in his life,' Emily said with a laugh. 'Of course he'd disagree with that, and he was single for at least a year before he went to America, but no doubt that's not the case now. I've met a lot of his actor and actress friends while growing up and they love to be the centre of attention – going to parties, having the spotlight on them – but he's always been the opposite and if he ever got into conversation with someone who didn't recognise him, he would never say what he does for a living.'

'Can you remember when we were little, Emily, and we were out and about and someone would say "are you Kennal Scott?" We both shouted, "no, he's our dad!" That always made him laugh. We were very protective of him but it was different when he was with my mum because she actually loved all the attention that came with being on his arm and being "the wife of Kennal Scott". That's why we're here now – she sees him doing well in the US and she wants a piece of it. Of course her dream would be for him to get back with her but as Emily and myself know, that's never going to happen. At least one good thing has come out of coming here – meeting up with my sister here and rekindling our friendship. I'm already looking forward to coming back and having time with both you and Dad,

163

Emily.'

'I'm pleased for all three of you that the family will be back together,' Sophie said as the sisters embraced.

'I have to admit, I've always wondered if there are more of us out there. There have been so many women in Dad's life!' Casey said with a laugh.

That was the cue for Sophie to say goodbye as she didn't want Emily to share her suspicion with Casey just yet. One thing was certain, the first thing she asked her mum when she got here would be what exactly the nature of her relationship with Kennal had been, and if there was any chance he was her father!

She would have loved to stay on the beach by herself but didn't want to offend the sisters so she told a little white lie about going to visit Graham.

Sophie said her goodbyes and headed off up the beach, spotting someone sat on a wall looking towards the sisters – Ramon.

'Hi, Ramon. Why don't you go down and say hello? I'm sure Casey would like that and I don't think Emily is a problem anymore. She's calmed down quite a bit ... well, for the time being at least.'

'Thanks, Sophie, but I don't think that's a good idea.' With that he jumped down and said goodbye.

Sophie could tell he was upset, which was such a shame, but then she turned back and looked at Casey and Emily on the beach and her thoughts drifted back to Emily's theory. Was this fate? Was she meant to be here to meet these two women? Could they possibly be her sisters?

Chapter 23

Today was a big day. Firstly, Velma and Casey were leaving – fingers crossed that they actually would because it would be Kennal's problem if they didn't! – and secondly, all Graham's furniture was due to arrive. Sophie was sad she wouldn't be able to get involved as she would be spending the day cleaning the villa in preparation for the next group of guests.

As she walked down to the main gate to pop to the bakery and stock up on energising snacks for the day, she could see Velma on the terrace. That was a good sign. She wasn't normally up this early, which must mean she was getting ready to leave. Sophie would have liked not to have to say goodbye, but that would be rude and at the end of the day Velma's problem wasn't with her, it was with Kennal. Sophie resolved to pop in and say farewell once she was back from the shop.

She was running through her plans for the day as she headed down the lane when coming towards her she saw Casey. By the looks of it, she had also been to the bakery. Sophie was glad to see her as it meant she could ask what time they were leaving.

'Hi, Casey. Great minds think alike as I'm also off to the bakery. It's become my favourite place since coming here to work.'

'I'm definitely going to miss it! I know I've already said this but I want to apologise again for my mum. It's nothing to do with you, she's just a bitter woman who hasn't gotten over the way my dad treated her. Not that that's an excuse for her being rude, of course.'

'Honestly, it's not a problem. I just hope you've had a nice holiday and been able to enjoy yourself. It must have been nice to catch up and spend some time with Luis after all these years, and of course to see and reconnect with Emily.'

'Yes, that was good as it meant I wasn't stuck with my mum for the whole holiday. Honestly though, as much as we had a laugh, I think the only reason he liked being at the villa was because you were around. He thinks a lot of you and I know you don't feel the same about him but perhaps you should give him a chance. His heart's in the right place ... it's just a shame about his head and mouth! Anyway, I'd better get going or else me taking my time will be something else my mum has to moan about. Will we see you before we leave?'

'Yeah, I was planning on popping in after I visit the bakery. Casey ... I mentioned to Ramon that you'd asked about him and I think it made him happy, but also sad. I know it's none of my business – and I don't know what has gone on between you both in the past – but would it maybe help if you chatted with each other directly?'

'Maybe, but he's had two weeks to talk to me and I haven't heard a peep so I don't think he wants to. Now, I'd better go. And remember, Luis really likes you!'

As Casey walked away, Sophie pondered what she'd said. She did feel the same about Luis but she just didn't see how it could work between them.

Enough of these thoughts, Sophie, you are in Tenerife to work, not to have a relationship! Now get a move on. You have a busy day ahead.

****

Once Velma and Casey were gone – Sophie had gotten a thank you from Velma, though no apologies for being rude – Sophie took a quick look to see what state they had left the villa in. Starting at the top, where Velma had slept, she was relieved to see that the rooms looked no dirtier than normal and all

166

the rubbish had been taken to the bins. It looked like today wouldn't be as hard as she'd initially thought!

Readying to get stuck in, Sophie heard her phone beep and saw a text from Graham had come through to say that the furniture had arrived and the delivery people were very helpful. As her phone was in her hand, she took the opportunity to message Kennal to say Velma had left. Even though Sophie had never met him, she knew that news would be a big relief for him.

The rest of the day flew by and she managed to clean everything in record time. All she had to do tomorrow was sweep and mop outside and do the shopping, and as the guests wouldn't be there till late, she wouldn't have to rush.

Sophie had just enough time for a quick shower before going over to Graham's to look at the new furniture, but as she was heading back up to the bungalow she heard the main gate opening. Oh dear. She wasn't in the mood for this.

'Hi, Luis, is everything ok? Was there something you wanted?'

'Hello, I was just wondering if you'd like to go out tonight for that meal we talked about?'

'I'm sorry but I have other plans. Perhaps another night?'

When she saw the defeated look on Luis's face, she found herself saying, 'Can I get you a drink while you're here? I was just going to have a glass of wine before going around to Graham's, why don't you join me?'

He nodded and followed her up to the veranda, taking a seat while she nipped inside and fetched a bottle and two glasses.

'Did you have a nice couple of weeks with your friends?'

'Yes, but it was difficult realising that Velma really doesn't let Casey think for herself. She also spends a lot of time slagging Kennal off. Ok, he cheated on her, but then, he was also married when he met her so it was exactly the same situation. Never mind. Casey mentioned she chatted with Emily, which is promising. They used to be so close so maybe they can be again, even though they live in separate countries.'

'I hope so. Also, the more I find out about Kennal, the more I'm intrigued to meet him.'

'I'm sure he'll also be very interested to meet you and give you the charm offensive. I've yet to meet a female who hasn't fallen for him.'

'I won't. For one, he's too old for me, and for another, why would I get involved with a man that just goes from one woman to the next? No thank you.'

'So what type of man are you looking for? Sorry, I shouldn't have asked that, it's none of my businesses.'

'That's ok. All I know is he has to be single and honest and not full of promises that he can't keep. Basically I'm looking for someone who is nothing like my ex, but saying that, I'm not sure I'm even ready for a new man at the moment. I'm enjoying being here and spending time by myself in the bungalow or on the beach. It's strange really, but I think I've changed so much since I've been here in Tenerife and that's a good thing. So that's my story, now it's your turn. What great things has Luis got in store for himself?'

'You tell me. I seem to just keep messing things up. I have no plans and am just going from one day to the next.'

Sophie didn't know what to say and figured they were best to leave it there. Explaining about Graham having the furniture delivered she said she needed to head off. Thankfully, he understood and took the hint that it was time for him to leave.

'So sorry I'm late! Luis turned up and wanted to chat.'

'You should have stayed and had a nice evening with him! You didn't need to come around here to check on me.'

'Don't be silly! I wanted to see what you've been up to. Lead the way to the furniture.'

'Have you seen the garden?' Graham asked as they moved through the villa. 'Javier came this morning and started to clear things up. He told me he'd worked on the garden before, with the other owners. What a stroke of luck that is.'

Graham paused outside the doors to the lounge, which were closed, he explained, as he didn't want Mable in there on the new furniture. Sophie knew all too well that once the cat found a comfortable seat she'd settle in for the long haul, likely bringing the kittens with her.

As he opened the doors with a flourish, Sophie was amazed by the way the room had been transformed.

'I know I was with you when you chose the sofas but don't they look good in situ! You must be so pleased. And the oak sideboard against the white wall... Oh, I'm over the moon for you, Graham.'

'Do you like the way I have the sofas now, or would you move one to the back wall and bring the other around here?'

'No, I think you've got it perfect and I can already picture you on that one with your feet up and Mable cuddled up beside you.'

'Exactly. Now the only thing left to do is find some cushions and put out some of my nice pottery. That's not going to be easy but I'll take it one day at a time. Now, come and look at the bedroom. I'm really glad I bought a new bed because that old one wasn't the most comfortable.'

After oohing and aahing over the bedroom, they went back to the main living space. If it had been up to Sophie, she would have been diving right into the boxes to find nice things to decorate the room with, but just to have proper furniture to sit on was such an achievement in itself.

Graham cooked a pizza for them, which they ate outdoors, and as they carried the plates back inside after they went through the lounge...

'You know, a nice table lamp in the corner would be good, providing just enough light in the evening to see by.'

'That's a good idea, and I have a few to choose from. I know it's late but if I can just find a lamp in the boxes that will be an achievement. Let's do it.'

Sophie was thrilled − what a leap forward for Graham! − and was quick to offer her help, diving into the box he thought held the lamp he was looking for.

****

'Oh my goodness, have you seen the time? It's nearly one forty in the morning! I've not been up this late for such a long time but I'm so proud of you. Everything looks so lovely, and the two side lamps are stunning. How are you feeling about it all? I know you've had a few tears tonight and it's been a little overwhelming at times, but are you happy with the result?'

'I *am* happy, but also completely drained. I feel a sense of relief, too. Thank you so much, I don't know how I'll ever repay your kindness.'

'I know a way, you can entertain my mother when she comes! No, I'm only joking, I wouldn't wish her on anyone.'

'Oh hush, she's more than welcome to stay with

me when she visits. That way you wouldn't need to share a room with her and I would be glad of the company. If she's anything like her lovely daughter, I'm sure we'll get on fine.'

Chapter 24

What an emotional evening, and a late one as well. Not what Sophie had planned but today was another day and she had loads to do before the next guests arrive. She was just getting all her bits together to head to the supermarket when her phone went. It was a text from Graham saying thank you and how lovely it was to wake up and see the new furniture. Sophie was relieved to hear he was still feeling positive about the changes. All her worries about pushing him too far had gone. And as for his suggestion of letting her mum stay with him? It was the perfect solution to her problem and she did think they would get on well together. She could just see him questioning Madeline all about the TV industry and its gossip.

****

Just as Sophie was walking into the supermarket, she passed Cristina, who was coming out with a trolley full of food.

'Hi, Cristina! You're more organised than me this morning, I had a late night and have a bit of a sore head; thankfully the guests won't be here until early evening.'

'I hope it was a nice evening. Was there a man involved? Anyone I know?'

'Very funny. There was a man though...'

'Oh! Tell me more. Does he have a friend?'

'Sadly no, and he's gay, so my evening wasn't the one you were obviously thinking,' Sophie said with a laugh. 'Shall I give you a call later once the guests have arrived and sorted themselves, so you can bring the food down? I'm sure if you talk to them, they'll agree to you preparing the other meals you have to cook for them at the villa instead of having to go to all the fuss of transporting them.'

'That sounds great!'

'Fab. Ok, I must run or else Ramon will be here before I've finished grabbing everything I need.'

'Now *that* is one gorgeous man.'

'What are you like, Cristina? There's more to life than men!'

'Really? I don't think so,' Cristina said with a wink.

Sophie laughed and headed into the market, list in hand. Any man that took Cristina on would certainly have their hands full. It was difficult to see what she had had in common with Luis or how they'd ever dated – they were like chalk and cheese! She was hip and full of life and he ... well, he was more of a plodder. But there must have been a spark there at some point as the relationship was on and off for so many years.

****

When Ramon arrived to pick her up from the supermarket a while later, Sophie noticed he wasn't his normal self, and she suspected she knew why. It had to be the Casey business. They obviously had a past together, but given how they couldn't even face one another, perhaps that's where things between them should stay – in the past.

'So, do you think Casey will be coming back at some point?' Ramon asked out of nowhere.

'I'd like to think so, but I suspect it won't be her choice, but her mother's.'

****

Once Sophie had packed away all the shopping for the guests in the villa's kitchen, she did one last dust around with a damp cloth and a final mop of the inside floors. Heading out to the pool area she was straightening out the sunbeds when she saw Luis coming in the main gate. He was dressed for work so likely wouldn't be hanging around for long, which was a shame as she would have liked to spend some time with him. She was feeling a bit guilty about rushing off to Graham's the day before to see the new furniture.

'Hi, Luis, how are you doing?'

'Fine, I was just wondering if you needed a hand with anything before the new guests arrive. I have a couple of hours before I start work.'

'No I'm all sorted, thanks, but do you fancy a coffee? I was just going to stop for one.'

That brought a little smile to his face and he nodded. They went up to the bungalow and Sophie used the excuse of Luis's visit to open a huge bag of cookies she'd grabbed for herself at the market.

'I saw Cristina when I popped into the supermarket earlier. This new group of guests are having her cook several times over the two weeks so I'll be seeing a lot of her. I have to say, I really don't see you two together – you're just so different from one another and yet, despite the fact you both say you don't want each to be together, you still have to know what the other is up to. It's all very odd. Combined with my own experience with Mark, I'm beginning to think the single life is the best way forward!'

'That's because you haven't found the right person yet. When you do, you'll think differently. Which reminds me, why don't you and I check the villa diary to see when you might be free for us to go out?'

Sophie laughed. 'You certainly are persistent, aren't you? Hold on, I'll grab it.'

They decided on a week on Saturday and Sophie

suggested they have a nice meal and then head to a lively bar afterwards. Luis looked like he was the cat that got the cream and Sophie reminded him this wasn't a date, it was just two friends spending an evening together.

'Of course!' Luis said, but the smile he gave her suggested otherwise...

Sophie rolled her eyes. 'Ok, you need to get to work and I have the patio and terrace to get ready for the new guests.'

****

Once Luis had left she got stuck in to all the final jobs and in no time at all she heard the sound of a vehicle pulling up outside the villa. She hurried down to the gate to say hello.

'Hello and welcome to Villa Kennal. I'm Sophie and hopefully I will be able to help you have the perfect holiday.'

'Hello, I'm Malcom, this is my wife Kate, and these are our two boys, Tom and Paul.'

The boys were definitely not boys – they were men. Both looking to be in their late twenties or early thirties, they were very handsome, not to mention extremely fit. A lovely bit of eye candy like this around the pool would certainly be very welcome and Sophie had to stifle a laugh when it crossed her mind that Cristina was going to be very pleasantly surprised by these new guests.

'It's nice to meet you all! If you'd like to follow me, I'll walk you up to the villa but there's just one thing first; I had it down that there were five of you – two couples and one single. Will the last guest be joining you later on?'

'No, Tom and his girlfriend had a falling out so she decided not to come,' Malcolm said, rolling his eyes.

175

Sophie could tell this change of plans had obviously not gone down too well so she quickly changed the subject and led them up the path to the villa, pointing out the pool deck and other amenities. She presumed Malcom and Kate would have the upstairs bedroom with the balcony, and the two brothers would take two of the downstairs bedrooms so once inside she pointed in the direction of the various bedrooms and then did a quick run through of the features of the kitchen and utility room. She then explained that all the shopping they had asked for was either in the fridge freezer or the cupboards. As Kate and Malcom went up the stairs, she showed Tom and Paul the other bedrooms for them to choose from. She could tell that both the lads were looking at her with interest and she could feel herself blushing. Time to leave and let them settle in.

As she went to return to her bungalow, Malcom came back down for the other suitcase and bags so Sophie took the opportunity to ask what time they would like to eat. Tom chimed in 'early as possible' because apparently he and his brother were planning to head off out to investigate the island's night life.

'What my son means, Sophie, is they're off to introduce themselves to the island's female population,' Malcom said with exasperation. 'But yes, we are ready to eat whenever you're ready for us.'

'Great, I'll give Cristina a call – she's the person who will be doing the cooking during your stay – and she'll be here soon I expect. In the meantime, I will leave you to settle in and I'll see you in a bit. If you need anything while you're here please don't hesitate to give me a call. My number is in the book on the coffee table.'

Malcom thanked her and Tom smiled and gave

her a wink, which yet again led her to blush. Once back in the bungalow, she caught the view of herself in the mirror and wondered if she should change before going back and helping Cristina serve the food. Oh flipping heck! She hadn't phoned her!

'Hi, it's me. The guests said they'll be ready to eat whenever you're ready. By the way, despite what the booking said there are only four of them, and none of them are children. Also, and I'm only telling you this as I don't want you to walk in and have your jaw drop on the ground, it's a mum and dad and their two sons ... who just so happen to be drop dead gorgeous and from what I've seen already they are quite flirty. I'm intrigued to see what happens when they meet you with your stunning figure!'

Cristina laughed and said she'd be right over with the food.

****

Sophie did end up changing her clothes and as she was going to be serving the food, she tied her hair up. Making her way down to the gate to help carry everything in, she smiled when Cristina pulled up wearing an outfit that wasn't what you'd typically expect for a chef. The summer dress was cut very low in the front and as for the heels on her shoes...

'I think I'd best carry everything. The last thing we need is you to be falling off those shoes, but then saying that, I'm sure there will be some willing hands to help you up.'

When they got up to the kitchen no one was around so Sophie got stuck into laying the table out on the patio while Cristina put the ovens on to keep the food warm.

First down for dinner was Kate, who said good evening and how blown away she was with the villa. Malcom appeared next with wet hair – he had

177

obviously had a shower – and Sophie asked if she could get them a drink. They both settled for wine and as Sophie went to get them each a glass, they headed down to look at the pool.

Paul was next to arrive and Sophie was certainly not disappointed with his reaction to Cristina. She actually wanted to laugh as Paul suddenly became all tongue tied. The same thing happened when Tom came into the kitchen, and the brothers seemed at a loss. They didn't need to flirt as Cristina – who was like a tigress eyeing up her evening meal – was doing it enough for everyone! Sophie had never seen her friend like this and found the whole thing hilarious.

Eventually the lads got a lot more confident and after a few bottles of beer you could see they thought they were the bee's knees and in with a chance. Cristina was very professional as she was here to cook, but saying that she had made it quite clear in those first couple of minutes where she stood, and that was done just with her eyes!

As Sophie served the dinner and topped up the drinks, there were lots of questions from all four of them about the best beaches, the water sports available, any restaurants they should go to and sights they really should visit.

'Of course the most important question of all – which both our sons no doubt want to know the answer to – is where the best night life is,' Kate said with a smile.

Sophie knew this was when Cristina would jump in but what she had to say wasn't at all what Sophie was expecting.

'Well, lads, you are in luck. You've arrived on the right night because once we've finished here both Sophie and myself are off out to a party. You're more than welcome to join us. Isn't that right, Sophie?'

Chapter 25

'Good morning, Kate, did you and your husband sleep well? I'll only be a few minutes here as I've just got the other side of the pool to mop and then it's all yours to enjoy for the day. There are plenty of towels in the pump room and you are more than welcome to take them to the beach. Just leave the dirty ones in the basket and I will collect them tomorrow morning.'

'Thank you. Did you have a nice night out with my sons? I hope they didn't drink too much, though I'm glad Tom is getting the chance to let his hair down now he's not at the beck and call of that girl he was seeing. Between you and me, Sophie, it's a huge relief she hasn't come with us.'

'Yes, we had a nice night, thanks. I need to get on but if you need anything just let me know.'

****

Back on the veranda of her bungalow, Sophie thought through last night's events. It had actually turned out very well and thankfully it wasn't a late night for her. As for Cristina ... that was another story. As Sophie put her coffee cup down, Mable arrived for a visit, clearly taking a break from the kittens. A quick look in the fridge and some tuna was found, which seemed to go down very well before she curled up on the chair in the sunshine.

'Oh, Mabel, it's so nice to have you back! I've had no one to talk to and seeing as I have fed you now, you have to listen to me going on. First, Tom and Paul, the new holiday makers, well ... what can I say? Cristina and Paul couldn't keep their eyes off each other – and something tells me it didn't stop at the eyes – but thankfully Tom didn't feel the same about me. He was missing his girlfriend back in England and told me that the reason she didn't come was because she can't stand being organised and bossed around by Tom's mum. They haven't actually split up but... Are you listening, Mabel, or have you fallen asleep? Don't get too comfortable because those babies of yours will be wondering where you have got to. Also, I have work to be getting on with. Come on, let's take you back to Graham's and I'm not carrying you either, you can walk.'

Sophie laughed as she went through the main gate because it was as if Mabel had understood every word, following behind dutifully, if a little hesitantly.

Arriving at Graham's gate Sophie called, 'Good morning! I've returned this little stop out who by the way has been fed. Don't believe her if she says she hasn't.'

'Morning! I saw her heading for the wall at the end of the garden and I guessed she'd be popping down to see you. Now Mable, go in and see if your kittens are ok; they're your responsibility after all. Have you time for a snack, Sophie? I've just been to the bakery.'

'Oh what do you think? Of course!'

While Graham went to make up a plate Sophie looked at the garden in front of her. Everything had been cleared away but it did leave a huge mess of dead grass and dirty paths and seating areas. There was much still to do but hopefully it wouldn't be too overwhelming for Graham. Thankfully he had help and Sophie was sure Javier wouldn't see him off.

'There you go,' Graham said as he deposited the pastries on the outdoor table. 'Now tell we what's happening down in the villa. Are the new guests nice or are you in for a hard couple of weeks?'

****

180

After a nice chat with Graham – and plans put in place for them to go to las Américas for some more shopping – Sophie headed back to Villa Kennal to work on paperwork and deal with some emails that urgently needed sorting. As she went through the gate she could see Tom and his parents down by the pool. No sign of Paul but that wasn't too surprising. If he'd had a late night with Cristina – as Sophie suspected – he was probably having a lie-in. But then she wondered – had he even come back last night? Not her problem. As long as he showed up at some point and Cristina turned up to cook the meals, all would be golden.

****

Four hours later the emails were sorted, the diary was updated and a number of taxi rides pre-booked with Ramon. Sophie was feeling very proud of how organised she'd become. Looking at her phone she saw there was a text from her mum to tell her to look online at some of the UK papers as there were a couple of features on her going back to acting. She wanted to know what Sophie thought of the photographs, looking for reassurance that they didn't make her look like mutton dressed as lamb as a stylist had picked out all the clothes.

Sophie Google searched her mum's name and clicked on the first link that came up. Her mum looked nice and the clothes suited her but the text that went with the photos was a little odd. It was true that her mum had given up acting to raise her and had subsequently became a business woman with her property company, but then it listed a load of hobbies that were clearly all made up and the final bit claimed that after finishing the series she was working on she would be 'taking time off to spend with my daughter, who is running a very successful business abroad'. Sophie laughed at first, but actually, she *was* running Villa Kennal, wasn't she? That feeling of pride came back, a little stronger this time.

She went to close the article but her eye caught on a name she recognised in a link at the side of the page – Kennal. She clicked through to find a photo shoot of the cast of the series he was working on in America. The accompanying article mentioned all the main characters with profiles on the actors playing them. Kennal's section was a brief paragraph saying he'd been enjoying filming but was looking forward to going back to his home in England when the filming took a break between the first and second series. There was no mention of his house in Tenerife but she respected that he kept his private life private.

Before she switched the laptop off, she printed out the villa's booking diary, which was looking very full for this year and next. She had even managed to fill the weeks in August, something she was very proud of. Reviewing the rest of the schedule she saw that there were two bookings that still hadn't paid a deposit. She had already emailed one but the other had minimal details and no phone number. As it was for ten days this was something she needed to mention to Kennal – if only to ask if he thought another wife and daughter might turn up! She attached the booking details to an email, along with the year's calendar so he could see what was happening with bookings overall, and then switched the computer off.

She was just about to go for a shower when the main gate opened and closed. She moved to peek through the bushes to see who it was but before she could step outside, she heard her little gate open and saw Luis step through.

'What brings you here?' she asked as she walked

out onto the veranda.

'What's going on with the people in the villa?' he asked abruptly.

'I don't know what you mean,' Sophie said, confused by his serious tone. 'They're a nice family – spotlessly clean and no trouble whatsoever. I wish all the guests were like them.'

'Did you know one of the blokes is seeing Cristina? He stayed the night at her place last night.'

'I really don't think it's any of my business, nor yours, come to that. Cristina is a free woman and she can see and spend time with whomever she likes.'

It was hard to tell from the look on his face if he was mad or upset.

'Was there anything else?'

'I'll bet you put her up to this, introducing her to the guests...'

'No I didn't. She came here and cooked for them last night and she and Paul just hit it off. It had absolutely nothing to do with me.' With that she turned and walked back into the bungalow, closing the door firmly behind her. Honestly, the nerve of him!

She was interrupted from her frustration with Luis by the sound of her phone beeping with an incoming text. It was from Kennal.

I'm sorry I forgot to tell you but that booking is for me. I'm coming back to Tenerife for ten days between filming and I'm really looking forward to meeting you, Sophie.

Chapter 26

The cleaning around the pool and terrace was all done very quickly the next morning and as the family didn't want anything doing inside the villa Sophie sat on her veranda thinking about Kennal. What if he was coming back to tell her she wasn't needed here anymore? To get herself out of her thoughts she decided to get ready for her shopping day with Graham and head over to his villa a bit earlier than planned.

On her way out she stopped to say hi to the guests and see if they needed anything.

'Are you enjoying your holiday?' she asked.

'Some are enjoying it more than others,' Tom said, looking at Paul and making a face.

'I meant to say, Sophie, if it isn't a problem to your plans, we won't be eating in the villa anymore. We've decided to go out to try the restaurants,' Malcolm explained.

The look on Kate's face said it all. Clearly, she wasn't impressed with Paul and Cristina's involvement.

'Not a problem at all,' Sophie said, leaving them to enjoy the sunshine.

****

'An atmosphere is developing in the villa and I'm beginning to think Tom and Paul's mum tries to run their lives for them because it seems that when they step out of line she isn't best pleased,' Sophie told Graham as they headed off to the bus stop.

'Oh dear, you'll have to keep me updated if there are new developments. In the meantime, can I ask you something? And I want you to be honest and not just say what you think I want to hear. Let me put it this way ... I haven't been a silly old fool, have I? The villa is starting to look fabulous and, well, it's too good for me. I don't need all of this and-'

'Graham, I'm not having this conversation with you again. You aren't the only person struggling...' At the shocked look on his face Sophie rushed to reassure him. 'I'm sorry! I didn't mean for it to come out like that. I just meant that you've come so far already and we want to keep you moving forward on your healing journey. Come on, let's get going. I think we both need a little boost of confidence today so what if we forgot shopping and everything else and instead have a day of being holiday makers? We could head over to La Caleta, where Ramon comes from. I haven't been there yet but he's always telling me how much I would enjoy it. Also, his mum has a gift shop. It will be fun!'

'You're right, it's silly not to focus on all the positive steps I've made. A day seeing the sights in La Caleta sounds perfect.'

Relieved that she hadn't upset him with her honesty, Sophie linked arms with Graham and they continued on to the bus stop.

****

The journey didn't take long at all and they both really did feel like they were on holiday discovering a new town.

As they walked towards the town centre Graham declared, 'I think I'll treat myself to one of those small cheese pie things. I've seen them in bakeries but have never tried them.'

'You are wild! Whatever next? Real cream on your hot chocolate, with sprinkles of chocolate and a flake? What are you youngsters like just throwing caution to the wind at every spare moment?' Sophie joked.

They both laughed and said this was definitely what they each needed – a day away from the villas and Los Kalanchoe. They found a little restaurant café down by the edge of the sea and managed to get an outside table. This was so different from Los Kalanchoe – very quaint – and for the first hour or so they didn't mention their lives or Villa Kennal, but eventually real life started to creep into the conversation.

'I just think that he's his own worst enemy,' Sophie said of Luis. Graham didn't know him personally but had seen him around and knew a bit of his history with the villa. 'I do believe if he stopped and thought before opening his mouth, weighed up the options instead of jumping right in, he would be a lot happier. And as for falling out with Kennal ... I reckon Kennal wouldn't be still relying on him for things if he was truly mad about the party.'

'Kennal is another kettle of fish though, isn't he? He intrigues me and I can't wait to meet him again now I know more about his history.'

Sophie couldn't wait to meet Kennal either. What was it about him that made all these woman fall for him? She was also intrigued to find out his thoughts on Emily and Casey. He obviously knew Emily caused problems when she visited the villa and from what Casey said he and she hadn't seen anything of each other since she was eighteen, but what was his take on each of his daughters?

'I have to admit, I've watched some of his film work and TV shows and he's very talented, not to mention handsome. The latest thing I saw was an interview with six of the cast members of this new show he's filming and I was very surprised how he came across. The other actors and actress were all fighting to be in the spotlight but not Kennal; he was more than happy to sit back and let them take all the glory. That makes me think he's quite grounded and I reckon it's just a job to him, a means of earning some money. Now, enough of all the Kennal talk, it's time for a walk to investigate what La Caleta has to offer ... and to build up an appetite for our next meal,' she said with a cheeky grin.

Graham laughed and insisted on paying, and then they headed off back into the little town. Walking up one of the side streets they could see very steep steps between the buildings leading towards the hill in the distance. Deciding a stair climb was not for them and realising that if they continued up the street it could possibly wind around without the steps, they continued on, stopping to look in a few shop windows. Thankfully, they were right and the road did take them above the little town and then across some rough ground until they could look down onto a very rocky cove, which looked like it was impossible to get to. Graham joked that at least it would be all downhill back to the harbour and going down they took a little side street that looked to have some cute shops.

'I know we said it wasn't a day for cushions but look at that shop over there – the window display is gorgeous! Shall we go in and have a look around?' Sophie asked.

'Absolutely!' Graham agreed and Sophie was almost taken back by how keen he was.

This was a completely different Graham and she wondered briefly if this was how he had been before Robert died.

The shop wasn't big but everything in it had colour – all bright greens, yellows, oranges and reds – from jugs and bowls to art work and of course cushions. They both fell in love with the selection of rugs and smiled at each other, knowing that they wouldn't be leaving this shop without spending money. A woman approached them to see if they

187

needed a hand with anything and Graham said how he loved the rugs but he wasn't sure he could manage to carry one back on the bus to Kalanchoe.

'That's not a problem. I can deliver it for free. Well, not me, actually, but my son. You just need to give me an address and when it would suit you to have it delivered.'

'If that's the case then I think I'll go and look at the cushions as well,' Graham said happily. 'I'm on a mission now, Sophie. Soon you'll be having to stop me!'

They happily spent ages matching cushions to rugs to see what combination worked best but it was difficult to choose as they liked everything. Eventually Sophie said perhaps Graham needed to choose his favourite rug first and then they could discard the others and work out which cushions went best. That was easier said than done though as Graham loved everything. Another twenty minutes or so and between them they had finally come to a decision. The shop owner was just wrapping up all their purchases when in walked a very familiar face – Ramon.

'So you have both finally come over to La Caleta, and more importantly, come to my mum's shop. I hope she isn't twisting your arm to buy things,' Ramon joked.

'No twisting of arms needed. If anything, I've had to stop Graham from buying more! We definitely should have come to this gorgeous little town a long time ago. We love it, don't we, Graham? Also, I'm not sure why we hadn't put two and two together. You said your mum's shop was very colourful so of course it had to be this one.'

'Yes, and now we've bumped into you perhaps you can tell us the best place to eat?' Graham asked. 'It has to be fish though as that's what we'd set our minds on.'

Ramon suggested a few options and then his mum jumped in and told them about one that she and the family had been going to since she was a little girl, which had been run by the same family for generations. Ramon agreed the food was lovely but said the place wasn't the best looking of restaurants.

'The food is the important part so I'm sure we'll love it,' Sophie said.

Ramon gave them directions once Graham had paid for the rug and they said their good byes and were just leaving the shop when Graham turned around.

'Why don't you join us, Ramon?'

With a little bit of encouragement Ramon said yes and they managed to grab a table outside the restaurant. Having ordered the food and a nice bottle of white wine – though Ramon stuck to water as he was driving – he talked non-stop about the town and how since his father died his mum had run the shop by herself, but she had always been the brains behind it. The creative one, she seemed to have a knack of knowing what would be fashionable before it actually was and so was always one step ahead. The only bad thing was that she was always tired because the business took up so much of her time.

When they'd finished their meal Graham sat back and gave a contented sigh. 'That was beautiful. Thank you for recommending it, Ramon.'

They ordered another glass of wine each and while Graham popped to the restroom Sophie turned to Ramon.

'I don't think I mentioned this but I've heard from Kennal and he's coming back for a holiday in a few weeks' time.'

'That will be nice. I'm sure you and him will get on well... Oh, but does that mean Emily will be coming to see him? Then again, she normally behaves when he's here.'

'I get the impression she plays on being the rebel just to wind people up. I have to say I saw a very different side to Emily the second time I met her, especially when she was with Casey.' Ramon flinched ever so slightly when she said Casey's name and she couldn't stop herself from blurting, 'You can tell me to mind my own business, but am I right in thinking you and Casey have a past together?'

'Yes, and it wasn't just Casey's relationship with her father that came to an end when she was eighteen, it was mine and hers as well. That's why it was such a shock to see her again when she was recently here, and why it was so difficult to work up the courage to speak to her. We used to see each other whenever she came to stay with her dad but then Velma gave Casey the choice – Kennal or her – and that was it. She left and never came back. It took years for me to get over losing her and having her back in Kalanchoe brought everything back to the surface. But I'm over it. It's well past time to move on.'

Sophie couldn't tell if he was lying to her ... or lying to himself. Because when it came to Ramon and Casey, things seemed anything but over.

As the waiter brought two more glasses of wine and cleared the dirty plates out of the way, Sophie glanced up the street to see someone walking down she recognised – Luis. She gave a little wave but he turned his head and walked by without saying a word. What was all that about?

'Oh dear. I think your admirer has put two and two together and made seven. He's not happy,' Ramon said with a chuckle.

'What do you mean? You don't think he thinks we're a couple, do you? Sorry, I didn't mean to sound horrified at the prospect,' Sophie added, causing them both to laugh. 'It's just so frustrating

190

that he gets himself in such a state, all because he doesn't stop to think through situations. Graham and I were talking about this earlier.'

'What have I missed?' Graham asked, picking up on the fact that something had happened during his absence.

Sophie explained about Luis walking by in a huff and Graham started laughing. 'I'd guess you're in for a few days of sulky Luis until you explain to him that what he saw wasn't what he thought.'

'I quite enjoyed the whole situation but I'm afraid I need to be going as I have an airport pick-up,' Ramon said.

Graham wouldn't let him pay for anything and so they all said their goodbyes and off Ramon went after first arranging a time for the rug and cushions to be delivered.

Graham and Sophie decided to have another little walk down at the water's edge before catching the bus back to Kalanchoe. The day out had been exactly what they both needed but they were both exhausted. Sophie suggested it was because choosing cushions was particularly tiring and they laughed all the way back to the bus stop.

****

'Thank you so much, Sophie, it's been another lovely day with you – they all are – but I'm sorry Luis got the wrong end of things and you'll have to explain. I do think it's quite funny though,' Graham said as they arrived home. Then, with a wave, he headed back to his villa.

'Oh I'm not worried. It's a daily thing with him now. Goodnight, Graham, I will see you with an update tomorrow,' Sophie called after him.

Shortly thereafter, just as she was about to turn her bedroom light off and go to sleep, a text came through from Cristina.

I need to speak to you. its urgent. can we meet up tomorrow?

Chapter 27

Sophie had had such a lovely day with Graham yesterday and she was glad she'd ignored Cristina's text last night because no doubt it would involve Luis and what he thought he saw. Luis really was his own worst enemy. She replied to Cristina with a *sorry I missed your message* and within seconds Cristina messaged back and they arranged for her to come up to the villa in a few hours. In the meantime Sophie would keep busy with some cleaning.

As she started sweeping one of the paths she looked up towards the top terrace where it looked like Paul and his mum were arguing. She couldn't hear what they were saying but Kate was waving her hands around a lot; both were standing and seemed tense. She quickly turned her back so they couldn't see her looking and decided to wait until they had gone before going up to clean that level.

****

As she was finishing cleaning the pool area, she noticed Paul and Tom going out the main gate and Kate and Malcom heading down towards her. She greeted them with a 'good morning!' expecting the normal response with details about where they'd eaten last night or what the weather was doing today – all the general chit chat – but today it was just a quick 'good morning' before settling in on the sun loungers. Sophie smiled and wished them a nice day before heading up to the top terrace to sweep and mop.

Something had gone off for sure.

Once she had put the pool towels from yesterday in to wash and gathered her cleaning things she went back over to the villa and started upstairs in the bathroom Kate and Malcom were using before going down to Tom and Paul's room. That was when she figured out what all the upset was about. Paul hadn't slept in his bed last night, which meant he had obviously been at Cristina's again, and that was why his mum hadn't been happy. Sophie smiled to herself because the fact of the matter was that the lads weren't teenagers, they were grown men and could do what they liked – and see who they liked – even if that wasn't how their mum saw it.

Cleaning done for the day, Sophie had a quick shower before Cristina popped in for a chat. No doubt it had something to do with Paul.

A summer of Cristina dating the visitors wasn't something that had crossed her mind as a possibility and Sophie suddenly found herself hoping the next guests that arrived had daughters and not sons...

'I'm really sorry to interrupt your day,' Cristina said once she'd arrived and the two women had grabbed a seat on the veranda. 'I don't know how to say this, really, because it's going to cause you a problem... You know I've been seeing a lot of Paul? Well, we've been getting on really well and he's asked me to go back to England with him to live. He has his own house and a good job and I'm sure I can find a job quite quickly, but that will leave you without a cook. I'm so sorry but I need to follow my heart.'

This was not what Sophie had been expecting but now all the arguing made even more sense.

'Have you told Luis?' Sophie found herself asking.

'No, but I have messaged Kennal because he's been good to me and I know I'm letting him down.'

'Don't worry about that, I'm sure it won't be a problem and your happiness is what's most important.' Though her words were supportive, in her head Sophie was thinking this was all very sudden and wondering if Cristina had really thought it through. Not that she would ever say that to her though.

'Thank you. I'm really excited and after all these years I do feel as if I have found my soul mate. It's made me feel silly for all the time I've spent being upset with Luis – did I want him or did I not – and strangely I now feel so differently about him. I've met Paul and ... to be honest this probably sounds so stupid because I'm not a kid, but I finally feel grown up, you know? I really feel as if I want to create a home with him and settle down, grow old together. Are you shocked because I am! I really don't think I've been this happy or content in all of my life.'

Cristina was radiating joy and Sophie couldn't help but be caught up in the romance of it all.

****

Two hours later and Cristina gone, Sophie had listened about how it had been love at first sight and all the little details that led to Cristina's life-changing decision. Sophie hoped she'd feel that content with someone someday. For now though, she was happy with life at the moment. The job was a dream and her time with Graham was very special. That was enough for now.

With Cristina leaving, however, she knew she had to find someone to cook the guest meals and she didn't know anyone that fitted the bill. She certainly wasn't capable of doing it herself so there was only one answer – she needed to email Kennal. He had lived in Kalanchoe for years and must have loads of contacts.

Once she had done that, she decided to go through all the reservations and make a list of all the meals that had been requested. Thankfully it didn't take very long as her filing system was really well

195

organised – another thing she could add to her list of accomplishments. As it was nearly six o'clock and she needed to clear her head she decided a walk on the beach and something to eat sat looking out to sea would be the perfect solution. She smiled. If only all the world's problems could be sorted just by looking out at the ocean.

The walk on the beach did clear her head and she thought about everything that had happened today. She was really happy for Cristina and she hoped she and Paul would be very happy together. She then found herself wondering what Luis would think about it. Would he be happy or jealous? Only time would tell.

Her stomach starting to protest, she made her way back to Kalanchoe and the little family restaurant she had got to know quite well.

Sat eating her pasta with a big glass of wine everything did feel better. She really was lucky to be living here with no one to answer to apart from Kennal, who was thousands of miles away and basically let her just get on with things. This cooking lark was really the only a hiccup and she wasn't going to let it spoil her time here in Tenerife.

****

She arrived back at the villa as it was nearing ten thirty and decided to do a quick water of her flower pots before turning in. She jumped when her phone rang out in the quiet darkness and was only partly surprised to see it was Luis calling. No doubt he wanted to ask about Cristina leaving. Here she was again in the middle of their domestic problems.

'Hi, Luis, how can I help?'

'It not about you helping me, it's about how I will be helping you, Sophie. Kennal has contacted me about the situation at the villa and I'm happy to share that I'm your new chef! I'm looking forward to us working together and hopefully you will feel the same ... and Ramon won't have a problem with it.'

Chapter 28

Kate, Malcom and the boys – and not forgetting Cristina – had been gone for just under a week. New guests were now at the villa and thankfully no cooking was required. In fact, Sophie had not had any contact with Luis since she had emailed him the list of dates he was required to cook as she had been so busy. The new guests had young children, which meant that the cleaning was taking ages each day – the glass a nightmare, dirty finger marks all over the place and the pool area a mess with all the toys and splashing – but thankfully there had been no dramas and the family were lovely, if high maintenance.

Sophie also hadn't seen much of Graham because he had been busy helping Javier sort out the garden, but tonight they were going out to eat and to discuss Madeline coming and staying at his villa. Shockingly, her mum had seemed happy to be staying with Graham and her only requirement was that her room had to be private and not overlooked. But before that it was cleaning time. Sophie put a smile on for the clients even though the place looked like a tip.

****

Four hours later the villa was as clean as it could be with kid's toys and clothes everywhere but the parents understood Sophie had done what she could and were happy with the result. After putting a load of towels in to wash, Sophie headed back up to the bungalow for a little sit down for the rest of the afternoon.

'Hello, Mable, and a good afternoon to you. Have you left those kittens unattended again? They won't be happy. As you're here already though, would you like some tuna? I think I have a tin open from when you were here yesterday. So, what have you to tell me? Oh, it's the other way around? Ok, well, I've not seen Luis for a few days – he probably still thinks I'm seeing Ramon but he can think what he likes ... though I would be interested to find out if he's missing Cristina... And off course, you're in for a treat as my mother's coming to stay at Graham's villa. She isn't a huge fan of cats so you might have to keep those kittens under control and out of her way, but if – like me – she chats to you, I would appreciate if you could tell me what she says because I don't think everything is that straightforward in her acting life at the moment. Are you walking away, Mable? So that's how it is, is it? You eat the tuna and then leave? That's put me in my place,' Sophie said indignantly ... before realising she was scolding a cat for not listening.

Sophie had a while before she had to meet Graham so she sat on the veranda and opened up the villa diary, which thankfully was full. As she turned one of the pages she saw Kennal's booking and realised it wouldn't be long before he came back. The excitement about meeting him had worn off a bit now and she was starting to get very nervous. For one, he was her boss – would the place be up to scratch? Was she doing a good enough job? – and for another, she had learnt so much about him and his family situation over the past few months, including some things he might not be comfortable with his employee knowing. Plus, she was living in his home, which now looked completely different to when he'd left it. With thoughts swirling, she decided to close her eyes and try to enjoy the sunlight for a few moments...

****

Sophie had unintentionally fallen asleep on the veranda and was late to meet Graham for dinner, apologising profusely when she arrived at his villa.

'I'm so sorry! Mable kept me chatting – well, I chatted to her – and then I did some planning and then one thing led to another and before I knew it, I'd fallen asleep and the afternoon had flown by! Now, how are you and where would you like to eat?'

'Sophie you are buzzing. Slow down and catch up with yourself. I don't mind where we go and as for chatting to Mable, you're not the only one. I've started talking to the kittens myself, asking them questions and such. You read about these crazy people and their cats ... I think I'm becoming one of them! Actually, I may have already been one of them...' he said thoughtfully, causing them both to break out in laughter.

Heading down the lane to the town they decided tonight was a pasta night. Once they had found a restaurant they liked the look of and had ordered, Graham told her he'd brought his writing pad to make notes of what he needed to get for Madelaine's stay. Sophie reassured him he wouldn't need anything as she would get the food and other necessary bits and pieces the morning of her arrival. All he would need to supply was the patience.

'My mum is high maintenance and now she's back acting I presume it's gotten even worse. The good thing is that the new television series hasn't come out so apart from publicity things in newspapers, her face isn't out there yet. Just wait until she's recognised in the street and supermarket! Actually, I could be wrong because I'm not so sure if she's enjoying being back in the spotlight all that much. We'll have to wait and see what she says about it all once she's arrived. Now, talk to me about the garden. How's it going? Is Javier working hard?'

'Absolutely. In fact, he seems to be trying to

prove something because when I first got him to help I told him that once everything was sorted and back to how it should be, I would maintain it myself. But I think he likes the idea of doing it himself so he's pulling out all the stops to prove he's the right man for the job. I do think looking after it all by myself might be a bit hard so perhaps I should take him up on the offer. Anyway, that's me. What news from the villa? Oh of course, you've got that young family there. Are they still making a daily mess?'

'Yes, but they're only children on holiday having fun and as it's all part and parcel of the job I don't mind too much. I'm just glad they don't want any meals cooked.'

'Talking of your new chef, have you seen him and told him you aren't with Ramon?'

'Nope, not seen him or told him. Ultimately it's his problem not mine, and if he wants to be childish, let him.'

'Don't you think that's a bit mean? Now Cristina has gone he's a free man – you should be having fun with him!'

Sophie blushed. 'The thing is, I'm beginning to think there will always be something Luis jumps the gun at. A relationship with him would never be straightforward.'

'I didn't say have a relationship with him, just some fun. They're two completely different things.'

The food arrived and that wasn't the only thing that happened – in walked Luis! He spotted Sophie immediately and she hoped that he wouldn't jump to the wrong conclusion yet again and think she was dating Graham. He went to talk to the owner before eventually coming to say hello, but before Sophie could reply Graham was on his feet.

'Hello, Luis, I don't think we've been formally introduced, although we seem to see each other a lot. I'm Graham, the eccentric man that lives up the lane with the cat. I just love that title; it means I'm not anybody. Please, why don't you join us? We would really like that, wouldn't we, Sophie?'

What could Sophie say apart from yes, but again that was the only word she got in. Graham was on a roll and poured Luis a glass of wine before ordering another bottle, all while trying to eat his pasta at the same time. Luis looked shocked but ordered the lasagne, which he said was already cooked in a big tray so he wouldn't have to wait long and they could all eat at the same time. The conversation was all very light and Graham asked Luis questions like how long had he lived here and had he seen lots of changes to Kalanchoe over the years? But Sophie wasn't daft. She knew Graham would eventually go in for the kill, she just didn't have a clue what that would look like.

'It's lovely to have company for a change, isn't it, Sophie? Well, more for Sophie really as she has so much to put up with, what with me telling the same old stories over and over again. But oh, she has been such a huge help sorting out my villa for me. I'm telling you, Luis, I couldn't have done any of it without her, she really has been a life saver. And we really do enjoy each other's company. In fact, the other week we went off to La Caleta and had a lovely day... Oh but you know about that already, don't you? Sophie said she and Ramon saw you walking by while I was in the bathroom. We had bumped into him when we popped into his mum's shop earlier on and so of course we asked him to come and eat with us. Now, talking of bathrooms, I think I need to pop off for just a minute. This is turning out to be such a lovely evening, don't you think?' His performance complete, Graham slipped away with a secret smile sent in Sophie's direction.

She really had to hand it to him – that had been very smooth.

'Graham was with you and Ramon in La Caleta...?' Luis's face broke into a sheepish expression. 'I've been stupid again, haven't I?'

'Yes and yes. If you could only see the look on your face just now when Graham told you... To be honest, I think he was very diplomatic – he could have been a lot blunter. And now you're going to ask me why I haven't said something sooner and my reply to you is why should I? You've been the silly one. Graham's on the way back,' she added, looking over Luis's shoulder.

'Have you both been having fun while I was gone?' Graham asked with a satisfied smile. 'I was only earlier saying to Sophie that she needs to have more fun.'

The record set straight, the rest of the evening was far more relaxed. Whether that was down to the wine or just the fact that Sophie and Luis finally knew where they stood with each other ultimately didn't matter. Luis was able to fill Graham in about the people that had lived in his villa before him, and to give them both some more insight into Kennal. It was a very nice evening but Sophie knew that was all down to Graham being there. What a different man he was compared to the one she'd first met when she arrived. As they stood outside the restaurant afterwards, Luis thanked both of them for a lovely evening and went to say goodbye but Graham was having none of it.

'The night is still young, why don't you two kids come back and have a night cap with me at the villa?' he said.

Though she didn't say it, Sophie wasn't sure it was a good idea, but Luis jumped at the opportunity and the three of them started to make their way up to the villas. It was very quiet as they approached Villa Kennal, which Sophie took to mean the screaming children must be in bed for the night.

That was unsurprising though, given that it was late.

She commented on the time, to which Graham replied, 'Yes, actually it is rather late, isn't it? I've suddenly come over all tired. Do you mind if I give having a drink a miss? But don't let that stop you two! I'm sure it will be nice sat on Sophie's veranda this evening now it's a bit cooler. Have a lovely time and remember, Sophie – fun!'

With that Graham was gone and Sophie and Luis laughed. They had been set up.

Sophie said they shouldn't disappoint him and invited Luis in for a night cap and he readily agreed. The relaxed atmosphere changed subtly and instantly to something a little more tense, and once through the gate and up the path to the bungalow Sophie took control and asked Luis what he would like to drink. She'd expected him to say beer or wine but he actually replied, 'A coffee would be nice, if that's no trouble?'

'Not at all. Back in just a moment,' she said as she went inside to get the drinks.

'There you go – one coffee. So now you've properly met Graham, what do you think of him?'

'I think he's fun and definitely not the man I used to meet in the lane. But like he said, that's all down to you, Sophie. You should be very proud, though perhaps that's not the right word... But you know what I mean.'

'Yes, but it's not just him that's changed, he's also been really good for me in so many ways, and made me realise all sorts of things about my own life and how much it's changed. And now your life's changing too, Luis, with no more Cristina. How do you feel about that?'

'Honestly? I'm fine and I wish her well. There's someone else who has been taking up a lot more space in my mind these days anyway...'

Sophie blushed at the loaded look in his eyes.

'Up until I was very stupid with the Ramon and you misunderstanding, I was starting to think one of the best things I have done was messing up last year with Kennal because if I hadn't and I was running the place, you would have never come here and we would never have met, and that would... Sorry, I don't know what I'm trying to say, really. Well, I do know ... I just can't put it into words.'

Silence fell between them but even if Luis couldn't put words to his emotions right now, Sophie knew exactly how she felt – happy. She stood up and went over to Luis and kissed him on the cheek. He stood and took her hands and kissed her on the lips, which made her even happier.

Luis leaned in to kiss her again but then they both jumped as Sophie's phone started ringing loudly. She told Luis to ignore it but it rang again and he said it must be urgent. Sophie sighed and looking at the screen saw that it was her mum.

'Hi, Mum, this is very late for a call. What's wrong?'

'Sorry I know it's late but this can't wait until the morning as I will be arriving tomorrow.'

'Tomorrow? But I thought your visit wasn't for a couple of weeks.'

'Well, it's not now. I will explain when I see you so please, no more questions for now. Will this be ok with your neighbour?'

'Graham will be absolutely fine with it. Text me when you land.'

Chapter 29

Last night's call from her mum had been the end of the evening for Sophie and Luis as Sophie couldn't relax and Luis had suggested it was best if he left her to make plans for her mum's imminent arrival.

It was still early in the morning and Sophie had barely slept. Something was up with her mum and it had to be something to do with the filming because why else would she be coming early? Had she been sacked?

Whatever it was, she would find out in ten hours' time when Madeline arrived. Looking at the time she texted Graham the news and also said that once she had cleaned the villa she would come around so they could put a plan of action together. Thankfully he wasn't bothered by the sudden arrival; he just said it was exciting, a real actress living in his villa.

Sophie's reaction to that was that it was definitely exciting, until you realised that what comes with the actress is drama.

The family still hadn't surfaced out of the villa so Sophie decided to start the day with a quick tidy up and clean down around the pool. Yesterday's beach towels were put in to wash and while she waited to get into the villa she pulled together a shopping list of things her mum might want to eat. As she sat on the veranda figuring out what to buy she heard the children running out the villa door and peering through the hedge she could see the family were gathering the inflatable toys from the pool area and heading down to the main gate. It looked like they were off to the beach, which was perfect timing as it would allow her to get the villa cleaned before her shopping trip.

'Thank you so much for picking me up,' she said to Ramon later that day when he picked her up from the market. 'Please could you drop me at Graham's and not Villa Kennal?'

'You are loaded up! Is he having a party?'

Sophie explained her mum was going to be staying with Graham then recounted what had happened at last night's dinner and how Graham told Luis what actually was going on over in Le Caleta.

'I have to say I'm a bit disappointed. I was hoping to carry the story on for a few weeks as it was so fun seeing Luis seething like that,' Ramon said with a laugh. 'So, you're friends again? That's good considering Luis is doing the cooking at Villa Kennal now Cristina has left, but then there will probably be something else that upsets him again soon, no doubt.'

'I hope not!' Sophie said as they pulled up outside Graham's. Ramon helped her carry all the bags of shopping in and Graham laughed, saying he was shocked how much Madeline ate. Sophie explained it was for him as well, and she wanted to give her mum plenty of choice as it minimised the chance of an outburst.

She thanked and paid Ramon and then got everything into Graham's fridge and freezer while he made them a coffee. Of course the minute she was by the fridge Mable appeared for a treat as she knew Graham always had something there for her.

'Job done. Now, I best try and explain – not that I really know what's going on. My mum called late last night and said she was arriving today. And her timing couldn't have been worse as thanks to your plan Luis and I were having "fun" right when she called. He left soon after.'

'I don't know what you mean,' Graham said slyly. 'Though my plan actually was rather good, wasn't it? I was quite pleased with how I orchestrated it.'

'Yes, you are very clever, but getting back to my mother, are you sure it's ok, her staying here with you? It's not going to be straightforward; she is very demanding and controlling at the best of times and now, with the TV programme under her belt, she will be worse, I'm sure.'

'Stop worrying! I have everything here ready for her and from tomorrow the pool will be filled. Ok the area around it isn't very nice but other parts of the garden are and if she's grumpy I will just leave her to herself,' Graham said confidently.

Sophie's phone beeped. It was Madeline to say she had just boarded but could Sophie arrange a discreet lift from Tenerife airport to the villa? A call to Ramon and it was arranged, and Sophie decided she had better go with him to meet her mum.

'Oh, one thing I wanted to just check, will you be eating with us when you're not working?' Graham asked.

'I hadn't really given it any thought but yes, if that's ok?'

'Of course! That would be lovely,' he replied.

****

'I remember picking you and your mum up from the airport the day you first came here. It was like answering a questionnaire with your mum,' Ramon said as he drove Sophie to the airport.

'I think it might be a little different today,' Sophie said, not knowing what kind of mood her mother would arrive in. 'Hopefully she hasn't brought tons of luggage.'

Ramon dropped Sophie off at the arrivals door

before going off to park the car. Sophie checked the arrivals board and though her mum's plane hadn't landed, it was going to be on time. Sophie went and bought a couple bottles of water as she thought her mum might appreciate that, and as she stood watching holiday makers coming out from the arrivals area she thought about the fact that these people were only here for a few weeks at a time. How lucky was she to be living here? But on a not so happy note, what would she do when the last guests left and she had to lock the place up? She really should start thinking about what was next for her, but best wait until her mother had left. One thing at a time and all that.

Looking up at the arrivals board she saw that the plane had landed. After a while people started to come through but it was those that only had hand luggage. But then Sophie noticed something odd.

Surely not...

It couldn't be ... but it was.

Sophie was more convinced than ever that something serious must have happened because her mother was not just carrying one small carry-on bag, she was also wearing a disguise – a wig, hat and glasses, paired with a baggy jumper and some jeans. She didn't think her mother even owned clothes like that!

'Mum! I didn't recognise you, why-'

'Questions and more questions. You never stop. Now, where is the car? Come on, before...'

'Before what, Mum?'

Madeline didn't answer so Sophie silently led the way to the car.

'Hi and welcome back to Tenerife, Madeline. I hope you had a good flight.'

Madeline remained silent so Sophie jumped in and explained to Ramon that her mum had a dreadful headache and just needed some quiet.

Whether he believed that, Sophie didn't know, but at some other point she would apologise for her mother's rudeness.

The journey to Kalanchoe was undertaken in complete silence. Sophie wasn't going to say a thing for fear of having her head blown off and she had plenty to think about to occupy her for the ride. Her mother's lack of luggage could be a problem but she presumed in the hand luggage was at least one change of clothes – though hopefully more. As they were nearly there she texted Graham and warned him that the atmosphere was dreadful, apologising in advance for her mother. He texted back and told her not to worry because everything would be fine. Sophie wished she had his confidence.

'So, here we are, and there's Graham by the gate waiting for us. Thank you, Ramon.'

'You are more than welcome! I hope you feel better soon, Madeline. The lovely Tenerife sunshine will help, I'm sure.'

Madeline made a noise that sounded like it could be a thank you, but could have been anything really. With an apologetic smile to Ramon, Sophie took her mother's carry-on bag out of the boot and carried it towards Graham. Introducing them, she was surprised to see a polite smile on her mum's face – the first one since she had arrived. Graham said how lovely it would be having her staying here and led the way into the garden. He pointed out that it was a work in progress but there was no reply. Then Mable appeared and – in a scene which was quite funny to Sophie – her mum and Mable just stood and stared at each other, both looking as if they didn't know what to make of the other. Sophie supposed she shouldn't be surprised given they were both very determined characters.

'If I go and put the kettle on, can you show your mum her room, Sophie? Now Madeline, would you like tea or coffee, or would you sooner get your holiday officially started and have wine?'

Madeline gave no reply so Sophie shrugged at Graham and ushered her mum towards the bedrooms.

Her mum said nothing about the guest room she was being offered, which was a first. Unnerved by her mother's continued silence, Sophie suggested Madeline sort herself out and come join them on the terrace when she was ready.

It was a good fifteen minutes before Madeline appeared. Gone was the wig, jumper and jeans. Now her hair was tied back and she had a loose summer dress on. The sunglasses had remained but then it was sunny out... Thankfully Graham took control of the situation and he asked if she would like a glass of wine.

'Thank you, that would be nice. White if you have it.'

Madeline plonked herself down on a chair facing the sun and Graham automatically poured three wines. This was it, a conversation had to start and it wasn't fair to leave it to Graham.

'I need to pop out later, Mum, so if there's anything you need for your stay – toiletries for example – just let me know and I'll pick it up for you.'

'It's clothes I need, obviously. Surely you've noticed I haven't come with any? Honestly! Sometimes I despair of you. Do you not have any common sense? Go get a note pad and I will tell you what I need.'

Unsurprised by her mother's demands, Sophie was about to get up when Graham spoke in a stern tone she hadn't seen or heard from him before.

'Madeline, I think before you continue I need to explain a few house rules – actually, just one: as long as you are staying under my roof, you will *not* talk to Sophie in that tone of voice. Whatever your problems are and whatever you are running away from isn't my business, but your daughter has been the best friend ever to me. She has pulled me from the depths of despair and given me my life back and so I will not accept you putting her down in my home. If you feel you are unable to do this you are more than welcome to leave and find a hotel. Now, while you two put together a list, I will go and make us a sandwich. There is cheese, ham or beef. Which would you like?'

They both asked for cheese and off he went into the kitchen. Not sure what to say after Graham had issued his edict, Sophie said she would go and fetch a note pad, but Madeline said it could wait until tomorrow as she wasn't in a rush for anything.

'But I could go for another glass of wine, if possible?'

Sophie went into the kitchen to fetch another bottle and also gave Graham a huge hug. She and her mum then sat in silence until Graham reappeared with plates of sandwiches, crisps and olives. He seamlessly took control of the conversation before mentioning how he loved the daily reports Sophie gave him about the guests in Villa Kennal. He recounted some of his favourites and when he got to the Rich and Mandy story Madeline was actually laughing aloud and appeared to be enjoying herself.

'Have you lived here long, Graham? And why Kalanchoe? I can imagine you would love to be somewhere busier, with more life.'

'If I'm going to tell you my life story – especially the Tenerife part – I best get us another bottle of wine because it's not a five minute story, is it, Sophie?'

'Why don't I get the wine and take the plates back in and you can start telling my mum all the details?' Sophie offered. 'And don't leave Mable out! She's a big part of the story,' she added.

Sophie took her time washing the dishes up and taking deep breaths. Thank goodness for Graham. How would she have coped if it was just her and her mum in that little bungalow? In short, she wouldn't have.

When she finally went back outside she could see Graham had got upset telling the story and Madeline was holding his hand while taking everything in. They were so engrossed that they didn't really take any notice when she topped their glasses up and sat down.

'So basically, you just existed from day to day and your life was on hold? That doesn't sound a bit like the chap who is sat here telling me this story right now.'

'No, I'm completely different and have come so far from where I was. Don't get me wrong, I still have my wobbly moments, but they're getting less and less frequent. It's honestly all down to Sophie; she has helped me take little steps that feel manageable and I'm finally happy, something I never thought I would ever be again.'

'I only pointed you in the right direction. You did everything else yourself.'

'Well, you two have certainly had a busy and not so straightforward few months with one thing and another, haven't you? I guess that just leaves me to tell you my story and, most importantly, why I'm here. *That*, at least, is straightforward – I have been suspended by the TV company until further notice.'

'I don't understand, Mum, what do you mean suspended? How can that happen while making a television programme? Aren't there timelines and schedules that are set in stone?'

'It can actually happen very easily, darling, and so it has. Apparently the other actors are finding me

213

difficult to work with and the producers are saying I'm not playing the part I'm being paid to perform ... basically, I'm no good and I've put everything in jeopardy as I'm the lead and the whole story revolves around my character. I'm sorry to be such a party pooper but would you mind if I went off to bed? I'm really tired. Thank you both for your kindness though.'

As Madeline got up and went back indoors Sophie and Graham looked at each other with the same question in their eyes – did this mean they might recast Madeline's part and end her second chance in the acting world before it even began?

Chapter 30

The following day Graham was up early, sitting on the patio reflecting on everything Madeline had told them. No wonder she was in a state – actors refusing to work with her, the producers not happy with how she came across on the screen... It was a right mess, but like he and Sophie had said to her, she was a major character in the programme and they couldn't just write her out. Plus, weeks of filming had already been completed and more importantly, a lot of money had been spent on the production. His phone beeped with a text from Sophie to say she would get all her cleaning done at the villa and then go into las Américas to get everything her mum needed. He messaged back to say there was no rush, he would encourage Madeline to have a rest in the sun all nice and quiet.

After making another coffee he could hear a door opening. It sounded like Madeline was up and he knew he needed to be positive with her. After many hours spent chatting about her situation last night, today she needed to switch off completely from everything, sort her head out and then make decisions. Though actually, it wasn't her that had to decide what to do ... it was the production company.

'Good morning! I hope you slept well. Can I get you a tea or coffee?'

'Coffee, please, Graham. I did sleep like a log but I think that's down to the wine. We drank quite a lot but thankfully I've not got a bad head.'

Graham was relieved. She seemed in quite a good mood and not upset like she was yesterday, but he was very aware that that could quite easily change. While he was in the kitchen he made some toast. If she didn't want it, he would eat it. He also wondered if there was a way of helping Madeline's situation. He knew he couldn't change what had happened but surely there had to be a solution.

'There you go, one large coffee and some toast if you fancy it. I've brought out some marmalade and jam but it's not a problem if you don't want it.'

'Thank you and please, you really don't need to pussy foot around me. I'm ok. Well ... I'm not, but I will be. And I know I can be awkward and a dozen or so other things as well so thank you for putting up with me. The toast does smell gorgeous.'

They settled into a comfortable silence and Graham could see Madeline was very relaxed. Mable had wandered outside, followed by the kittens, who now were getting very brave and adventurous, although she wasn't happy if they wandered too far away from her.

Madeline's phone beeped, interrupting the stillness, but after taking a look at the screen she put it right back down. Graham thought this was good in a way as she wasn't obsessed by it. He took the empty plates back inside and made them both another drink, wondering how he could get around to talking about her suspension without asking questions that upset her.

'Can I get you anything else?' he asked as he joined her outside again.

'No I'm fine, thank you. This is so peaceful here now, with no road noise and plenty of gorgeous sunshine. I could cope with this twenty-four-seven.'

'I hope you enjoy it while you're here for the break and do whatever you want to do.'

'The thing I don't want to do but have to is read the email that's just come through from the production company. I still haven't got it sorted in my head that the cast got together and said I was difficult to work with and they've had enough of having to work long hours because of me. All I wanted was my scenes to be the best they could be. I knew my lines every time but I just cannot get my head around how there isn't any rehearsal. Basically, you leave your dressing room, walk on to the set with the other actors who are in that scene with you and just ... do it Everything is done so fast.'

'It does sound terrifying but surely the company can't complain just because you wanted to give it your best. And if that means doing several takes, I would think the other actors would be ok with that as surely they'd feel the same.'

'Yes, but it wasn't just that. They've also said that when I played the character all those years ago she was different from how I play her now. I've explained that there have been a lot of years in between and she would have changed – grown up and become a completely different woman – which they understand and is what they wanted. But they've said a grown up version of the character is not what I'm delivering and showed me clips of my character now and in the past to make their point. To be honest, I wish they had never contacted me about the show.'

'Can I ask, Madeline, were you excited to go back after all these years? Was the buzz for acting still there?'

'Yes, it was. I never really knew how much I had missed it as I suppose life got in the way, and as the years passed the yearning went as well. If only I could nail it, give everyone what they want, it could lead to a few acting jobs now and again, which would be lovely. I've also loved doing all the publicity stuff and being back in the industry bubble as I do feel I belong there. I know I need to sort myself out if I want to avoid it all slipping away, but the million dollar question is ... how do I do it?'

Graham suddenly had a thought and decided to go for it.

'Out of curiosity, when you watched the two

clips – the old one and the new one – could you notice a difference between the two?'

'I guess ... the younger one came across far more relaxed and at ease, whereas when I'm acting now I feel more conscious of things. I have the clips on my iPad. Would you like to see them?'

Watching the footage, Graham could see exactly what the producers and directors were saying, as there was a clear difference between the Madeline from the original show and the Madeline in the new scenes she'd shot in recent weeks. He had to agree with the producers claim that she was acting completely differently and he had to be honest with Madeline without being brutal and knocking her confidence even more. He needed time to think things through and thankfully his phone rang with a call from Sophie, asking if he needed any food shopping. He couldn't think of anything so said he would see her later on.

Turning to Madeline, he took the opportunity to say, 'Speaking of people changing, I sense that Sophie is a lot different now than she has been the last few years. She told me the boyfriend story and I've explained to her she shouldn't feel guilty as she did nothing wrong apart from fall in love and that's no bad thing. Thankfully, she seems to be getting over him and moving on.'

'Yes, I've been thinking a lot about it since she told me and so much now makes sense. I wish she had confided in me years ago as I feel sure I would have sussed him out and maybe it could have ended sooner, causing her less pain. I do think you're right and she's moved on though. I've not asked if she's met anyone here on Tenerife yet. That nice taxi driver Ramon would be suitable...'

'Oh, no, they get on very well, but just as friends. My money is on Luis. I think they are well suited.'

'You mean the one who looked after the villa for

Kennal? Surely not! Aren't they always falling out?'

'Yes, all the time, but I think it's just because there's passion there.'

This made Madeline laugh.

'On that note, I think it's time for an early glass of wine and then you can fill me in on the other important man in Sophie's life – Kennal. I want to know everything there is to know.'

'That would take a month! And besides, there's just one word I need to sum him up perfectly: charming. He's a total charmer to everyone he meets.'

'First, wine, and then the dirt on the lord of the manor ... or the villa,' Graham said, returning hastily with a bottle and two glasses.

'His downfall, as I'm sure you've already figured out, is beautiful women. He falls in love very quickly, marries, then ends up getting a divorce and marrying the new woman he's inevitably fallen in love with. Thankfully I sussed him out years ago, when we were both very young, and saved myself the heartache of being charmed by him. I have to say though, he has always been there for me and he really has been a good friend. I've not seen him in the flesh for a while though and I'm not sure I'll still be here when he comes back in a few weeks' time.'

'You are more than welcome to stay as long as you like. I think the two of us could have a lot of fun together. In addition to all the Kennal stories I also want to know all the show business gossip.'

'The biggest bit of gossip is that an aging actress who is trying to make a comeback actually can't act her way out of a paper bag.'

'That's not true! You just need to figure out what it will take to get yourself back on track.'

What Graham didn't say was that he already knew what the answer was. He just needed to find the right words and the right moment to tell her.

With that, Sophie walked through the gate with bags of shopping in her hands. It was clear that Mable, who was right at her side, thought that the bags meant food, but Graham knew the cat would soon be disappointed as the bags were likely clothes and toiletries for Madeline instead.

'Hi, you two, having a nice day? Mum, I'll put these in your room and if there's anything you don't like I can take it back. As I was walking up the lane the family who have been staying at the villa were getting into a taxi to take them to the airport so I thought I might get stuck into the cleaning this afternoon to get it out of the way, even though the new guests aren't arriving until the day after tomorrow. You both don't mind, do you? It would be useful to have the extra time to clean the children's sticky handprints off of things but also I thought it would free me up so that we could have a nice day around the pool at Villa Kennal tomorrow and perhaps a barbeque. And I might invite Luis, if that's ok.'

'That works for me,' Graham said, looking to Madeline who was also nodding. 'I'll cook dinner around eight to eight thirty tonight, shall I?'

'Sounds great, thank you,' Sophie said before heading off. Graham couldn't help but wonder if Sophie's desire to spend the day cleaning was actually to get ahead on the work, or to avoid spending time with her mum, but then, it wasn't his business to judge.

'You know, Graham, my daughter has taken to running the villa like a duck to water. I'm so pleased for her and if Luis is coming to dinner tomorrow, we'll get a chance to see if your theory is correct. Right, I best look at this email and see if the suspension has turned into a sacking. I just don't know what to say if they ask me if I've sorted myself out.'

'Madeline, can I say something? Firstly, can you put reading the email off for a bit? I know I'm not a producer or an actor or director, but I am a viewer and I think I can see what the issue is. When you created the character all those years ago you were her – every bit of her was spot on and all the things they wanted her to be – but now, and I'm sorry to say this but I think it will help if I'm honest, I think you're playing yourself rather than playing the character. Yes, you're saying the words she's meant to say, but you're doing so as you – Madeline Mundey – rather than as the character. If you could move on from that and focus on bringing the original character back to life, I think you will be brilliant. The script is undoubtedly good, so it's just a matter of losing the Madeline to allow the character to shine.'

Chapter 31

Sophie was up early, excited about a day at Villa Kennal without any guests. The cleaning yesterday had taken for ever and there was still more to do tomorrow before the new guests arrived. She hadn't even had time to go back to Graham's last night for dinner but both Graham and her mum said they understood that work had to come first.

She was just putting all the cushions on the sun loungers by the pool, readying for a day spent relaxing poolside, when her phone beeped. It was Luis to say he would love to come for a barbeque but wouldn't be able to get there until seven that evening. As Sophie was getting clean towels out the main gate opened and she saw it was her mum but no Graham. That wasn't really the situation she wanted.

'Hi, Mum, you've good timing. I've just got everything ready so pick a spot before the crowds arrive. Only joking, it will just be the three of us until Luis gets here around seven. Is Graham coming to join us soon?'

'He's just nipped to the bakery for fresh bread to have with the barbeque. He said he wouldn't be too long. He's very nice and you really have changed his life, darling. I can't imagine what he was like when you first met him; you must have had to tread very carefully.'

'Honestly, I only pointed him in the right direction. He made most of the decisions himself. He's also been good for me with all the Mark business but enough of that. Can I get you a coffee or a tea?'

'A coffee would be lovely, thank you, but would you like me to make it for myself?'

'No, it's ok, I can do it,' Sophie said. 'I need to

take some things out of the freezer up at the bungalow anyway.'

As she walked up she could tell her mum was a lot more relaxed and not at all like the woman who'd arrived on Tencrife a couple of days ago. Whatever Graham had said to her seemed to have worked.

She also wondered if now, well they were alone, she should mention Emily's suggestion about Kennal potentially being her father. Oh she knew he wasn't, deep down, but it would be good for her mum to confirm that. Though 'confirm' sounded the wrong word...

'Thank you, darling, this is lovely by the pool. Do you get many days between bookings to do this?' her mum asked when Sophie joined her back at the villa.

'No it's very unusual but a nice change. Did you have a nice evening with Graham? I bet he wanted to hear all your show business stories from years ago.'

'We had a lovely evening and he's been very helpful. He took time to listen to all the problems that have brought me here and he was very honest and constructive. A lot of what he said was exactly what the producers and directors have been saying but he talked it through with me and took his time – not like them, where everything is bang get it done. Filming these days is nothing like all those years ago. I know the technology is so much more advanced but sometimes it feels as though the first word and the last word in a scene are just seconds apart. Of course I'm not blaming all my problems on that, but I do think the speed doesn't help.'

'I'm glad you've found talking to him helpful.'

'Yes, but finding out the problem and sorting it are two different things, and I think the only way that can happen is if I go back and spend time with the rest of the cast.'

Sophie was a little confused but didn't want to ask any questions that would upset her mum. Thankfully she was saved from having to say anything because Graham came through the gate with a huge bag from the bakery. Actually, it was more than one bag.

'Have you bought up the whole place?' she asked.

'No, I just thought it made sense to get morning pastries for right now, cream cakes for this afternoon and fresh rolls for the barbeque. All essential items for a day at the pool!'

Sophie laughed and went off to make him a coffee and take the goodies into the villa, thinking how much her life had changed. Not just spending time with her mother and living and working here, but also the differences in Graham, who was now full of confidence, laughing and joking with her mum.

Back on the sun loungers the chit chat was all about Tenerife, the villa and Sophie's daily routines. Madeline commented how Sophie was so organised and no doubt Kennal was over the moon with her work.

Graham picked up on the Kennal conversation and asked how Madeline had met him initially. Madeline explained that they'd frequently worked as extras together – or as they call it now, 'supporting cast' – and a lot of their time was spent hanging around doing nothing so they got to know one another quite well. She'd made lots of friends that way and several had even gone on to become famous actors and actresses.

'Graham, I was telling Sophie how helpful you've been. Everything you said was right and I have lost the essence of the character. I need to go back to the UK and prove to the production company I can bring her back to life for viewers.'

'And do you think you can do that, Mum?'

'Well, I won't know until I try and get acting back on set.'

'But do you need to be back on set?' Graham asked.

He went quiet for a moment and Sophie could see he was thinking.

'I have it! The solution! Madeline, you have the scripts on your phone, right? Why don't I read the other characters with you so you can rehearse? Sophie could film you on her phone so that you can watch your performance back and then, if you're happy with it, we could send it to the producers. What better proof is there that you are more than capable of recreating the character than seeing you in action?'

Sophie thought it was a great suggestion but what if her mum couldn't do anything different? Yes, she knew how the part had to be played, but actually doing it was another thing. Either way, there was only one way to find out, and come the end of the day it would either be joy and happiness or tears.

Madeline agreed to Graham's plan and she and Sophie went up to the bungalow to print off the script so that Graham would have it on paper and not have to read his lines off a phone with the sun shining on the screen.

'Oh, darling, this is different!' Madeline said as they walked into the bungalow. 'How bright and cheery you've made the place. You did say Kennal gave you permission to do it, right?'

'Yes, he was fine with it. Now, let me get the printer on. You find the scripts that you think you can work on and we'll get them printed off. Perhaps it would be a good idea to print a couple of different episodes in case you feel you want to continue tomorrow or the next day?'

****

It took ages to get the phone and printer to work together and that was meant to be the easy part of the day! As they'd decided to do it down by the pool, Sophie put up the umbrellas and fetched them all extra bottles of water. Graham was very excitable and was asking who he was playing and the background to the character, which he didn't really need to know as all he had to do was read the lines, not act it.

But when Sophie mentioned this he replied, 'What? Not act? When will I ever get an opportunity like this again? I'm ready to give my Laurence Olivier!' Sophie knew all his messing around was to try and relax Madeline into the part because the three of them knew this was serious – a make or break moment for her mum.

'Right, could I have the cast on set? Lights, camera, action and … rolling!'

****

This was the first time Sophie had seen her mother act in person and she couldn't take her eyes off the scene unfolding in front of her. Graham was in the zone, as they would say, not just reading from the page but acting the scene out, which must be helping her mum who was word perfect. After two hours, and with three different scenes shot, they decided to take a break and view them back. Sophie said she would go and sort out some lunch while her mum and Graham reviewed the footage.

'Lunch is ready,' she called soon after. 'I've decided we can sit up on the top terrace as I never get to do that. There are sandwiches and crisps and I have a sweet flan and ice cream for dessert.'

'Darling, you haven't asked what the result was. Graham says the third one we filmed was spot on and he couldn't see me in any of that scene. I think after lunch we should do a little more filming and then I can send the scenes to the producers and see what happens. Shall we have a glass of wine with the food? I'm sure one glass wouldn't hurt...'

****

One glass led to three and then it was back down to the pool for more filming, the wine seeming to help Madeline, taking off the edge and making her acting feel more real and convincing. Sophie knew alcohol wasn't the answer in the long term but it would hopefully get the results her mum needed for now to convince the producers she was still the right person for the role. The second round of filming went so quick and they got some amazing footage.

'Mum, I've just looked at a few of the clips and am so proud of you, I really am. I think you should email the best clips off now so you can relax and enjoy the barbeque. You've done all you can for now.'

'Thank you, darling, that means so much to me. And you're right, it's time to send them off and see what the producers have to say.'

'Good luck! I'm off to get ready. Luis should be here in an hour.'

As Sophie walked back up to the bungalow she hoped the production company would be able to see her mum was making a significant effort to sort things out and address the issues that had been raised.

****

As she was drying her hair Sophie felt nervous. She wasn't sure why but it kind of felt like she was going on a date. But then, her mum and Graham would be there as well, so an unusual date at that.

Pull yourself together. You know you won't get a word in edgewise with your mum asking Luis a thousand and one questions.

Just checking herself in the mirror one more time she heard the main gate open. She decided to go right down to get there before the inevitable interrogation started, but she was too late. Her mum was alone with Luis as Graham was on his feet and heading inside the villa to get the drinks.

'There's your phone, Sophie,' he said as she joined him, pointing to where it was sat on the table. 'The email has been sent and we ended up attaching four clips. They are so much better than the original ones she showed me and I really hope the producers also see the difference because if they don't, your mum's going to be so upset. It's just a waiting game now though. By the way, your young man is looking very nice and he smells gorgeous.'

'He's not my young man,' Sophie said with a laugh. 'Now, while you take him his beer, I will fetch us another bottle of wine. We need to hurry though, before my mother scares him off!'

'That's not going not happen. Nothing is going to stop him being here tonight,' Graham said with a warm smile.

Madeline was on form tonight, doing just as Sophie had suspected and asking one million questions about Luis's past. Thankfully there was no mention of his mess up with Kennal last year.

Sophie suggested they move from the pool up to the top terrace just as Madeline said perhaps she should go and change.

'Don't worry about it, Madeline. We probably won't be staying that late so there's no point,' Graham argued.

'Why aren't we staying late?'

'Because you've had a long, tiring day and these two young people don't want us hanging around for the whole night, spoiling their fun.'

Sophie could feel herself blushing but looking at Luis he had a large grin on his face.

'Um, I'll go and get the barbeque ready,' Sophie said, desperate to change the subject.

'I can do that,' Luis offered, immediately heading to one of the store rooms to get the coals.

'Well, darling, he's certainly not the same young man who was rude to us when we first arrived here. He really has taken a shine to you; he can't take his eyes off you and he smells so lovely.'

'What is it with you two and how Luis smells?'

Graham and Madeline laughed.

'Smelling nice is important!' Graham said.

'Well, make the most of it because once he starts cooking on the barbeque, he will smell of meat.'

'There's nothing wrong with a fit young man smelling of meat is there, Graham? I think you are in for a very pleasant evening, Sophie.'

Sophie rolled her eyes.

'I'm going to lay the table and sort the salads out.' She left Graham and her mum giggling away. She could see Luis was getting organised so she went and fetched him another beer.

'Your mum and Graham are like a double act, when one stops for breath the other one takes over. It's very amusing, really.'

'I'm happy for both of them that they've clicked and enjoy each other's company so much. I'm also glad they're so honest with each other and can be themselves, flaws and all.'

'Do you think we put on an act with each other? More importantly, do you think we click? I'd like to think we do, even though I have so many flaws.'

'You don't have flaws, Luis, it's me that is screwed up; I'm the one that has messed my life up. All you did was invite a few friends to the villa for a drink. You couldn't have guessed things would get out of control the way they did.'

'Forget about the past, Sophie. What about us here and now? Can you see us having a future together? I know that's what I want and I'm hoping it's what you want too.'

Sophie was shocked at how earnest Luis was being and didn't have an answer. Did she see a future with him? She really didn't know what to say and so panicked and changed the subject.

'I'll go and fetch the meat to put on the barbeque,' she said before rushing away.

Of course Luis had his flaws but so did she. They also had a lot in common – her relationship with Mark had been odd and his with Cristina hadn't been straightforward ether – but did she want him deep down? She didn't entirely know.

****

The table and food were ready and Sophie hoped Graham and her mum's double act would kick in and carry the conversation. She wasn't disappointed.

Graham started them off by asking Madeline which of the famous people she had acted with was her favourite. Her first answer had them all laughing as she said it had to be him this afternoon, and the conversation flowed from there.

Luis was putting the last few sausages on the barbeque as Sophie topped up the wine after what had been a lovely evening. Her mum was looking tired and starting to nod off so she was sure it wouldn't be long before she and Graham left and it would just be her and Luis. How should she handle the situation? She was startled from her thoughts by the sound of a phone ringing.

'Mum, it sounds like it's your phone.'

Madeline dug her phone out of her bag and looked at the screen. When she saw it was one of the producers she started shaking but knew she had to answer it. She stood up and walked away from the table.

'Hi, Madeline, it's Ron from production.'

'Hi, Ron, how can I help you?'

'I got your email and I have to say ... I'm blown away by the videos! This is just what we've been looking for from you and we need to send a huge thank you to you for putting in this extra effort and to whomever you've been working with to achieve these results.'

'Thank you, that's very kind of you to say.'

'Now, I've talked it over with the rest of the production team and we wondered if you could be back on set a week on Monday? We want to get started reshooting some of your scenes. There's a lot of work still to do but if you keep doing what you're doing, everything will be fantastic.'

'Of course! I'll absolutely be there and I just want to say, again, that I am truly sorry for everything, I really am.'

Madeline said goodbye and ended the call before bursting into tears. Graham stood up and went and put his arms around her as Sophie moved to hand her a tissue. They waited for her to compose herself and tell them all about the call. Eventually, she wiped her eyes and had a glass of water, ready to fill them in.

'They loved it! That was one of the producers and he said my performances in the little videos were exactly what they've been trying to get out of me all these weeks. He also thanked me. Gosh, it should be the other way around as I'm the one who should apologise. Oh, what a huge relief.'

'That's amazing! So what happens now?'

'They've said I need to reshoot some of my scenes but I'm sure I can do that by myself and they can cut them into what the other actors have already done. I've got another week here before I have to go though.'

'That's such fabulous news, Mum! I'm so happy for you. And as for you, Graham, how brilliant you are to have come up with the idea.'

'Graham you got a mention in the call – they wanted to thank the clever person who I have been working with.'

That caused a laugh.

'Perhaps when Kennal arrives back you should work with him as well?' Sophie suggested.

'That might not be a good idea though as he could end up being the next Mrs Kennal!' Luis joked.

'And on that note, I think your mum and myself will leave you two in peace. Come on, Madeline, let's get you back and see what Mable and the kittens have been up to. Thank you for a lovely day, Sophie. We've had such a laugh but I am absolutely tired to death and your mum must be as well.'

'I am, and like Graham said, it's been a lovely day. Hopefully before I go back to the UK we can have a few more days like this. And thank you for cooking tonight, Luis, the food was gorgeous. Have a nice rest of the evening, both of you!'

'And remember our magic word,' Graham whispered to Sophie with a wink.

'Goodnight, you two,' Sophie said on a laugh.

As Madeline and Graham headed down to the gate they both looked a little worse for wear, which had Sophie and Luis laughing.

'I've really enjoyed the evening as well,' Luis said. 'But what was that about a magic word? I didn't quite understand what Graham meant.'

'Oh, Graham is just always telling me to have fun.'

'And are we going to have fun tonight?'

'I think we are, Luis.'

Chapter 32

What a day yesterday was, but Sophie had no time to think back on it. Today was yet another busy day and with new guests arriving at lunch time, she needed to get organised. She checked the flight times and although the plane hadn't taken off yet, it was still on schedule so that gave her six hours before they should pull up at Villa Kennal. The booking was for three couples – all with different surnames – and Sophie had fingers, toes and everything else crossed that they wouldn't be rude and demanding like Mandy. Only time would tell, but today she felt she could cope with anything that was thrown at her as she was on a high from last night with Luis.

After a few hours the inside of the villa was ready. Now to tackle the outside. Sophie remembered then that it was a Javier day. She needed to let him know a few of the paths were starting to get narrower with the plants coming over the edges.

'Good morning, Sophie,' Javier called as he came through the gate just then. 'Sorry I'm late, I went in to see Graham to find out what he needed me to do next and we got chatting and the time just flew by. Then I met his guest. I was trying to figure out how I know her and then it clicked – I remembered she stayed here with Kennal once. I think he was between wives at the time as I'm sure it was only the two of them here.'

Sophie stopped in her tracks. She wanted to ask a dozen questions but then ... Javier had kind of already answered all the questions she might have. Her mum had been here with Kennal. Alone. Before she could ask how long ago that had been – recently or many years ago – Javier supplied the answer she was looking for.

'It was three years ago because I can remember we chatted about a tree I was planting and that tree has been there three years,' Javier said, clearly proud of his memory.

Not knowing what to say about the bombshell that Javier had just dropped, Sophie simply explained what work she wanted doing today, which he was happy to get on with.

Her head was all over the place but Sophie had to concentrate on getting the villa ready for the guests and only once they had settled in could she stop to think through the Kennal and her mum situation. Why had Madeline never mentioned she had been here before? Why did she feel she needed to keep it a secret?

Forget about it for now, Sophie. Get the pool swept and mopped and sort all the fresh beach towels out. Hurry up or you'll soon be running late.

****

Three hours later Sophie was ready, and Javier had done a really good job with the paths; they now looked crisp and sharp.

Before taking a quick shower she returned Graham's text inviting her for dinner, saying of course she would love to join him and her mum. She had nothing else to do as Luis was working and so wouldn't be able to pop in until later tonight, once he'd finished.

****

'Hello, welcome to Villa Kennal!' she greeted the guests as they disembarked from the taxi van. 'I hope your journey has been ok. I'm Sophie and if you need anything while you're here my phone number is written in the information book in the villa.'

The three couples were all middle aged and Sophie hoped that meant they wouldn't be loud and raucous like Rich and Mandy's group had been at the start. She offered to help with the luggage but they said they were ok and as Sophie led them up the path to the villa it was clear that they were over the moon with the complex and excited they had their own pool. Once inside she explained the bedroom situation with the one upstairs and the others down. The couples decided to toss a coin to decide who got the upstairs room, saying it was the only fair way of doing it. She chatted a little about the villa cleaning times, the area shops and bus time tables, and reminded them that if they needed any food shopping, she would need twenty-four hours' notice.

'Thank you so much, Sophie, I just know we're going to have a lovely time here and I think we will be more than capable of fending for ourselves. We plan to eat out every night and can take turns going to the bakery each morning. You won't even know we're here! We've all come to switch off from our busy lives and relax in the peace and quiet.'

'I hope you all have a lovely holiday and like I said, I'm only in the bungalow the other side of the hedge so don't hesitate to ask if you need anything.'

As she walked up to the bungalow she wanted to scream and shout with joy. They seemed as though they would be the perfect guests and she just knew they would not be messy. She was in for a good, easy week, which after the last family was a real treat. Right, paperwork time. There were emails to answer and the villa diary to update but first of all she sent a text to Luis with just two words: *missing you*. He quickly texted back *missing you more*. She was going to reply but she knew the back and forth could go on for ever and she had work to do. And then there was that other thing on her mind – Javier's revelation about her mum and Kennal. Why hadn't her mum mentioned she'd been here before? And more importantly, was Kennal maybe actually her father? For the second time today, Sophie had to pull herself together and concentrate on her work. Everything else could wait.

*****

Looking at the time she saw it was seven thirty. A quick glance at her to-do list and she was pleased to see that she had done most of the jobs. The one thing she still needed to do was check with Kennal if he wanted to put a calendar for the year after next up as people were already enquiring about availability then. She also needed to ask him if he might want to consider extending the holiday rental season at the villa. She'd had countless emails asking for winter breaks as the weather in Tenerife was hot all year running and she'd thought more than once that it was a missed opportunity to close the villa down in October. Though perhaps he used the villa during that time, or just didn't need the money? There was only one way to find out – by asking.

Packing up for the day, she headed over to Graham's villa for dinner.

'Hi, Sophie, how are you and more importantly, are they nice guests this time?'

'They seem like they're going to be the perfect customers as they just want to be left alone for some peace and quiet. Is my mum not here? I thought she would be lying in the sun.'

'She's just this minute gone in to have a shower.'

'Can I ask you something? Has she ever mentioned being here in Kalanchoe before? Because

Javier said he recognised her from staying at the villa. I know the day we arrived and walked through the main gate she had an odd look on her face, but if she'd been here why not say anything?'

'She's not said anything but leave it to me. I have ways of working questions into a conversation. Now, pour yourself a glass of wine and then you can tell me the exciting news.'

'Exciting news? I don't have any.'

'I think you do, because when I was going out the gate this morning, on my way to the bakery, I saw someone coming out of Villa Kennal with the same clothes he had on last night. I take it some 'fun' was had?'

Sophie could feel herself blushing but it wasn't as though she and Luis had done anything wrong. As Graham went to grab the wine and some nibbles Sophie realised she was feeling happy in a way she never had ever before. She had a fabulous job, lovely new friends and a fella. What was not to love about her life?

'There you go,' Graham said, handing her a glass. 'While your mum's getting ready, I have to say she is a completely different woman than the one who first arrived. First thing this morning she had an email from the TV company with the filming schedule and a list of scenes she'll have to reshoot, plus the scripts, and she seemed happy with it all. I asked if she wanted to run through a few scenes but she said no, she knew where she was with everything that had been going wrong and was fine. She's booked her flight back to the UK but I've invited her back to stay whenever she likes. I enjoy her company.'

'Hi, darling, how has your day been? Did the new guests arrive ok?' her mum asked as she joined them.

'Yes, all good, thanks, and Graham told me

you've heard back from the TV company. You must be so happy. Is the schedule ok for you?'

Madeline said it was as Graham went to get her a glass and the three of them chatted about all sorts. Thankfully for Sophie there was no mention of Luis, though Graham did mention that Javier had come in this morning, just to see if he got a reaction from Madeline. There wasn't even a flicker of the eye but she is an actress, Sophie thought. Perhaps she should mention Javier had recognised her? No that wouldn't guarantee that they got the full story out of her.

'I'm going to start the cooking and as we had all that meat from the barbeque last night I've chosen seabass for tonight, if that's ok, with a few vegetables and sauté potatoes. I will leave you ladies to chat.'

This was the opportunity for Sophie to ask her mum every question she had in her head but she couldn't just come out with them one after another, so how should she start? The moment reminded her of the old days when she spent the odd weekend with her mum and they both tip-toed around things. It was so stupid really, but that was how their mother daughter relationship had always been.

'Mum, tell me about Kennal. I've heard so many stories from different people. What should I expect when he comes to stay in a few weeks?'

There was a silence and Sophie knew her mum was thinking of the perfect answer but would the answer bring her any closer to finding out about Madeline's relationship with Kennal?

'He is a charmer and that hasn't really changed over the years at all. He will be a breath of fresh air when he walks through the gate.'

'That makes me feel quite nervous as he's my boss.'

Madeline smiled. 'You have nothing to worry

about. You'll get on wonderfully with him and also he will be so proud of the job you're doing here.'

'What have I missed?' Graham asked, topping the drinks up.

'Nothing really,' Sophie reassured him.

'Good. Dinner will be twenty minutes.'

Sophie was no further on finding out about her mum's past with Kennal and whispered as much to Graham.

'Leave it to me. We just need to get your mum relaxed and comfortable and she will open up eventually.'

****

Dinner was gorgeous and what was so lovely for Sophie was that she could see how happy Graham was. He was the perfect host, something that seemed completely unthinkable a short time ago. Dinner over, Graham insisted on clearing everything away and while he was gone Sophie dove in with another question. This time, she was going to ask about Kennal's wives and find out if her mum knew more about any of them.

'I knew Velma more than the others, but there was also an actress friend I had when I started out ... she was with Kennal on and off for a while. She was lovely but they never married as they were far too young at that point.'

'Who is far too young?' Graham asked, confused as he'd missed the initial question.

'No one we know, Graham. Mum and I were just chatting about the many wives of Kennal.'

'Oh he fascinates me.'

'Do you know if Casey and Emily are his only children? Given that Kennal had had a lot of wives it would only make sense if there were lots of children ... or grandchildren, come to that. And have you ever spent time with Kennal's children?'

With the last question Madeline looked at both of them as though she knew there was more to the questions than Sophie was letting on. When she excused herself without answering and went off to the bathroom, Graham whispered, 'We're starting to get somewhere! We'll soon have found everything out.'

'I'm not so sure...' Sophie hedged.

With that Madeline came back carrying a new bottle of wine and an odd expression on her face. It was clear something was coming. Had they pushed her too far?

'Let me just top these glasses up and then I can begin to answer the questions you are both skirting around. And there are really only two, aren't there? The first being, was I ever one of the many wives of Kennal? The answer is no, but I could have been if I had chosen to. And then the second question will likely be, is Kennal your father? The answer to that is the same – no, but he could have been.'

Chapter 33

Sophie was up early and out on the veranda with a coffee. She was feeling so happy. Last night's answers from her mum had helped. She'd never really believed that Kennal was her father but to have it confirmed was reassuring, though she wasn't entirely sure what her mum had meant when she'd said Kennal 'could have been' her father. Her mum had quickly changed the subject after her surprise declarations and there was no chance to ask her more about her almost relationship with Kennal or her having visited the villa before.

'Good morning, you, why didn't you wake me?' Luis asked from the bungalow's doorway.

'Because you were tired. You had a long day working yesterday and you have another one today. Have a seat and I will make you a coffee.'

'I was hoping to wake up with you beside me, not to an empty bed.'

'Sorry, but I was awake and couldn't just lie there. Would you like something to eat?'

'No, but I would like us to go back to bed...' he said suggestively.

'Coffee it is then,' Sophie said, making Luis groan.

She smiled to herself as she went back inside. Luis was another reason she was happy. Actually, he was the top reason. Her phone beeped with a text from her mum to see if she would be around later today for a chat. Sophie suggested her mum come over to the villa around one o'clock as she'd have all her jobs done by then and could do them a little lunch.

Sophie took Luis's coffee out to him and said she had to get on and sweep and mop around the pool before the visitors were up and about. He looked sad

241

and she thought that perhaps when she first woke up she should have woken him as well so they could spend some time together. That would certainly have been a nice start to the day.

As she got her cleaning stuff together she told him to help himself to anything before he had to go.

'Ok, boss. How about I try to get off work early tonight and we could go out for a drink or something to eat?' Luis offered.

'That would be nice.'

****

The cleaning took no time at all as the guests didn't want their rooms doing and said the kitchen was ok as well, and Sophie was back in the bungalow by eleven o'clock. Luis had already gone but not before saying goodbye with a cheeky kiss.

She had a quick shower and then sent an email off to Kennal to check his arrival time. She also took the chance to enquire about who might be staying with him when he visited, saying she wanted to make sure she had everything he and any 'guest' he brought with him might need.

'Hello, darling,' her mum called out as she came through the bungalow's gate. 'You don't mind me coming around here, do you? I know I answered your questions about Kennal but I also know the answers I gave were very vague and undoubtedly opened up a few more questions, and so I thought we needed to have a chat.'

Madeline made herself comfortable in the shade, as it was getting really hot now at mid-day, as Sophie went to make them a cup of tea. This felt strange, her mum coming to where she lived and not the other way around, and thinking about it, this little bungalow really did feel like home now.

'There you go, Mum, were you ready for lunch

yet or would you like to drink your tea first?'

'Thank you, darling, tea and a chat first. I thought I best explain my relationship with Kennal, which as you know goes back many years. You know how we met and my history in show business, but I expect you are wondering where Kennal fits into it all.'

Sophie nodded.

'As you know, when I got pregnant your father didn't want anything to do with me or our baby.' This was something Madeline had told Sophie about when she was a teenager and neither she nor her mum had issues with it because Madeline always said she was happier without him in her life and why would she want to be with someone who didn't want to be with her or her new baby? 'When Kennal found out I was expecting you, he wanted to protect me and so he offered to marry me and bring you up as his daughter.'

Sophie gasped. 'And you said no? Were you not tempted to take him up on the offer? Sorry ... that sounds wrong, but you know what I mean.'

'I didn't have to give it a second's thought; the answer was always no because I knew him so well – he was one of my best friends – and I knew what would happen sooner or later. He could never have stayed faithful to me. He loved women too much and with all these up and coming actresses throwing themselves at him? He couldn't have helped himself. No, I wanted him in my life not as a husband, but as a best friend. I'm also a strong woman who didn't – and doesn't – need protecting. I was more than capable of looking after you and myself and I have to say I think I did a good job of it as neither of us ever went without.'

Sophie needed a moment to think through what her mum had just said so she suggested going and fetching the lunch. As she chopped the salad she realised she was no longer nervous about meeting Kennal, in fact, she was kind of excited to meet the man who had been willing to do whatever it took to help her mum in her time of need.

'Here we go, a delicious vegetable tart made not by me but the bakery. I don't know if everyone in Kalanchoe could survive without that business, I think I must eat something that's come from there every day of the week. The salad was put together by me though.'

Sophie had more answers now but her mum still hadn't mentioned anything about her visit here three years ago.

'So, Mum, I presume Kennal and yourself pop in and out of each other's life from time to time? You aren't like two friends that meet up every week or month.'

'That's right, and we can go years without any contact but when we do catch up – I will say its normally when he's between wives or girlfriends – it's just like old times and that's what happened a few years ago. When Villa Kennal was finally finished he invited me over to see it. He wanted to show it off as he was so proud of his new home. Darling, do you think I can have a glass of wine, please? And by the way, lunch is lovely, thank you.'

So it was no big secret why her mum was here three years ago after all. Kennal wanted to show the villa off to a friend, just like anyone who had achieved something like this would.

'Now, where did I get to? Oh yes, my first visit to Kalanchoe. I mean, what's not to love? The little town is just so wonderful but the highlight has to be this villa. It's perfect! How could anyone not want to be here? I had the upstairs bedroom with the balcony when I stayed. For three weeks the weather was gorgeous and I was in and out of the pool all day. The food – which Kennal cooked most nights out on the barbeque – was just to die for. Everything was just so special and I was so happy and relaxed, but there was one niggle in my head. Of course I knew what it was before I even stepped on the plane to come here – what if Kennal wanted more than just our friendship, which I didn't?'

'But, Mum, had you not ever thought that if he was with you, he could be trusted? Weren't you even tempted to give the relationship a go?'

'I suppose there was a time, and it was during those three weeks that I was here. Kennal wanted to dress up and go out for dinner one night so we went to one of the lovely restaurants in Del Duque and had a fabulous evening. The food was out of this world and we laughed so much about the old days when we both started out on the acting journey. We came back here and sat on the villa terrace with a brandy afterwards. The sky was full of stars, the candles were lit and it was just such a wonderful end to a special evening. And then Kennal asked my thoughts on the villa – if I had been designing it, would I have done anything different, that sort of thing. Of course I said no, the villa is perfect, and then he just came out with it and said he had built it for me.'

Sophie could see her mum was trying to compose herself so she picked the dirty plates and dishes up and took them back into the kitchen, hoping to give her mum time to sort herself out. Sophie knew her mum had obviously turned down any offer he'd made after saying that, because she would be living here if she hadn't. But then, was that why Kennal had asked her to come and run it for the summer? Was it his way of trying to get her to fall in love with the villa?

'I'm sorry, darling, I didn't mean to get upset. I was of course very flattered and a touch overcome with what he said, but I knew the villa and Kennal would come with more baggage – the ex-wives and girlfriend, Velma, coping with Emily and all her dramas ... and that was only the things I knew about! So at the end of the day, the answer had to be no because if I had loved him I wouldn't have had to think about it at all, would I?'

'I don't think he's given up trying to win you over though. That's why he asked you to come and run the place while he's in America. Surely that means he really does want you in his life?'

The two women were left in silence as Madeline considered what Sophie had said.

Chapter 34

'Good morning, Graham! Another lovely day and I must say, I know I haven't been here that long but the difference in the garden from when I arrived is staggering. It's really taking shape and I shall miss seeing its progress – and being here with you – so much when I'm back in the UK.'

'But you know you are more than welcome to come and stay whenever you like. The room is yours so feel free to leave clothes and toiletries rather than carry them to and fro all the time. Now, go and have your last morning in the sunshine. You need a restful day before your busy filming schedule begins.'

Graham could tell Madeline was a lot more anxious today, which was understandable as when she'd left everyone was complaining about her and now she was going back and having to prove herself to them. All the nerves must be kicking in and he could understand as it was one thing saying her lines in front of him but to go back and perform in front of the cast and crew was another matter entirely. He knew he was in for a day of building up her confidence and he wouldn't have Sophie there to support him as she had agreed that the three couples could stay in the villa a bit later than usual. It would mean a tighter turnaround for her as the next guest would be arriving later today, so she likely wouldn't have a chance to join them.

'Here you go, my dear, one glass of juice to give you your vitamin c and a coffee to fill you with caffeine. The perfect start to the day. Also, I have some bacon in the fridge. How about a bacon and egg sandwich? I'm having one.'

'Go on then. Thank you, Graham, you have spoiled me since I've been here. I've not really lifted a finger to do anything so far so would you like me to do the sandwiches?'

'Of course not. For one, no one interferes in my kitchen, and for another, you're my guest.' As he stood watching the bacon under the grill, he thought how lucky he had been to have Madeline here these last few weeks. She had been a real tonic for him and though they had never met before, it was as though they had known each other for ever, which was so lovely.

****

Breakfast eaten, Madeline said, 'That was gorgeous! Thank you so much. Do you know, I've been sitting here in the beautiful Tenerife sunshine and I've been pondering, like you do, and I was thinking how well we both get on. We have really gelled in such a short time and it's been lovely but I do feel guilty because I arrived with all my problems, which you sorted out for me. I am very lucky and the offer to come back is very kind. I have to admit I do feel very comfortable here, right at home.'

Graham could feel himself welling up. He tried to stop the tears but he couldn't so Madeline got up and put her arms around him. There was no need to speak and after a few minutes Graham calmed down a little and Madeline sat beside him at the table, holding his hand.

'I'm sorry about that. When you said the word "home" I think it felt like a relief. I don't really know what I'm trying to say, I'm just a silly old gay man. Take no notice of me.'

'You are not silly and certainly not old, my darling. But you are gay and that's what makes you so special. Now, we both need to be very British and pull our shocks up and show the upper lip, or whatever the silly saying is. Let's go out for the day somewhere so I'm not thinking about the stupid acting. We can walk the bacon sandwiches off and build up an appetite for a late lunch or early dinner, and then we'll grab a taxi home. Where would you suggest?'

Graham didn't have to give it a single thought. 'Let's go to La Caleta. It has shops, people watching, a gorgeous view and fabulous food.'

Decision made, they both got dressed and were on the way by eleven.

****

'This is so lovely,' Madeline said as they explored La Caleta. 'I can see now why you suggested it right away. Did you say this is where the taxi driver lives? Talking of him, I must apologise when he takes me to the airport tomorrow. I wasn't at all friendly to him when I arrived.'

'I'm sure he's already forgotten,' Graham reassured her.

'That's a relief. Now, time for a glass of wine, I think. There must be somewhere down on the water's edge.'

Graham knew the perfect spot for them to sit and while away a few hours and suggested they go to Ramon's mum's shop later on. Madeline thought that would be a good idea as she would like to get Sophie a little gift. They sat at the café in silence for a while, both consumed with their own thoughts going around in their heads, before Madeline finally said she could quite easy live here, enjoying time spent in the sunshine by the sea.

'There's nothing stopping you from visiting frequently. In fact, you could quite easily live here in Tenerife between jobs and as you said you have a property agent that looks after the houses you rent out, there's really no reason not to live the dream, is there?'

'Oh, I do think this job will be the last as the thought of going through it all again... No, this was – or is – a one off.'

'But what if it's a huge success and producers come knocking at your door? Are you going to turn them away?'

'When the series came out all those years ago it was a hit, but it didn't have to compete with anything then. Now there are hundreds of channels for people to choose from. It will be shown over six to eight weeks and then forgotten, mark my words. Here today, gone tomorrow, although ... if it was commissioned for a second series, which is what the production company want, there's scope to take my character further. She could become quite the villain.'

'And would you like that? Say it goes on for years and you had the opportunity to stay with it, could that be where your future lies?'

'Ohhhh I don't know. But enough of TV make-believe land. What's your future, Graham?'

'Mine's an easy answer – I'm staying put in Kalanchoe. No more moving for me, thank you, but talking of the future, how about Sophie? I know we keep avoiding the subject when I chat with her but come October she's out of a job and now's she's met Luis and – after several false starts – they do seem to be getting on very well.'

It had been on Madeline's mind as well.

'Perhaps a helping hand is needed, but then everything would ultimately be down to Kennal and what his plans are. Will he love America so much that he stays there? Or will he miss Tenerife and want to come back? The one thing that I didn't want to happen is for Sophie to run back to Mark.'

'That will never happen. No, Sophie's life will be here in Tenerife regardless of what Kennal's plans are. We're thinking too much, Madeline. Come on, let's visit some shops and find Sophie a gift. We are living here in the present and not the future – that can take care of itself down the road. By the way, I don't want to alarm you but there is a chap over by the sea wall with a camera and he seems very interested in us. Do you think the press know you're here?'

'Even if they do, what have I to hide? I'm just an actress on holiday. I might even give him a wave... No, I won't, but can you see the headlines? You will no doubt be named as the secret man in my life. Isn't that fun?'

With that they paid the bill and headed up the sides streets towards Ramon's mum's shop. As they walked, Graham noticed the chap with the camera was following them but when he told Madeline her reply was that she would have been so disappointed if he hadn't. Eventually they got to the shop and Ramon's mum recognised Graham and welcomed him back, saying her son wasn't around today. Madeline was in her element in the shop, which was again full of fabulous things, and then she saw the perfect present over in the leather section – a collection of beautiful purses in every colour imaginable. One would be just the gift for Sophie.

As she was trying to decide, Graham noticed the man now outside the shop. This was all very strange to him but Madeline was just taking it in her stride.

She ended up buying two purses and a lovely leather wallet before they bid Ramon's mum goodbye and considered wandering along the street.

'Time for something to eat, Graham, I think my stomach is rumbling.'

He suggested the place he, Sophie and Ramon had ate at last time they were here, which was fine with Madeline and so he led the way. Once there, Graham said it was probably best if they sat inside away from the long lenses but Madeline was having none of that and said, 'Let's give the gentleman the shot he needs.'

Graham wasn't so sure it was a good idea but went along with it anyway. They ordered a glass of wine and started to look at the menu but before the waiter walked away Madeline called him back and ordered a beer, asking if it could be taken over to the man across the street with the camera.

The chap seemed very uncomfortable as the waiter pointed out to him that it was from Madeline and when he looked over, she raised her wine glass. He raised the bottle of beer in a silent salute of thanks before walking away. After his departure the lunch tasted even lovelier to Graham.

'Food and wine both seem to have been a big part of my stay here on Tenerife. I'll definitely have to cut back on both when I get back home and I'm working. Also, I can't believe it's nearly five thirty, where has the day gone? Shall we finish off here and get a taxi back? I can't have a late night because my flight is quite early and I will need to see Sophie before I leave.'

****

Back at the villa, Madeline went off to her room to have a lie down while Graham sorted Mable and the kittens out and then took a cup of tea out on to the terrace, dozing off soon after and being started awake some time later by Sophie's arrival.

'Hi, Graham. Sorry, I didn't mean to startle you. I thought you would have heard the gate open.'

'Not at all! I was just having a quick few minutes of shut eye. What's the time? Oh, maybe not so quick – it looks like I've been asleep for over an hour! Your mother has worn me out, but in a good way. I've really loved having her here as we get on so well.'

'The reason he's tired is because he's not stopped fetching and carrying for me,' Madeline said as she walked outside to join them. 'I'm telling you now, when I come back the rules will be reversed! Now, can I get either of you anything while I'm on my feet? And how has your day been, darling?'

'I would have said ok, Mum, until I started to get ready to come up here. As I was walking out my little gate there was a man by the pool with a camera. When I demanded to know why he was there he said it was ok as he had come to see Madeline Mundey. I said no one by that name was staying at the villa and he got all snappy with me so I then threatened him with the police and he stormed off.'

'Oh dear. He followed Graham and myself around Le Caleta all day. He must think I'm staying in Villa Kennal. I thought I'd given him the photos he needed and he'd leave me alone now but I guess that's not the case. Hopefully the pics the magazine or newspaper uses will be flattering and not one of me eating. I emailed the TV company and warned them I've been spotted in Tenerife but they said it would be good publicity as long as I wasn't caught in a compromising situation. I explained I was shopping with a gay friend and if they mistakenly think Graham's my other half that's absolutely fine – the world thinking I have a handsome man by my side will be lovely.'

'And on that note, this handsome toy boy will go and fetch us some nibbles and a drink for your last night here,' Graham said as he popped inside.

****

The evening was lovely. They laughed about everything and anything – Madeleine's stories from her early acting days, holidays when Graham and

253

Robert first got together – they nibbled on cheese and biscuits and they fussed over the kittens. It was the perfect end to Madeline's stay.

It was getting on for eleven thirty when Madeline's phone rang. She told them it was one of the TV company's press team and Sophie could tell the call was serious as her mum just sat there and listened with the odd 'yes' and 'no'. Finally she came off the phone.

'Is everything ok?' Graham asked.

'Well, you won't be in the press as my handsome toy boy, I'm afraid, but I will be in one of the tabloids tomorrow and you will both be able to read the piece along with the rest of the world. It basically says I'm an aging actress who hasn't worked for many years and I've been living with my aging actor lover, Kennal Scott, here in Tenerife. But now, as we're both working again, our Tenerife home is being looked after by our daughter, Sophie. So, darling, until the newspaper prints an apology, the world is going to think you're Kennal Scott's daughter.'

Chapter 35

As Sophie walked back through the villa gate after waving her mum off, she was feeling hopeful that despite the fact that the world was about to be incorrectly informed that Kennal Scott was her father, her life would get back to some level of normal now her mum was headed back to the UK. All she had to do was think about her job and of course she now had time to spend with Luis and she knew from the text he had sent her last night that he was looking forward to it just as much as she was. They had the rest of the summer together and this made her very happy, but seeing him would come later. For now, she had a villa to clean first, which shouldn't be that difficult as the group of couples had departed and there was now just one guest, which meant just one bedroom to keep clean. He also didn't look the type to be untidy.

After a sweep and mop around the pool she could see the villa doors were opened so he must be up, which was good as it meant a nice early start for the cleaning, which would then mean an early finish.

Sophie was just sorting the pool towels out when her phone beeped with a text. Her mum said she was all checked in at the airport and she would let Sophie know when she was home. Putting her phone back in her pocket, she could now see the guest – Jeremy – sat on the terrace with a book. It was the perfect opportunity to ask if she could clean the inside of the villa.

'Good morning, I hope you had a good night's sleep and everything is ok for you with the accommodation. I was wondering if it was convenient for me to do the cleaning now?'

'Hi, Sophie, everything is perfect but I really don't think you need to clean anything as all I've done is sleep and any dirty glasses and cups I've put in the dishwasher. Why not leave it for today? Actually, there's something you could do instead – tell me all about Kalanchoe and the surrounding area,' he added, gesturing for her to join him.

Sophie sat and chatted about all the tourist things he would need to know. Of course top of her list was the bakery. He laughed and said perhaps that was somewhere he actually needed to avoid as the last thing he wanted was to put on weight. After giving him a rundown of all the other main sights in the area, Sophie wished him a happy holiday and told him if he needed anything just to give her a call.

'You've been really helpful, thank you. I'll probably take a walk most days and take in the views as I don't want to be wasting my days lazing in the sun.'

'There's nothing wrong with that as you're on holiday specifically to relax. Well, I'll leave you to plan your day.'

****

Back in the bungalow she checked her emails, hoping for one from Kennal as the article about her mum was now out in the UK press. Unfortunately there was nothing but her phone beeped with a text from her mum to say she was home and would call tonight after she had spoken to the TV company about the story.

As Sophie went to put the phone down it rang and though she didn't recognise the number she answered it in case it was Jeremy in need of something.

'Sophie speaking.'

'Hi, Sophie, it's Casey. Are you free to have a chat?'

'Yes, hi, Casey, is everything ok?'

'It's just ... I've seen something in one of the UK newspapers today...'

'I know. It's a load of rubbish. My mum is hoping her TV company will put out a statement to make it clear that the story is not true.'

'Ah, sorry you've gotten caught up in one of the downsides to our parents' profession – the press interest.'

'That's ok, I'm sure it will soon be sorted,' Sophie said.

'By the way, I'm coming to stay again when my dad comes back from the US, and Emily is coming as well.'

'I think that's just what the three of you need – some time alone to chat. I'm looking forward to seeing you again too. Dare I ask what Velma has to say about you coming to stay?'

'I just told her I was going and that was it.'

'Good for you! I'm sure she will come around eventually; she won't want you not in her life.'

'That's what I'm hoping. I need to go for now but I just wanted to let you know about the article and check you were ok.'

'Thank you but I'm fine. I'll see you soon and if there's anything you want me to get for your stay just text me.'

Sophie was pleased for Casey and Emily – some time with their dad would be perfect and just what they both needed. Now to enjoy a little bit of early evening sunshine on the veranda before going up to Graham's.

I suppose I'll have a lot of time to enjoy on the veranda with this guest here as the cleaning in the villa will take no time at all. She smiled at the fact that this job went from one extreme to another – family with children and finger marks and toys everywhere, to middle-aged couples to a single man who didn't need anything. *Maybe I'll even be able to spend more time with Luis before Kennal arrives...*

****

'Sorry I'm late, Graham, I don't have an excuse apart from I have been day dreaming and before you say anything the answer is yes, it was Luis that was on my mind.'

'I wasn't going to ask that because I'd figured it out already,' Graham joked. 'First things first, have you heard from your mum and what has Kennal to say about all the newspaper stuff?'

'Mum's back in the UK and going to call me later, and I've heard nothing from Kennal but Casey called to say she and Emily are coming to stay when he's back so that will be nice for all of them. In the meantime, I'm glad you and I are back to our old routine of just me, you and Mable.'

'I think you're forgetting something – we have not just the kittens but also Luis! And on that note, it's wine o'clock time.'

As Graham went to get the wine Sophie grinned to herself. Yes, she did have Luis, didn't she. She was looking forward to seeing him tonight. Thinking of Luis she suddenly wondered what Kennal would say when he found out they were a couple.

Wait, did she just think about her and Luis as 'a couple'? *Come on, Sophie, stop running ahead with yourself! It's still very early days.*

'One glass of wine and a selection of nibbles,' Graham said, presenting them with a flourish. 'I'm so pleased we were able to help your mum out as she certainly left a different woman than when she arrived. I did wonder if she was just saying she would be back but I really think she will be, which is nice as I've loved her company. We've had a lot of laughs in between the TV drama stuff.'

'Oh, there's my phone, she must have heard you

talking about her!' Sophie said as she pulled her phone out of her pocket. 'Hi, Mum, everything ok? Were the producers upset with your press coverage and are they going to ask the publication to print a retraction?'

'No one's upset, in fact it's the complete opposite – both my production company and Kennal's are very happy with the publicity. And there's been no communication yet but both PR companies are chatting about it and putting together a joint statement.'

'That's good news then. And how are you feeling about going back to filming?'

'I'm ok. I think I just need to get the first few scenes out the way and then I'm sure everything will be ok.'

'I'm sure you'll be great and feeling more confident in no time.'

'How is Graham?'

'He's fine and already looking forward to you coming back.'

'Tell him I can't wait to be back in Tenerife either.'

'I will. Sleep well and let me know how the filming goes, will you? Bye for now.'

Sophie explained to Graham what her mum had said, both of them relieved that the article hadn't been too damaging.

'Let me top your glass up. I have a pizza in the freezer, shall we go halfsies on it with some chips on the side? What time did you say Luis would finish work?'

'Pizza would be lovely, thank you, and Luis won't finish work until at least ten thirty so I have hours yet before I need to head back to the bungalow. Do you want me to do anything to help?'

'Not to worry, I've got it,' Graham said, heading into the kitchen to get the food into the oven.

Sophie sat back in the late sun with her feet up, enjoying her wine. Taking a brief glance at her phone, she saw a notification for a new email from Kennal.

Hi Sophie,

Sorry about the article. The PR company are on to it and I can't say I'm all that surprised. I knew it would only be a matter of time before people found out I had a home in Tenerife and I'm ok with that.

I hope you had a nice time with your mum while she was there. Such a shame our visits couldn't overlap.

One last thing, when I come to stay Casey and Emily will be visiting, which I'm really looking forward to. I will also be bringing my girlfriend with me and she will need a few things there when she arrives. I will send you a list asap.

Kennal

So Kennal is bringing a girlfriend after all. That likely won't be straightforward with his daughters also present but it ultimately wasn't her problem to worry about.

The thing she *did* worry about was the fact that her boss was coming and would be checking up on her. Was he planning on coming back to live in the bungalow sooner than expected?

'Are you ok, Sophie? You were miles away. Day dreaming about Luis again?' Graham asked.

'Not this time. Just overthinking everything as usual.'

Chapter 36

After last night's email from Kennal, Sophie was concerned. Had he told Casey and Emily about bringing a girlfriend? Should *she* tell them? But then, it was none of her business. She was just an employee after all.

'Sophie, you've done it again – got up and left me asleep alone. I wanted to be the first one to wake up so I could entice you not to get up.'

'Sorry, the minute my eyes are open I just have to get up and moving. Shall I make you a coffee and some toast before you go off to work?'

'Ok if I have a quick shower first?'

'Of course,' Sophie said, heading for the kitchen.

****

Having said goodbye to Luis, Sophie got herself ready to clean around the pool and terraces. As she headed down to the pool she could see Jeremy on the top terrace, reading. She gave him a quick wave and a shouted good morning.

As she was prepping her cleaning equipment her phone beeped with a text, which was from Emily.

My dad's texted me to say he's bringing a friend with him. I've texted him back and asked if I should plan to call her mummy. I thought that might make you laugh!

Sophie messaged back with a crying laughing emoji and then finished off the cleaning and headed back to the bungalow. After getting ready she had a think about what she wanted to do for the rest of the day. She decided a walk somewhere would be nice, perhaps to Del Duque for a little lunch and then a slow walk back, stopping for some treats for when Luis comes around after work.

****

She couldn't believe how busy everywhere was in Del Duque now that they were in the peak of the summer holiday season, but that's what she loved about Caleta and Kalanchoe – they never got overwhelmed with holiday makers. As she knew all the cafés and restaurants would be full she decided to walk a little further on than usual and hopefully she would find somewhere a little quieter to stop and eat. Finding herself near Playa Del Bobo, she came across a beach café that looked promising, still busy but not packed. Sitting in the shade she didn't need to look at the menu as she knew exactly what she was going to have – a club sandwich and a small beer, which she ordered from the waitress. While she waited for it she checked her phone. No emails, just a text from Luis saying he was looking forward to seeing her tonight and asking if she was having a nice day. She sent a text back saying she was looking forward to seeing him and she had come out for a walk and a snack. As she was putting the phone back in her bag, the waitress brought the beer and said the sandwich would be just a few minutes. As Sophie nodded she caught sight of someone she knew walking towards her out of the corner of her eye.

'Hi, Tony.'

'Hello, Sophie, I think I owe you an apology.'

'Honestly, it's all forgotten. We had different outcomes in mind for the evening and there's nothing wrong with that.'

'If that's the case, can I sit down and join you? It's my favourite place to eat at lunch time and I promise you I don't have any ulterior motives.'

Sophie had been enjoying her alone time so was hesitant to say yes but as they both knew where they stood with each other she couldn't see the harm in being polite. Settling in next to her, Tony asked her

262

about the job and if she was enjoying it, then told her he was now running a bar in Playa de las Américas and felt very settled for once in his life.

'I feel the same, to be honest. I love working at the villa and it would be nice to come back next year and do it again.'

'That won't go down well if you do though, will it? I think Luis gets the impression that now he's behaved himself Kennal will give him the job back.'

Sophie figured Luis hadn't yet told Tony about them seeing each other and she certainly wasn't going to.

'That said,' Tony continued, 'if you didn't want to go back to the UK once the villa work is finished, I'm sure I could find you something. If it's not in my bar I have lots of contacts who have shops and restaurants. Just give me a call; you have my number. Actually, you probably don't anymore. Under the circumstances I wouldn't blame you if you deleted it.'

They both laughed and Sophie got her phone out of her bag and put Tony's number in. They finished their food and Tony headed off to get the bar ready for the evening but as Sophie was in no rush she ordered a coffee. She wouldn't want to work with or for Tony, but at least she might have the opportunity to stay in Tenerife after her contract was up at Villa Kennal, and that would mean she would get to stay here with Luis – a thought that made her very happy.

*****

Six hours later, Sophie was sat waiting for Luis to arrive. She had wine and beer chilling, nibbles and crisps in bowls and candles lit on the veranda. She had also showered and put on a nice dress. She was excited for the night ahead and when her phone rang she was delighted to see it was Luis.

'Hi, are you on the way?' she asked.

'Where did you go today?' he asked abruptly.

'Sorry? I went for a walk and stopped for something to eat. How come?'

'By yourself?'

'Yes, by myself. Luis, is there something wrong?'

'How could you be by yourself if you were having lunch with Tony? He's told me everything – how you two are friends again and how, once Villa Kennal is closed for the season, you're going to work for him. He says you'll be the perfect team.'

Sophie sighed. Of course Tony had managed to mess things up for her. 'Luis, you have got it all wrong.'

'No, I don't think I have, actually.'

With that he cut the call off and Sophie flopped down in the chair. The perfect evening she was hoping for clearly wasn't going to happen because yet again Luis had put two and two together and made five.

Chapter 37

Sophie hadn't slept well. She was upset with Luis for making her feel as if she had done something wrong when all she had done was have lunch with Tony, especially as she hadn't even wanted to eat with him in the first place.

She'd already tried calling Luis this morning but he wouldn't answer.

'Perfect timing, Mable, now what would you do in this situation? Should I apologise to Luis?' When the cat – predictably – made no answer, Sophie sighed. 'Fine, I'm going to see Graham. Perhaps he'll have some advice for me.'

Mable was most put out that she had to go back to those very playful kittens, but of course Graham was glad to see Sophie and hear everything she had to say. Thankfully, he did think she had done the right thing and told her not to worry about Luis as he would come around eventually. He also told her not to give in and apologise in the meantime.

'By the way, have you heard from your mum if everything went ok with the filming yesterday?'

'Yes, her text said she was all good and that she'll call me when she has five minutes free, so that's one less thing for me to worry about. Now, I need to build myself up for my boss coming with his girlfriend, not that I have anything to do other than keep out of the way as I'm officially on holiday while he's here. Although I do need to go through the villa paperwork with him and see what his plans are for the future.'

With that, Ramon came through the gate carrying a box. An excited Graham told her it was some pictures Madeline had liked in Ramon's mum's shop. He'd ordered them for her room as a surprise for when she next visited.

'Hi, Ramon, I'm glad I've seen you as I have news – Casey is coming to stay in the villa! Her mum isn't coming – thank goodness – but Emily will be here along with Kennal, who's coming back from America.'

'I'm pleased for Casey to be able to see her dad and thank you for telling me but I don't think I will be seeing her unless they need a taxi. By the way, did your mum get home ok? I get the feeling from what she said she will be popping over here quite a bit from time to time.'

'Oh, yes, my mum and Graham have become quite a team. I think Tenerife needs to watch out as they will no doubt be the new party animals!'

'Please let them know I am more than willing to chauffer them around. Talking of the taxi, I need to be off. Have a lovely day.'

Back inside, Graham was excited to get the pictures unpacked and up on the wall, hoping they would look just right. Eventually – with a lot of 'to the right', 'a little higher' and 'just down a bit' – the pictures were up and they looked great. Graham asked Sophie what her plans for the rest of the day were and as she didn't have any she asked, 'Do you fancy going out for the day? I don't mind where. A walk to the shops? Anything.'

'Yes, but only if it involves food. Actually, do you know what I would really like? Sausage, egg and chips with lots of ketchup.'

Sophie's face lit up. 'Yes, but to get a good old British meal like that we would have to go to Playa de las Américas. Should we call Ramon, get a bus or walk?'

'Definitely walk and then we won't feel guilty about eating it,' Graham said.

While Graham got ready, she Google searched the best cooked breakfast in Playa de las Américas, not really thinking anything would pop up, but it did. She knew the place was right in the centre by the big fountain displays and so they headed off. They were on a mission like two young children heading off to McDonalds for a Happy Meal.

****

'How good was that? We shouldn't have had the large one with three sausages though, we've made right pigs of ourselves,' Sophie said as they left the restaurant.

'No we haven't and later on, before we go back to Kalanchoe, I will require an ice cream. Anyway, once Kennal is here you are on your holidays and we could be doing this every day. I'm only joking but I was thinking if it gets complicated, you being in the bungalow, you could come and have your mum's room.'

'Do you know what? I think I might take you up on that offer. The last thing I need is being in the middle of all the family friction. I'm glad I have a day in between Jeremy leaving and Kennal returning to get the villa ready and to mentally prepare myself for his visit.'

'Also a day to make up with Luis, perhaps?'

'That would be nice but I can't see it happening. Now, are we jogging back to Kalanchoe to work off that breakfast?' she joked.

There was no jogging but instead a nice steady stroll to an ice cream parlour on the sea front before eventually heading back to Graham's with a nice slow walk. It was very enjoyable but tiring and a very welcome cup of tea on Graham's terrace was followed up with the both of them napping in the early evening sunshine. The perfect end to the day.

****

'Are you sure you don't want me to cook anything? The freezer is full,' Graham said after they'd both awoken.

'No, I'm fine, thank you. The snacks were more than enough and to be honest I just want my bed. I'm worn out!'

'Oh, but it's far too early for bed.'

'You know what your problem is? You've had too many late nights partying with my mum. You need to get back into a routine,' Sophie said with a laugh.

'You're probably right. So, what are we going to do about you and Luis? Yet again he's got hold of the wrong end of the stick, though I'm sure he's not going to walk away from you and he will come around at some point. But then what? I think you two are perfect for each other and it's not just Luis who wants you to stay in Tenerife, it's me as well. I don't want to lose you so I hope you know you are more than welcome to stay here with me until Kennal has you back next year. And don't go saying he won't because of course he will. You've run his business like clockwork.'

'That's very kind of you. I know I don't want to go back to the UK and I know you understand that because when Robert died that wasn't something you could consider either, but – and there is a big but – even if I do stay and get a job to see me through to the villa opening again, I couldn't stay unless Luis was in my life. Because the thought of seeing him and not being with him would be too much and I couldn't cope with that. I think I'm going to go back to the bungalow, if you don't mind, and I will try talking to him. Oh, and Graham? We are far too good of friends for me to leave you here. I'm with you for ever. Goodnight and thank you.'

Chapter 38

Several days had passed and Luis was still refusing to answer Sophie's calls but she had other things to worry about. Jeremy had gone the day before yesterday and now was the time she had been both anticipating and dreading – the return of Kennal and his family. She did one final check around the inside of the villa, using a damp cloth to wipe up any dust that had settled overnight and doing a check in all the cupboards. She stopped when she realised she was just needlessly going over things time and time again. She needed to stop worrying.

Everything done, she had a quick shower and then the waiting game began. Sophie was nervous Kennal would be here soon but everything was ready for him. Ramon was picking them up from the airport, the shopping had been done and double checked and she'd done all she needed to do, apart from have a conversation with Kennal about bookings and her future here at some point during his stay. Otherwise, she was on holiday and most of her time over the next few weeks would be spent with Graham. She'd decided she might actually stay in her mum's room in his villa as that way there would be no bumping into any of them in the villa complex. Checking her phone she saw that the plane was on time. One last walk around, picking up the odd leaf, and she was pleased to note that everything was looking perfect. Her mum had told her on the phone not to worry; Kennal was so laid back he wouldn't even notice anything and he certainly wouldn't be walking around inspecting everything.

Ramon was kind enough to text her as they were leaving the airport and with just half an hour to go she was at a bit of a loss as to what to do with herself. Should she check the cushions on the terrace again? No, they had been plumped to within an inch of their lives. Maybe she should wait at the main gate to greet them? Yes, of course.

Pull yourself together, Sophie, everything will be fine.

Every minute seemed like an hour as she waited. She could see a leaf in the pool and wondered briefly if she should get the net and fish it out. But no, they likely wouldn't be going into the pool this evening and she could grab it first thing.

A car stopped outside the gate doors, interrupting her spiralling thoughts, and in no time at all the gates were opening.

Here you go, Sophie, this is it.

'Hi, welcome home to Tenerife, Mr Scott.'

Oh my goodness she was not expecting this...

A supermodel had just got out of the taxi! Well, perhaps not a supermodel but a very gorgeous twenty-year-old with legs that went up to the sky. Sophie just knew this wouldn't go down well with Emily and there would be drama and fireworks to come.

'Hello, Sophie, it's lovely to finally meet you in person and my goodness you look like your mum – and that's a good thing! And it's not Mr Scott, it's Kennal.'

'Thank you, it's nice to finally meet my boss.'

'Excuse me, are we going to stay out here talking all day? I'd like to see my room and freshen up if that's ok,' the supermodel interjected.

'Sorry, darling, I will lead the way. Sophie, can I introduce you to Lara? And Lara, this is Sophie. She manages the villa for me.'

Lara wasn't interested in anyone apart from herself and she followed Kennal through the gate while Sophie helped Ramon with the rest of the luggage.

Ramon whispered to Sophie, 'Wait until Emily

meets her! I think ... no, I *know* there will be fireworks.'

'Yes, I think you're right. But thankfully I will be out of the way behind that big wall in between the villa and Graham's.'

'Very sensible of you.'

Ramon put the bags down just inside the patio doors and said goodbye. There was no sign of Kennal or Lara – they must have gone upstairs – and Sophie thought it was only polite to wait until one of them reappeared. She was surprised there was so much luggage as she knew Kennal had suitcases of clothes in one of the outhouses that he had packed up before going to America. It must be all Lara's things.

She could hear footstep coming down the stairs – it was Kennal.

'Thank you so much for getting everything ready for us. It's so good to be home; I've missed this place so much. Now, you need to head off as you are officially on holiday. The cleaning will be my job and stupidly I have missed sweeping and mopping around the pool. What are your plans for the next few weeks? Are you going back to the UK or on holiday? If so, we could catch up on things before you go or when you come back. Whatever works for you.'

'No, I'm not going anywhere. Well, I *am* going to the other side of the wall as I will be staying with Graham next door.'

'The cat man?'

'Yes. He's changed a lot since you were last here but it's a long story and I won't bore you with it. You have my number so just text me to let me know when you have a spare moment and we can have a chat about everything. In the meantime, I'll let you get settled back in. I'll be up in the bungalow all evening if you need anything.'

'Bungalow? That's a bit posh. I always refer to it as the shed,' Kennal said with a laugh.

'Oh no, it's much more than a shed! It's gorgeous and I love it. The veranda is my favourite place to relax... I think I can hear Lara calling you so I should go. Have a lovely stay, Kennal, and welcome home.'

****

One extra-large glass of wine with a massive bag of crisps and a cheese and tomato sandwich later, Sophie sat on the veranda enjoying the perfect end to the day, and of course reflecting on the last hour. Kennal was very nice but she hadn't really seen the charm all the women fell for yet. No doubt that would come but what of Lara? High maintenance to say the least but so young. The text to her mum would have to be along the lines of 'Kennal's friend is in her twenties and on a scale of one to ten, she is a ten in the glamour stakes with teeth and hair to die for. Emily is going to freak.'

Speaking of texts, she would have loved to be reading one from Luis but she knew that wasn't going to happen. He was finished with her and she wasn't going begging or apologising as she had done nothing wrong. Coming back out from topping her glass up in the kitchen, she could hear her little gate squeak. It had to be Kennal. Not what she was planning tonight as she'd wanted time to be organised with everything before going over the books with him. Or was he coming to check the changes she'd made to the bungalow?

'Hi, Kennal, is everything ok? Can I get you something?'

'No, everything is fine. Lara's got a bit of jetlag so as she's having a sleep, I thought I would pop over and have a chat. You can tell me how your mum's getting on with the filming and also it would be nice to get to know you a little better. But first I have to say what a wonderful job you have been doing and not just how spotless the place is – it's honestly never been this clean – but also the organising of everything.'

'Can I get you a drink?'

'A glass of water would be perfect.'

She grabbed him a bottle from the fridge and refilled the bowl of crisps then asked about the flight and how he was liking being in America. Adding that it would be nice to have Emily and Casey here, she realised she wasn't actually taking a breath or letting him speak, so she stopped herself.

'Sorry, if that had been my mum sat there she would be shouting "why all the questions, Sophie?" at me. Let's start over. Is it nice to be back?'

'Oh yes. I've missed this place so much. Don't get me wrong, my life in America is lovely but just so different from here. I miss throwing a t-shirt on and just walking somewhere and not being recognised. Also, the work is long hours and if I'm not filming I'm doing promotion stuff. But I can't knock it. I'm earning very good money, which I never really believed would ever happen, and it's not exactly hard work, is it. Now tell me, are you really enjoying it here or is it just a job?'

'I love it. Everything about being in Kalanchoe is great,' Sophie enthused. She talked about her friendship with Graham, and the guests she'd had, which led her to mentioning Cristina.

'So what does Luis have to say about that? He is a good lad and all his problems in the past have revolved around Cristina so I think her leaving will be good for him. And by the way, is he behaving himself?'

Luis was a subject she didn't want to talk about so she brushed it off, just saying he'd been helpful.

273

Kennal then mentioned the drama when Velma arrived and it crossed Sophie's mind that that would be nothing compared to when Emily met Lara.

Kennal was evidently thinking the same as he said, 'I think there could be a few fireworks when Emily meets Lara, in that she won't approve and, well ... they are like chalk and cheese. I was hoping to come back by myself but with the chance of a trip to Europe there was no stopping Lara. I think I have got myself into a little situation and the only way out is by upsetting someone.'

'It's worth saying that I do think Emily is only wild because that's what people expect from her. She's playing a part and no wonder, with two actor parents, acting is in her DNA! I'm sure you'll all have a nice time and a lovely holiday while you're here.'

'You know as well as I do that that's not going to happen. The big question is who will be the first to walk out and leave? But enough of that, tell me about you. For a start, I'm loving the changes you've made to the veranda with the pots and the comfy cushions. Would I be allowed to look inside? I'm sure it's a lot nicer than when I left it.' Seeing the look of concern on her face, he quickly added, 'I promise you I'm not out to inspect it, just intrigued.'

'Feel free.'

He popped his head in the door and said he couldn't get over how big and bright it looked – not to mention how clean it was – but most of all how homely it felt. Sophie thanked him and was pleased there wasn't a problem with what she'd done.

'How about I stay here and you go down and stay in the villa when Emily arrives?' he joked.

'I'm sure everything will be fine, Kennal. It's good that Casey and Emily are reconnecting with each other, isn't it?'

'Yes, you're right. Now, Sophie, am I like you

expected? No doubt you've heard so many stories about me. How does the real me compare?'

'Well, you're charming, which everyone talks about, and in my head I always thought you were laid back and I can sort of see you are. I would think you take everything in your stride. I also knew you were creative and had an eye for things because of how the villa has been designed and furnished. So yeah, no big surprises.'

'Did they also say he's always got a new girlfriend?'

'Of course that goes without saying,' she said, and they both laughed. 'I've heard much about "the many wives of Kennal". Sorry, I've probably overstepped the mark there.'

'No, you haven't. I find that very funny and I think I'll have to use it if ever I write my autobiography. It's the perfect title!'

'It really is. Would you like another drink, or something else to eat?'

'I'm not really hungry but another water would be great. I do get myself tangled up with women,' he continued, 'and it always ends in tears. That's why your mum won't take me on. But I have to say I disagree that my eye would wander the way it does if I was with her. I would be happy and would have no reason to go looking elsewhere. I've been trying to convince her of that for years... But enough of that. Now, tell me, are you enjoying the job so much that you might want to come back next year? I'm contracted to stay in America for at least three years so the job is yours if you want it.'

Of course she wanted the job but not just for the summer season, she wanted it fifty-two weeks of the year! This was her opportunity to say something but at that moment her gate opened and coming through it was Emily.

'Hi, Emily, darling, I didn't think you would be

here for a couple of days.'

'Dad, please tell me that woman sat on the terrace isn't your new girlfriend. She's younger than me!'

Chapter 39

No coffee on the veranda today for Sophie. Instead she was staying in the bungalow with the door closed as she was not getting involved in Kennal and Emily's argument. But on the other hand, she would have killed to be in the villa when Kennal and Emily went back last night. Perhaps Kennal should call his autobiography 'The Many Wives *and Children* of Kennal Scott'...

She needed to pack her bag and escape next door to Graham's and let them all just get on with pulling each other apart. But there was actually one thing she would like to do during the next couple weeks – try and get Casey and Ramon chatting.

As she made another coffee she could hear her gate squeak. If she kept quite whoever it was would hopefully think she was still asleep. She stood perfectly silent and still as she waited but there was no knock at the door, which was good as it meant they'd gone away.

Throwing things in a bag was a quick and easy task and it didn't matter if she forgot something, she could always pop back. Looking at the time she saw it was nine thirty. Graham would be up and about so she would head around to his now. A little wave to whoever was on the villa terrace would be sufficient and later on today she would message Kennal to arrange a meeting to go over the diary and everything else connected to the villa – and most importantly, to see if he was willing to rent it out fifty-two weeks of the year. One last check convinced her she had everything and putting her phone charger in her bag she was off.

As she opened the bungalow door though, there was Emily sitting on the veranda.

'Oh! Good morning. Sorry, you just startled me.

Is everything ok?' Sophie asked.

'Hi, I hope you don't mind me sitting here. I just had to get out of the villa and clear my head. I was going to go for a walk but it was so peaceful here I decided to sit for a minute.'

Sophie said it was fine and thought it only polite to offer Emily a drink, which she accepted. Putting her bag down, she went in to make some coffee. No doubt she would now find out what happened last night.

'There you go, one coffee. Can I get you anything to eat? A pastry or some toast?'

'No, I'm fine, thank you. You'll be happy to know I didn't lose it last night. I surprised even myself as I was calm and even welcoming towards Lara. I could tell how uncomfortable my dad was but there's something else. The way the two of them are together isn't normal and I don't get it. We sat down for an hour or so with a drink and I'm not being horrible but she can't hold a conversation. I asked her about her life in America and what she does and from what I can gather she spends the day getting herself ready to go out at night. She has no interest in my dad's work, only what famous people she can be introduced to. It's sad because he and I were chatting about all sorts and she really wasn't capable of joining in.'

'But if he's happy surely that's what's important? Perhaps you should give her the benefit of the doubt as she could be feeling a little lost here in Tenerife.'

'But he's clearly not happy with her and I was so much looking forward to it being me, him and Casey. I just know everything will revolve around Lara and he will become a little puppy dog.'

Sophie tried to reassure her but Emily was having none of it.

'I guess once Casey arrives we can spend time

278

together away from Lara, get to know each other better. At least there's going to be one positive side to the stay here at the villa,' Emily acknowledged.

'Absolutely. Now, apart from that, how is everything with you? The job, to start with?'

'I hate it and I'm fed up living where I am but that's boring. What I want to know is what is happening with Luis? Have I got a wedding to look forward to in the near future?'

Sophie explained no wedding and not even an engagement party. She filled Emily in on everything that had happened but the other woman wasn't a bit surprised.

'That's such a typical reaction from Luis. The sooner he grows up, the better. Once Casey arrives we need a night out, just the three of us.'

'What if Lara wants to come out with us?'

'I don't think she will. Could you see her going from bar to bar? Actually, walking in itself would be a huge problem for her... And on that note, I need to get back to the villa and play the game. Thank you for the coffee. By the way, are you off somewhere with that big bag?'

'Yes, while your dad's here I'm on holiday and please don't laugh but I'm going the other side of the wall. I'm going to be staying with Graham for a few days but you can text me if you want to do something as I've no plans.'

'I will, now it's time to put the smile on. Wish me luck!'

****

Once Emily left Sophie headed up to Graham's. He was on the phone laughing and joking when she arrived.

'Sorry, that was your mum on the phone,' he said after hanging up. 'She was full of excitement as the filming is going well and the cast are being friendly towards her – she's even been out for dinner with several of them. She's excited about next week as all the photographs are going to be taken for the press – there is a real hype around the programme – and the best bit of news is that the day after all the filming is finished, she's coming over to stay! Now, why don't you take your bag into your mum's room and I will make us a coffee. Then you can fill me in on the many wives of Kennal.'

'Not just wives, Graham, daughters as well! My mum thinks she's in a drama? She should be down at Villa Kennal, it's far more exciting. Oh, there's my phone ringing... Hi, Kennal.'

'Hello, Sophie, I was wondering if you were free today to go over everything? Emily and Lara are going shopping for the day and I thought it would be the perfect time.'

'Of course. What time?'

'Shall we say in a few hours?'

'That's fine. It'll be good to have it all out the way before Casey comes so you can have a relaxing holiday with your daughters. I'll see you in a couple of hours,' she said, hanging up the phone.

'You're off to enter the drama then, Sophie?'

'No drama, just me and Kennal and the villa paperwork. Emily is taking Lara shopping – I expect they are off to the posh shops of Del Duque – so I think that's where the drama will be.'

Graham insisted that bacon sandwiches were in order though he had no real reason for them apart from that's what he wanted.

'You spoil me with these sandwiches and if I'm here for the full ten days I think we might need to stop having them or else I will be piling on the pounds.'

'Nonsense! You're on holiday and treats are allowed. Now, what have we planned for this evening – for the rest of the week, come to that – because if you are on holiday, then so am I. By the way, if you are having a business meeting with your employer, shouldn't you wear a suit so it's all very professional?'

Sophie jokingly told him to shut up. She was nervous as it was and he was only making things worse. She did think she would change out of her t-shirt and shorts and put a nice summer dress on though, and perhaps a little make-up. The good thing was that she had had weeks to prepare for this meeting and knew she had crossed every t and dotted every i. The villa accounts had been balanced, the diary was up to date and she just needed to persuade Kennal to keep the place open year-round. If she wanted a full time job here in Kalanchoe she had to really sell the idea to Kennal.

****

As she walked through the main gate there was no sign of Kennal, which was good as it meant she could go and fetch all the paperwork from the bungalow and then head over.

She walked down the path from the bungalow and headed up to the villa. She could see Kennal had come outside and was sitting at the big dining table.

'Hi, Kennal, everything ok? I've brought everything over as I thought there's more room here for us to spread out.'

He agreed but looking at him she saw he looked more tired than when she had chatted to him last night. Perhaps he was worried about Emily being out with Lara as anything could happen? Sophie put all the paperwork down on the terrace dining table and opened her notebook to the page where she had made a list of the order she wanted to go through things. Of course the last thing was the topic of potentially keeping the villa open for rentals year-round.

'To be honest, Sophie, this review seems a waste of time as you're doing such a fabulous job organising and running everything. You don't really need my input.'

'I do though. It's your business and so I need to know I'm doing things right. Also, seeing the figures you might decide you want to make changes – put the prices up and all sorts of things.'

'You have a point. Shall we begin?'

Sophie began by going through the diary for the rest of the year and the following one, both looking quite full as there had already been lots of enquires.

'Financially, with my work in America I don't need to rent this place out, and I know if my acting dried up I would still be ok, but I'm not quite ready to come back and live in it full time. Though that was actually my goal when I started planning Villa Kennal. I wanted Tenerife to be my final resting place. Strangely, we talked about it last night. Lara was shocked and asked why. Of course she just wants life in the Hollywood Hills. That's never going to happen for me though. Sorry, I'm digressing.'

Sophie didn't answer as she wasn't here to sort out his relationship problems. Bringing the focus back to the villa, she went on to the money side of things. She had printed off bank statements and created an incoming and outgoing spread sheet along with a list of wages that had been paid, which was really only her, Javier and a small amount for Luis when he had undertaken some minor jobs.

'Talking of Luis, I know it's none of my business but Emily mentioned – actually it slipped out – that you and Luis are, shall we say, getting on very well together.'

'Yes, for a short time we did get on very well but Luis had a change of mind and now our relationship is purely professional and it looks like that's the way it will stay. Now, getting right back to the running of the villa, I have an idea I'd like to run past you.'

She had practised this speech over and over again in her head for weeks. Would he go for it?

As she started to present her proposal – and it really felt like a professional presentation – Kennal started to smile, which was very disconcerting.

When she finished, he said, 'You've obviously given this a lot of thought and put so much work into it. I won't keep you in suspense, the answer is yes. It's something I should have been doing already as winter is a very busy time on the island with people seeking out the Tenerife sunshine. The reason I hadn't is simply that I was lazy. But now I have you to look after it all, if you'd be happy to stay on full time? If you do, please don't feel you have to work every week of the year. You're entitled to paid holiday so choose a month or so to close and take time off – maybe go back to England and see your family and friends. Now, was there anything else we needed to discuss? I'm happy – actually more than happy – with everything.'

Sophie closed the books and put them in a pile. She was shocked that Kennal was so laid back about everything. She had gone to all that trouble to convince him and now she realised all she'd needed to do was send him a short email, something she could have done months ago. Her mind was starting to race, her life was changing and she was now going to be living here in Tenerife full time. There were so many decisions to be made... She needed to clear her head and looked forward to sitting and chatting things through with Graham.

Looking at the time on her phone she saw she had been here at the villa for a couple of hours already. The gate opened then and in walked Lara followed by Emily but neither were carrying any shopping bags. Odd, as she had thought there would be loads.

'Hi, darling, have you had a nice time? Did Emily take you to some lovely shops? Del Duque has some gorgeous ones.'

'Kennal, can I see you upstairs, please?'

Lara didn't seem happy and as Kennal stood up he threw Emily a look as if to ask what had she been up to. Knowing Emily, she would have said something and definitely thrown a spanner in the works.

Once they were alone, Sophie asked Emily if she'd had a nice time and waited for a very smiley Emily to sit down.

'Yes, thank you. Let's just say that it's been a very productive day and it will be a huge surprise to anyone who knows the Kalanchoe Emily, as I have just been full to the brim with love and kindness to our visitor from America. I've chatted about everything nice about Tenerife and of course I've said how much my dad loves the island and especially his villa, which he spent years designing and building, and how there is nowhere on earth he would sooner live when he retires, especially because it's quiet. He doesn't have to mix with people, he can just be himself in a scruffy pair of shorts and a t-shirt. He really is at his happiest when he's here and with that I think I deserve a large gin and tonic, don't you, Sophie?'

Chapter 40

It had been two days since Sophie and Kennal's meeting and Sophie had been steering clear of the villa. She and Graham had not ventured out – well, that was a lie, she *had* been to the bakery and the supermarket – and she had spent most of that time working hard sorting out the villa website diary. She had added all the new dates it was available to rent out and the response was unbelievable. One booking was for a month, over Christmas and New Year, and then another for the following January and February was for the full two months. She wanted to discuss these longer rentals with Kennal in terms of pricing, and she also felt they needed to discuss putting the rental prices up for certain weeks of the year when the villa was in high demand.

First thing this morning she'd had a text from Emily to say Lara was leaving. Apparently Tenerife was not for her and she had friends in Paris so she was flying there today. The best bit of news though was that Casey was arriving from England, so they would all be able to have a meet up in the coming days.

'That will be nice, a girl's night out,' Graham said when Sophie mentioned the news to him.

'I don't know if I should go though. I don't want to get involved as the time at the villa is meant to be for Kennal and his daughters. It's better if I stay here with you, eating all the wrong for you foods and having fun. If that's ok?'

'Of course! I love having the company,' he said warmly.

They decided they needed to make an effort to do something today – perhaps go out for lunch and a walk to get some exercise and burn off some of the calories they'd consumed? The big question was

285

when they left Kalanchoe and got down to the sea wall, should they turn to the left or right? To Del Duque or to La Caleta?

'We're probably not glam enough for Del Duque,' Sophie worried.

'Speak for yourself. I'm glamorous to the tenth degree and when your mum and I go there it's like the parting of the waves, people just stand to one side to admire us. Actually, that's not what happened, that's just a dream, but anyway I'd like to go to Le Caleta. As well as finding something to eat it would be nice to pop in to Ramon's mum's shop – and why do we keep calling it Ramon's mum's shop? She must have a name. Could you please text him and ask what she's called? Then at least we can greet her in the right way. I'm also in the mood to dress up a little smart, though still comfy.'

'That's fine by me and I'll do the same and wear a dress. But I'm not walking both ways, we'll take a taxi back.'

****

An hour later they were both dressed and ready, looking very smart. After lots of nice compliments to one another they headed off down through the town and out the other side to the rocks and the splashy sea. They then turned to the right and both insisted it was a slow stroll not a march as they were out all day and didn't need to be rushing back.

They had walked for about half an hour and were nearing a little sitting area that was out on a point when all of a sudden Sophie recognised someone.

'Graham! Quick! Look over there, it's Luis ... and he's not alone. There's a girl with him. I don't recognise her, do you?'

'No, but there's only one way to find out who she

286

is. Follow me.'

Going over there was not what Sophie wanted to happen but she couldn't walk away now, she had to follow Graham. This would certainly catch Luis off guard.

'Hi, Luis, and ... sorry, I don't think we've met, young lady. Are you both having a nice day?'

Luis looked very uncomfortable as he introduced the girl – Julie – who had an English accent when she spoke. Sophie guessed she was a holiday maker that he had chatted up in the restaurant or one of the bars. Thankfully, Graham wasn't out to embarrass any of them and so it was 'hello' and 'goodbye' all within seconds. On their way to La Caleta once again, they walked in silence, nether mentioning Luis or the girl. Sophie's phone beeped with a text from Emily saying two words: *she's gone.*

'Lara has officially left Tenerife. It will be nice for Emily to have the day by herself with her dad before Casey arrives late tonight.'

Finally they reached Le Caleta with its big stainless steel sign, and although it was a cooler day they were both now hot from the walk. They had also worked up an appetite so lunch was the first stop of the day before an afternoon looking in the shops. They both settled for a small beer to quench their thirst, and to eat with it, a tomato omelette each, with chunky chips. Sophie already knew that would be followed later with a huge ice cream. Sophie justified it as she was on holiday and Graham said his reasoning was he was old.

'So how long before I should mention Luis and the girl?' Graham asked, a look of concern on his face. 'I guess she must be on holiday as she didn't really have much of a tan, so definitely doesn't live here on Tenerife.'

Their food arrived before Sophie could answer

and they got stuck into their lunch. The timing was perfect because now she didn't have to comment on Luis and the girl. To make sure Graham didn't circle back to the topic, she let him know that Ramon had messaged back and said his mum's name was Marta, which rang a bell to her. And then it clicked – that's what the shop was called. She had to laugh as neither she nor Graham had sussed it out.

After lunch they decided to have a little stroll around other shops before going to Marta's as no doubt between them they would buy something and they wouldn't want to be carrying it around. As they turned up one of the side streets, coming towards them was Emily and Kennal. Sophie introduced Graham to them and described him as the 'mad cat man', which caused a laugh all around.

'Graham, I have to say that you don't look the same man I used to see in the lane. By the way, thank you for being the perfect neighbour and sorry about all the noise that comes from Villa Kennal, most of it likely caused by my daughter, isn't that right, Emily? I'm only joking,' he added, putting an arm around her.

'To be honest, I rarely hear anything because of the wall and trees, although the woman who is running the place does get a little loud with all her wild parties in the little bungalow,' Graham joked.

'Enough of that,' Sophie said with mock outrage. 'Are you excited about Casey coming today?' she asked, turning back to Kennal and Emily.

'Absolutely. I'm a little lost for words to describe what it means to have both my daughters staying. It's wonderful and so lovely. You two must come around and say hello. How about I have a party? Emily, you know how to party better than anyone. Why don't you organise? It would be the perfect end to my stay, a last hurrah before I go back to the States.'

288

'That would be fine, Dad. I'll get on the case when we're back at the villa. But for now I'm hungry. Would you guys like to join us for some lunch?' Emily asked.

'We've actually just eaten but thank you for the offer.' Sophie could tell Graham would have jumped at the chance but he would have asked Kennal a million questions about Hollywood and she wasn't having that.

Taking the opportunity, she said casually, 'It would be nice to invite Ramon to the party as he's so important to Villa Kennal guests.'

Kennal agreed but Emily just gave Sophie an odd look before they said goodbye and went their separate ways.

'What was that with the Ramon thing? What you are trying to do, make Luis jealous? That's not the way to win him over,' Graham said.

'No it's nothing to do with Luis. It's all about Ramon and Casey. I just feel they need a helping hand. Now, shall we head to Marta's shop?'

As they walked through the little streets all Graham could talk about was the party. Sophie tried to convince him it would only be a handful of people – very laid back, nothing glamorous like he was imagining in his head – but he was having none of it. To him, it would be the party of the year.

They finally got to the shop and were surprised to find Ramon behind the cash desk. He explained that his mum had had a fall and hurt her leg and back and so was having to stay at home. A few of her friends and family were helping out at the shop and it was his turn to do a few hours today. Before Sophie could say anything, Graham blurted out about the party and said Kennal would probably invite him as he does so much for the guests at the villa.

'I don't think so, Graham, and even if he did

invite me I wouldn't go. It's not my thing, really. Sorry, I have a customer. Please excuse me.'

Sophie realised it might not be as easy as she'd thought to set Ramon and Casey up with each other. They looked around the shop, Graham saying he was looking for things to enhance Madeline's bedroom. Eventually they decided between them on a set of three wicker baskets with lids. They would be perfect as Madeline could put all sorts of things in them. They paid and said goodbye to Ramon, who explained that with this latest set-back his mum was thinking she might sell the shop, worried she was getting too old to look after it on her own.

'That would be such a shame though!' Graham exclaimed. 'We love coming here. Couldn't she just get a manager in?'

'She could, and that would be fine, it's just difficult finding the right person who would have a passion for it,' Ramon said with a shrug.

As they left with their shopping they walked up towards the bus stop, deciding it was time to head back to the villa, and as they turned the corner who was walking towards them but Luis and the young woman from earlier. The path was narrow so they couldn't cross over the road or even pretend they hadn't seen them. This was going to be awkward.

Thankfully, Graham took control of the situation and conversation.

'Hi again, Luis, we're off to the bus stop as our feet are tired. We've walked too far today.'

Before Luis could reply, the girl chirped in to the conversation.

'We're off to the buzzy bars and clubs along the coast. It's party time for us, isn't it, Luis?'

To her surprise Sophie found herself saying, 'Have a lovely time.'

Luis gave her an odd look and they all said goodbye.

As they walked on, Sophie gave Graham a look that made it clear she did *not* want to discuss Luis. Once at the stop she looked at the bus timetable and was pleased to find they had only about fifteen minutes to wait. Her phone rang.

'Hi, Mum, is everything ok? Graham and I are in Le Caleta.'

'It's a quick call, darling, but an exciting one. A magazine wants to do a story on me – well, not just me but both of us! A mother and daughter thing. It will be so fun with lots of fabulous clothes and loads of photos. Isn't it exciting?'

'No, sorry, Mum, I can't. Actually, no, it's not that I can't, but that I don't want to. That's your life, not mine.'

'Sophie! We would be getting paid very well for it.'

'I don't need the money and there's nothing you or any PR company will say that will convince me to do it. Look, the bus is coming, I need to go. Goodbye.'

'Is everything ok?' Graham asked as soon as they were settled in their seats on the bus.

'My mother wants me to do a mother-daughter photo shoot and an interview for a magazine. I couldn't think of anything worse! It's not happening.'

Chapter 41

It had been a few days since Sophie had bumped into Emily and Kennal, and she still hadn't seen Casey, but that was all going to change today as she was having a girls' day out with them. Emily had texted to say Kennal was tied up all day with online meetings with his agent and interviews so she and Casey were going to the beach and then for something to eat. The other person she hadn't seen or heard from was Luis, but she was off to have some fun so was determined not to think about him.

As she was walking to meet the girls her phone rang and she knew exactly who it would be – her mum. It was probably the fiftieth call from Madeline in the last twenty-four hours and she planned to ignore it just like she had ignored the other calls and all the emails from her mum's PR company. The thought of being in a photographic studio and then having to do an interview with answers the PR company no doubt would have prepared for her was so unappealing. It wasn't happening.

Sophie waited by the main gate as she didn't want to go up to the villa. This was the family's time and they should have the space to themselves. That was a huge part of why she was staying at Graham's – to give them privacy.

'Good morning and welcome back, Casey! I hope you're having a nice holiday so far.'

'I am, thanks. It's certainly a very different holiday to the one I had with my mum! I can't wait to hear all your news. Have you and Luis got it together yet? Also, my dad's told me you're going to be overseeing the villa year-round and not just the summer months anymore. How exciting!'

Before Sophie could answer Emily joined them and said if they didn't get a move on the day would be gone, and that they could chat on the beach. Her interruption was a welcome relief. Sophie didn't mind talking about staying in Tenerife all year but she wasn't in the mood to talk about Luis.

****

They stopped at the bakery for supplies to get them through the day and once on the beach they grabbed three sun loungers and an umbrella and settled in. By this time it was nearly the hottest part of the day so they headed into the sea to cool down. There was a huge difference in Casey, which Sophie knew was down to Velma not being around, and as for the wild and argumentative Emily? She was nowhere in sight. She was just lovely, friendly, Emily now. Sophie smiled and said to herself, 'All is good behind the walls of Villa Kennal.'

Once out of the sea and drying off on the loungers, Sophie was waiting for the Luis questions to reappear and she was ready for them. She would just say that she wasn't interested in him and likewise he wasn't in her. Of course that was a lie, as she did like Luis and being around him made her happy, but she wasn't going to say that to Emily and Casey. Perhaps she should jump in with the questions first to try and control where the conversation went...

'How have things been since you returned to England, Casey? And dare I ask how your mum is?'

'Mum's actually ok and a lot of that is down to her feeling sorry for me as I've had problems at work the past few weeks. The company I work for are streamlining the business and so basically there are about a dozen of us who have to apply for three jobs, though the minute they said that I could quite easily tell who the three people were going to be and I'm not one of them. It all kicks off in a few weeks and then they will start making redundancies. Ugh, I don't want to think about it. I'm on holiday and I'll worry about it when I get back.'

'What do you actually do for a living?' Emily asked. 'I know it's in retail but that's all.'

'I'm the merchandiser for a large chain of department store. There's essentially a me in each shop with a team of staff, but the company now want one merchandiser to cover four shops. The wage will be better but it will be a lot of traveling, and to be honest, even though I know I won't get the job, even if I was offered it I don't think I would want it. Now, where are the pastries? I'm starving.'

Sophie asked how the last few days had been without Lara and Emily said Kennal had been so laid back and relaxed.

'Though he was a little uptight this morning about all the video calls he has to do for the show, but at least he hasn't had to be in America for them,' Emily added. 'The thing with my dad, though, is that he's not good by himself. He hates being in the villa alone and I reckon it's the same when he's in America, which is how he ends up with all these girlfriends and wives. Casey, I think we need a rota system so we don't leave him alone. That way we won't get another mum.'

'Sounds good to me, as long as I have the Tenerife bit. I would hate to be in his American bubble with him. I'd be tongue tied the minute I met all the actors and actresses, and then there's all the press intrusion. No thank you!'

With the article about her mum fresh in her mind – the PR company having finally put out the statement correcting the lie that Kennal was her dad – Sophie couldn't agree more.

They continued chatting about their lives and the past, though nothing about the future as none of them really knew what was ahead. Emily hated her job and Casey was losing hers and as for Sophie, her job looking after Villa Kennal was perfect, it was just her personal life that was a mess. If she did get together with Luis, which felt very unlikely at this point, he would be so possessive and every bloke that stayed at the villa that she smiled at or was friendly with would cause him to go off on one. How could she make him realise that it was her job to be friendly and welcoming to the guests?

'Right, ladies, it's nearly six o'clock. I've just texted my dad and asked him if all his interviews are finished and he says he still has three more to do so he suggested we get ourselves something to eat before we go back to the villa. I know the perfect place and it's just a taxi ride away in La Caleta.'

Sophie was all for it and in the back of her mind she thought they could pop in to Marta's shop as Ramon might be there. Casey said they weren't really dressed for going to a nice restaurant but Emily said it was such a laid back place and there would be lots of people like them who had just come off the beach. They got their things together, did a quick sort out of the hair and put on a little bit of make-up, and then they were off to get a taxi. It did cross Sophie's mind to phone Ramon but no, this was all Emily's idea and she didn't want to come across as trying to take over.

****

The taxi dropped them off just down the street from the restaurant and they headed towards it, Sophie and Casey following Emily.

This will be perfect, Sophie thought. *Once we leave and walk to get a taxi back to Kalanchoe we'll have to pass Marta's shop.*

Once inside the restaurant, which was very quiet as it was still early for people to go out to eat, they were sitting at the perfect table and Emily took control. She ordered the wine and then talked about the menu, sharing what she and her dad had eaten when they were last here. Once the food was ordered and the wine started going down a little too fast, Emily went in for the kill.

'Now, Sophie, how are we going to solve your little problem?'

'My problem? I didn't realise I had one.'

'Luis. He wants you and you want him so there has to be a solution to get you to a happy ending.'

'Don't worry about me. I have my happy ending regardless of Luis – well, for the next three years anyway. Because as long as your dad's in America working, I'll be living here in Tenerife. I really don't need anything else and I'm very happy as I am. I don't need a man in my life to make me any happier. And what about you? You've admitted the Emily the locals see isn't the real one so what does the real Emily want? Where does she see her future?'

'You sound like my dad!' Emily laughed. 'The answer is I don't know. Yes, I'm bored with my job and my life but until I find a new challenge that's my lot. How about your future, Casey?'

'I don't know, I've worked so hard to get where I am and I love retail and the excitement when new stock arrives every season. I suppose I'll look for something along those lines. Now enough of this, none of us want to talk about the future. We're here having fun so what shall we plan for the rest of our holiday? And how are you getting on with organising the party, Emily?'

Emily started to laugh and couldn't stop. Eventually she explained that she hadn't even thought about it, let alone organised anything. This got both Casey and Sophie laughing as well.

'Tell a lie, I do have the date – it's next week on Thursday ... or is it Friday? Oh dear, I'm useless. I promise tomorrow I will start getting it all together.'

'You have to make it good as it's going to be the highlight of Graham's year, even though there will only be a few people there,' Sophie said.

With that, the food came, and all three of them shut up and got stuck in. Another bottle of wine was ordered and Sophie thought to herself what a lovely day she'd had with these two girls. She also thought the party was going to be a disaster if left to Emily. She'd have to tell Graham not to be too disappointed as basically it would just be a drinks party at the villa with a few snacks.

As they were finishing off the meal the restaurant was starting to get busy and all three agreed they were a little out of place in their beachwear and perhaps they should make a move. This was it. Sophie was hoping her plan of action would work.

They paid the bill and agreed they would have a little walk around the town before getting a taxi back. They first headed down to the sea wall. It was getting cooler and there was a lovely breeze so Casey suggested they walk along and get a taxi at the end. To get to Marta's shop Sophie needed them to walk back through the little streets, so she had to think quick.

'Would you mind if we walked back the other way? I think I need to get a bottle of water and there will be taxis at the top of the street.'

The other two said that would be fine and so they headed up towards the little supermarket they could see in the distance. They passed restaurants and shops and Sophie was counting down in her head as they would soon be at Marta's shop. She could see it in the distance and in a few seconds they were there – and it was closed! Sophie was hugely disappointed, especially when Casey spotted it and went to look in the window. If only it was open, this moment would have been perfect.

'What a gorgeous shop! So much colour ... it's such a shame it's closed.'

'Yes, Graham and I have bought quite a few things from here. I know the owner has hurt her back, so that's probably why it's closed. While you're looking in the window I'll just nip and get my water. Do either of you want anything?'

'I'll come with you,' Emily offered. 'Casey will be happily entertained remerchandising the window display in her head.'

In the supermarket, both Sophie and Emily picked up a few things they needed – treats for Graham and Kennal, plus some sweets and snacks for themselves – and as they walked back to meet Casey Sophie noticed someone coming out of Marta's shop. It was Ramon, and he had noticed Casey.

'Emily,' Sophie said, putting out a hand to stop her. 'I think perhaps we should get a taxi by ourselves. I think Casey has got her own taxi driver...'

Chapter 42

'Good morning, Sophie, and how are you this party eve? Any news from the villa? What are your plans for today? Have you thought about a new dress for the party? I think you should wear something glamorous that stands out, something striking.'

'That's a lot of questions to answer,' Sophie said, marvelling at Graham's enthusiasm so early in the day. 'I really hope you're not going to be disappointed with the party tomorrow. As I mentioned, it's more of a casual drinks get together and I doubt there will be more than a dozen people there. I do have good news though, Emily told me that Casey has been out a couple of times with Ramon since we left her with him in La Caleta last week. I did feel bad about it, and of course she complained we were matchmaking, but secretly I know she was pleased. It will be very interesting to see them together at the party and as for a new dress I will get something, I promise you, not because of the party but just to shut you up. I'll go into Playa de las Américas this afternoon but first I need to do some of Villa Kennal's admin. Can you hear that? What's all that noise? It's coming from the lane...'

Graham went to have a look and came back very excited. 'It's a huge lorry and the men are carrying chairs and tables into Villa Kennal! Plus, if I'm not mistaken, on the lorry is a mobile bar. It looks to me like Emily is taking this party much more seriously than we expected. I will have to rethink my outfit! Bring on the glamour...'

Sophie was intrigued. Tables, chairs and a bar? How many people would be coming and what people were they? Perhaps she should find an excuse to go back to her bungalow so that she could see what was going on? Yes, but before that she had work to do.

As she turned her laptop on she could see Graham was on his mobile, which was odd, as the only person he ever talked to was her mum and that was always in the evenings.

****

She had been at the laptop for three hours but hadn't achieved much as her mind was flipping from one thing to another. First Graham, who was acting a little odd with all this business about buying a dress when she had lovely dresses already, and now the unexpected delivery of the tables and chairs. Had she missed an email or a conversation? Was something going on that she didn't know about? No, that was daft. She knew everything about the villa ... or did she?

'I'm off to buy the dress,' Sophie said after putting her work away and grabbing her bag for a walk into town. 'But first I'm going to nip into the bungalow as I want to have a nosey and see what's going on.'

'Do you think you should? I wouldn't. Let it be a surprise tomorrow evening instead! And as for the dress, get something bright but make sure it's not too casual or fussy as you don't want it to clash.'

'Clash with what? You know I'm beginning to think I've missed a big part of this jigsaw puzzle, but let me tell you something, within the next hour I will find out what's going on. See you later.'

As she walked down the lane she could see Javier's van parked outside Villa Kennal. That was unusual as it wasn't his usual day to do the gardens, but perhaps he could be the person to find things out from. But first she would go up to the bungalow. As she went through the gate she could see Emily talking to a woman with a clipboard. So, she had handed the party over to a company to organise and obviously they had talked her in to having a grander affair. That made sense.

As she went through her little gate she saw Javier was moving the pots off the top terrace and it looked like the event team were carrying them down to the pool area. She unlocked the bungalow and closed the door behind her, sitting on the sofa to think things through. Emily had obviously talked her dad into having a big flashy party, which he would hate, but to avoid upsetting his daughter he would go along with it. But how did Graham factor into all of this and what was all the fuss about what Sophie wore?

After fifteen minutes she'd made no progress and so she decided it was time to go. As she locked up and headed down to the main gate she saw there were some men carrying in huge planters full of flowers, which were magnificent. As she headed out through the gate she ran into Casey, who was dressed very smartly and was clearly off out somewhere.

'Hi, Sophie, how are you?'

'Hello, Casey. I'm fine, thanks, though a little shocked by all of this. I didn't realise what a huge party it was going to be. It looks like it will be all very Hollywood; Lara would have loved it.'

'Yes, my dad and Emily have been planning it together. They asked if I wanted to get involved but I haven't the time. You see, I've been helping Ramon out at his mum's shop as she is still poorly.' Seeing the question in Sophie's eyes, she added, 'And yes, we're getting on well together, not that we've had that much time alone together as I'm in the shop and he's working in the taxi. But I'm excited he's agreed to come to the party and hopefully his mum will be able to as well.'

'That's nice for you and what do you think of the shop? Isn't it gorgeous?'

'Oh yes. Marta has a real knack of stocking the right things. I'd best be off or else I'll miss the bus to La Caleta. See you tomorrow at the party! I think it's going to be quite exciting.'

As Casey left and Sophie headed off through the town she thought to herself, *exciting? I'm not so sure. It's more of a mystery than anything else.* She was happy for Casey and Ramon though. They were so well suited.

Once in the main shopping area of Playa de las Américas she knew exactly where she was heading. There was a lovely shop that sold things you didn't normally see anywhere else.

****

Two hours later she had found a dress and in another shop a nice pair of shoes. She was sorted and hopefully everyone would be happy she had gone to all this trouble. Deciding she deserved a treat for doing what she was told, she stopped for a coffee and a fancy ice cream in a bowl before heading back to Graham's.

As she was crossing the road to the ice cream parlour she spotted Luis, who just like her was carrying bags. He spotted her at almost the same time so they would have to speak or at the very least acknowledge each other. She was nervous but excited at the same time. She had really missed him and it was all so silly, the whole misunderstanding. She told herself to smile and look relaxed.

'Let me guess, party clothes?' she said in greeting.

'Yes, I had a message from Emily to say I needed to look smart for the party and that my normal jeans and t-shirt wouldn't cut it. I offered to work the barbeque but apparently they have caterers. It's all a bit over the top, if you ask me, and I don't really know what all the fuss is about.'

'I'm not sure either. As long as Graham has a nice time, I'll be happy.'

As a commotion erupted across the road at one of the big hotels, Sophie tried to use it as an excuse to say goodbye, but Luis wanted to have a look as well. They both crossed over and Luis asked a woman what was going on. She said a car had pulled up with two famous actresses from America in, though she didn't know their names. Luis and Sophie looked at each other and at the same time said, 'Do you think this has something to do with the party?'

'I know some of the staff that work here,' Luis said. 'If you want to wait a minute I'll go and see what I can find out.'

As she waited Sophie decided this must all have something to do with Kennal's new TV show. *So, the party was going to be a big affair after all. Graham will be beside himself with excitement.*

It wasn't long before Luis was back. He had spoken to a receptionist he knew who told him their names. 'Time to see who they are,' he said, pulling out his phone and opening Google. A quick search confirmed that both women were on the same TV show as Kennal. 'I wasn't looking forward to the party in the first place and I'm looking forward to it even less now it's a glitzy Hollywood party. It's just not my kind of thing,' Luis said with a shrug.

'Mine either, and to tell the truth, nor Kennal's. He hates all the fuss that goes with his acting career.' On impulse, she added, 'I was just going to get a coffee and an ice cream. If you aren't in a hurry, would you like to join me?'

Why had she said that? If he said no she would feel so awkward but if he said yes what would they talk about?

'Sure,' Luis said breezily.

They headed to the ice cream parlour, which was busy, but they managed to find a table and ordered two coffees and an ice cream each. They chatted about the party and what they both thought might go on, but really they would have to wait and see. Sophie asked him about his work and talked about Graham and the villa but everything was a little tense and matter of fact between them. Oh how she wished they could go back to when he was staying at the bungalow. The smiles and the laughter, that's what she wanted back most of all. She wanted to feel the way she did back then again.

'I can't believe you've been here so long already, Sophie, the season is flying by. It won't be that long before you close Villa Kennal for the year. If you need a hand shutting the place up feel free to call me. I'm sure I'll be keeping an eye on it for Kennal during the winter again anyway.'

'Oh, um, actually Villa Kennal isn't closing for the winter. Kennal has decided to keep it open to guests year-round and I've agreed to run it for the next three years while Kennal works in America.'

'But you can't,' Luis said, looking nonplussed. 'That's my job. Kennal has punished me and I've learnt my lesson so now it's time for me to return.'

With that he stood up and stormed out of the ice cream parlour. Sophie was gobsmacked.

Chapter 43

It was party day but Sophie was already wishing it was tomorrow so it would all be over. It wasn't just tonight she wasn't looking forward to though, it was spending the day with Graham going on and on about it, and then hearing nonstop talk for the next week straight. All she wanted was to get back to work running Villa Kennal.

'Your face is a picture,' Graham said as he walked into the kitchen. 'It says, "all I want is for today to be over with". Am I right? No, you don't have to answer. One thing you should be pleased about is that the party will be busy and not just a handful of people. You can get lost in the crowd and even slip away without being noticed. I will say that I won't be doing the same, which makes me laugh as it was only a few months ago I couldn't even say hello to anyone and now I want to go and mingle with everyone. In fact, I can assure you I will be the last one to leave no matter what time it is. Oh, there goes my phone.'

Sophie had never heard Graham's phone ring as much as it had in the past few days. It had to be something to do with her mum. Perhaps she was trying to get Graham to persuade Sophie to do the interview?

'That was Emily saying it would be a good idea to keep Mable in tonight as all the noise from the party would probably scare her.'

Of course Sophie didn't believe his excuse. Emily didn't really know Mable at all so it was unlikely she'd be concerned for the cat's welfare. Sophie decided it was best to change the subject.

'What do you have planned for the day?'

'I'm going to keep myself busy. I'm going to strip the beds and get the sheets in the wash, and then there are a few bits of shopping I need and, of course, I'll need to give myself plenty of time to get ready.'

'Why not leave the bedding until tomorrow? Have a lazy day save your energy for the party.'

'No I need to be on the go and keep myself busy. It would be a help if you could strip your bed though. I have clean bedding all ready to go on.'

Sophie counted to ten in her head. Things could be worse. She could be in her bungalow with all the comings and goings of the event organisers. At least here she was out of the way. So, she did as Graham asked and took the dirty bedding off and put it ready to wash. She asked if he needed anything from the shops as she was going to get a few things, and between them they wrote a list and off she went.

As she walked she decided that before getting the shopping she was going to sit in the bakery with a coffee and cake, talk to no one, watch the world go by and try and switch off from all the party stuff.

****

As she was sitting with her coffee and cake, scrolling through her phone, she noticed Kennal coming in. He waved and walked towards her, asking if he could join her. Of course she said yes.

'This bakery has always been like a magnet to me. When I first came here to live it was just a small little building – and only selling bread – and I've watched it grow over the years. Now, with the huge extension and this café part, it's wonderful. If something can be made out of pastry, you'll find it here.'

'I completely understand. This is where I spend the bulk of the wages you pay me!' She laughed. 'Are you having a nice holiday? Emily and Casey seem to be enjoying themselves, which is nice for all three of you.'

'I've loved just staying in at night, cooking and chatting, just the three of us. It's been special. I could do without tonight's party – not my thing at all – but once that business with the paper came out... Ah, well, a few photographs and everyone will be happy. And it's nice to see Emily taking on the responsibilities with the party planners, which I have to say she seems very good at. But thankfully tomorrow it will all be over and life will be back to normal. I bet you can't wait to get the villa back and me gone. I don't blame you.'

'Yeah, the party isn't my thing either, but I have enjoyed meeting you and of course Casey and Emily coming back is nice. As you've been in the villa and seen it all being set up, dare I ask what tonight will entail?'

'I can answer that quite easily, there will be a set plan by my American publicist – photos after photos, and for every fifty to one hundred taken one will be used. I guess they're going down the route of Tenerife is my home and where I spend time with my two daughters, all sugar and spice. If only they knew the truth! Emily will be fine with it but Casey will be worried what Velma thinks once the pictures are printed in magazines. Talking of photos, one of the girls mentioned the magazine she works for wanted you to go back to England and do a photo shoot with your mum. Surely that would have been fun? A nice little earner with a few smiles, especially now you and your mum are getting on so well together.'

'You sound like Graham – and Emily, come to that – and with the amount of hassle it's caused... I should have probably just said yes.'

'Perhaps it's not too late and you can still help her out. Now, I best get back and make sure my gorgeous Tenerife villa hasn't been turned into a

Hollywood palace. Can I ask one thing before I go though? Please enjoy tonight and take it for what it is, just a bit of fun. Another few days and it will all be back to normal for you.'

With that Kennal left. Sophie was starting to feel bad about the way she had argued with her mum, but apologies could wait until tomorrow. For now, she needed to put a smile on and try to enjoy tonight.

****

'You look very handsome, Graham I will feel very proud on your arm and you never know, we might end up in one of the magazines! I can see the headline now; they'll say you're my sugar daddy.'

'Very funny, now shouldn't you be getting dressed? We have only half an hour before we need to leave.'

Sophie explained she only had to put her dress on and some lipstick, but Graham said not to worry about the make-up as there would probably be a make-up artist there to do it before the photos were taken.

His phone went off again then so off she went to get dressed.

But as soon as she walked into her room, the penny dropped. A make-up artist at the event, Kennal and his daughters doing a photo shoot, Graham's phone constantly ringing, the pressure to buy a new dress, Kennal telling her the party was all a game... Was all of this a set-up to trick her into doing the mother-daughter interview? Perhaps she should pack her bag as she would probably be sleeping back in the bungalow tonight as someone else would need this room – her mum.

She quickly got dressed and as she looked in the mirror she gave herself a little talk. *You have scrubbed up well so now you just have to play the game. Smile in the right places and it will soon be over and you can get back to normal ... whatever that is.*

'You look gorgeous, Sophie, you really do. Far too lovely to be on my arm. But what's with the bag?' Graham asked when she walked out of her room carrying her overnight bag.

'Oh, come on, I've worked it all out! Changing the beds, the need for a new dress and as for the week of non-stop phone calls ... my mum's obviously coming back and more to the point I will be walking into a photo shoot. At least I've not had to travel back to England for it, I guess. She can have her room back and I will stay in my bungalow.'

'I knew you would guess, but I promise it will be fine! A few snaps with your mum, that's all the PR people want, and you never know, you might actually enjoy it. Shall we get going? I don't want to miss a single moment.'

Sophie agreed they should head down the lane but first she sent a quick text to her mum to say they were on the way and let her know she knew she was here at Villa Kennal and more importantly, the photos weren't an issue with her.

****

'Here we go,' she said as she and Graham approached the gates where two gorgeous looking men were waiting to greet guests. 'I'll have to ask Kennal if they can stay – we could have one each!'

'Oh no, now your mum's here I already have someone to party with,' Graham said as Madeline came down the path from the villa to join them.

Sophie could also see a woman with the clipboard walking towards her. *Deep breath, Sophie, smile and give the impression you're excited.*

'Hi, I'm Penny and I'm in charge of the magazine shots. I'm aware you likely don't have a clue what's going on so I'll summarise it very briefly as there is a lot to get done. Both your mum and Kennal's PR companies are following up their response to the newspaper story by doing a joint PR campaign. All you need to know is that the five of you are all good friends and have been for many years. Right, Madeline, Sophie, this way please.'

There wasn't time for Sophie or her mum to even chat to each other before they were ushered into a roped off area – the team had clearly been at pains to ensure no one touched anything or messed up the setting for the photos.

Photo after photo – her mum on her left, then the right, then both sat down, then both standing – there were so many different poses to get through. Goodness knew what they would look like, but there was one set of photos she was hoping would come out nicely – the ones with her, her mum, Kennal, Emily, and Casey. Although they weren't a real family, they were good friends and that made her feel nice.

Three quarters of an hour later she was waiting for her next instruction when the photographer said that it was a wrap. The rope was removed and thankfully she could get back to Graham and at last be able to actually drink the drink that was in her hand without being told it's only a prop.

'Let's walk over to the end of the terrace, Mum, away from everyone. It will be quiet and we'll be able to talk.'

'You aren't too mad at me, darling, are you? I wanted to tell you.'

'No, Mum, it's fine and I'm sorry about being difficult. But saying that, if I had come over to you in England, you would have missed the party.'

'Agreed. It all worked out perfectly. Now, I need

to sit down. My feet are killing me.'

Sophie found a table and called Graham over. As he interrogated Madeline on who was who, Sophie walked to the bar, bumping into Casey, who gave her a kiss and a huge hug.

'Thank you, Sophie. I'm so grateful.'

'Grateful for what?' Sophie asked, confused.

'Throwing me and Ramon together! It's been amazing reconnecting with him and it's actually changed my life. You see, I'm going to be living here – well, not here in the villa, but over at Le Caleta – and I'm going to be running Marta's shop! I'm so excited and it's all down to you. Oh, here comes Ramon and his mum. I need to go but we'll chat later and I'll tell you all about it.'

Sophie was so happy for Casey and Ramon. They were perfectly suited.

As she got to the bar, she turned around to see Graham and her mum holding court with at least a dozen people hanging on their every word. She asked the barman to take their drinks over, as she didn't want to get sucked into it all, and picking up her drink she headed over to Kennal and Emily.

'How are you doing?' Kennal asked. 'Sorry you've been tricked into all of this.'

'It's not a problem. As long as the piece that goes with the photos gets all the facts right, I'll be happy. And hopefully it will only be sold in the UK and not here on Tenerife.'

Kennal's phone rang out just then. He answered it, said no, he couldn't talk, and then said goodbye. Within seconds it went again but before he could answer it Emily took the phone off him and switched it to speaker once she'd answered the call.

'No, I'm sorry, Mr Scott isn't available to talk.'

'But we need to ask him a few questions,' the voice on the other end of the line pleaded.

'He would be happy to give an interview but

311

please follow the correct procedures.'

'Who am I speaking with please?' the caller asked, their tone turning sharp.

'I'm his publicist. My name's Emily Scott, goodbye.'

'Thank you, Emily, that's the way to do it! I think I come across too nice so they try to press their advantage. Perhaps you should come back to America with me and run my life. You would be the perfect person for the job.'

'Ok, I will. But don't think you're in for an easy time. I'm high maintenance, though I guess you're used to that. One other thing, I will be vetting any guest that stays overnight. If I'm going to be getting a new mother, *I* will choose who she is.'

This caused a lot of laughter.

'Well, that's both my daughters sorted – one running a shop here in Tenerife and the other running my life in America!'

'You're right, Dad, so that just leaves Sophie to sort out. I wonder what the future has in store for you? Perhaps I should dig the old Emily out – you remember, the bossy one? Come with me, Sophie, I need to get serious and a little forceful.'

With that, Emily grabbed her hand and took her down to the pool where Luis was sat by himself. Before he could say anything, Emily said one line: 'Sophie, Luis, you both want each other. Sort it out. Here. Tonight.'

Sophie didn't know what to say as Emily walked away from them, but eventually she asked, 'Why haven't you brought the girl friend you were with in La Caleta?'

'She's not a girlfriend, just the niece of the owner of the restaurant I work in. He asked me to keep her out the way for a few days and evenings. Hanging out with her was all very boring and it looks like I'm not the only one who jumps to conclusions.'

They both laughed lightly.

'I guess we're even now, aren't we?' Sophie said, leaning towards him and kissing him on the lips.

'I'm sorry,' Luis said when they pulled apart. 'I'm sorry for not giving you a chance to explain that it was just an innocent lunch with Tony and I'm sorry for claiming you stole my job. You didn't – you couldn't – because it was never really mine in the first place. It's clear that you were made for the role and I can't wait to see you excel at it for the next three years, if not longer, because Kennal would be crazy to let you go.'

'Does this mean we can start again?'

'If that's what you want. I know it's what I want. I'm crazy about you and I'm ready to stop jumping to conclusions. Instead, I want us to be open and honest with one another.'

'Well that makes two of us because you're all I think about.'

They kissed again, losing themselves in the sensations until someone coughed and they sprung apart.

'Luis, would you be kind enough to get me another drink?' Madeline asked. He was off in a flash and her mum pointed to Casey, Emily and Kennal up on the top terrace.

'Darling, don't they look good together, the three of them? It makes me think perhaps I made a mistake and he would have been a good father to you and a lovely husband to me.'

'Possibly, but we will never know. Mum, can you remember when we were sat on the plane waiting to come here and you made me read all that information about Villa Kennal? The last page wasn't right. It said the job was for eight months but now it's for three years, also there was nothing saying I would fall in love with the person whose job

I had taken over and still manage to live happily ever after. Thank you, Mum, this has been one special summer in Tenerife.'

The End

Printed in Great Britain
by Amazon

21537183R00183